Praise for **GIFTED**

"*Gifted* is a page turner and the characters are totally enticing. Have not read a book this exciting since Harry Potter! Did not want the book to end. Great read!"

– Lynn Rossi, East Haddam,
Connecticut, Dream Builder Coach

"…a fun and easy read. I love the teamwork between the characters. Balchazar draws you into the story instilling in the reader the idea that you can do this too. And when the book ended, I wanted more."

– Andrea Munden, Health Care Professional,
San Diego, California

"…hooked from the onset, and thoroughly enjoyed watching the pieces of this story come together. I see a little part of myself reflected in each character of this book as they traverse their way through a beautifully choreographed adventure."

– George Jerjian, Journalist and Author,
The Spirit of Gratitude, Crises Are Opportunities

"This brilliant work of fiction gives you the understanding of the mental faculties as powerful and transformative tools innate in all of us."

– Matt Curfman, Co-owner and Founder,
Richmond Brothers, Jackson, Michigan

"*Gifted* takes the reader on a fun-house ride to understanding how we create our reality. With a combination of Universal Laws and unlimited imagination, the characters go through their own hero's journey and come out the other side realizing they had the power all along."

– Corinne L. Casazza, International Best-Selling Author
of *Walk Like an Egyptian* and
The Adventures of Blue Belly and Sugar Shaker

Published by
Hasmark Publishing
www.hasmarkpublishing.com

Editor: Corinne Casazza
corinnecasazza@gmail.com

Illustrator: B. Merzlock
bmerzlock@msn.com

Cover & Book Design: Anne Karklins
anne@hasmarkpublishing.com

ISBN 13: 978-1-989161-42-5
ISBN 10: 1989161421

Unwrapping
the adventure
one **magical**
thought
at a time

GIFTED

KIM GRIFFITH and **PAUL KOTTER**

SPECIAL CREDIT GIVEN

It is with gratitude and appreciation that we acknowledge the contributions of the following people and organizations. Thank you for sharing your words.

- Hay House, Inc., Carlsbad, California, and Wayne Dyer, *The Power of Intention*, copyright December 15, 2005

- Henry Ford Foundation

- Napoleon Hill Foundation, *Think and Grow Rich*, Napoleon Hill

- Earl Nightingale and Nightingale-Conant

- Penguin Random House, New York, New York, *The Memory Book*, Harry Lorayne and Jerry Lucas, copyright 1974

- Penguin Random House, New York, New York, *Practical Magic*, Alice Hoffman, copyright August 5, 2003

- Bob Proctor

- Rubik's Brand: Rubik's Cube® used by permission Rubik's Brand Ltd. www.rubiks.com

- Werner von Braun

- Warner Brothers Entertainment, The Wizard of Oz

- Turner Entertainment

DEDICATION

TO BOB PROCTOR

Thank you seems inadequate to describe the gratitude
we feel for your message of a fuller life, which has
changed our world.

Through your coaching, a new foundation was constructed
in the minds of these two authors. On top of which
a beautiful new super structure now exists, inspired by your
encouragement to believe in the creativity that lies within.

Your passion and example made it easy for us to believe.
Your consistency and training made it possible to free our minds
from the confining prison of negative belief.

Your ability to help and support goes beyond expectation.
Words cannot describe our heartfelt thanks for your declaration
that we can do, and become, anything we desire.

Bob, God has used you as an instrument in our lives.
From day one this book was dedicated to you.
You are the spark that ignited the flame, fanned our creativity,
and encouraged the dream.

Without you, there is no direction of our imagination,
no controlled impression on the subconscious, and no book to
dedicate. We celebrate and share your teachings in its pages.

Thank you for generously giving.

FOREWORD

BY BOB PROCTOR

Over the years, I have accumulated a personal library that contains what I consider to be some of the best books ever written on the subject of the mind, thought, and universal law. *Gifted: Unwrapping the Adventure One Magical Thought at a Time* is a wonderful story that incorporates all of these topics well.

For over a half century, I've taught people how to use their mind to change their results. Kim Griffith and Paul Kotter are two such individuals and like me, they have seen lives changed, goals achieved, and dreams fulfilled. It all happens by law.

The first thing you need to know when it comes to working with the law is that everything begins in your mind. You have a wonderful and marvelous mind. As an added bonus to being human, you were gifted six unique mental faculties or gifts: Imagination, Intuition, Memory, Reason, Will and Perception.

The purpose and power of the six mental gifts are inseparably weaved into this narrative. It is also reinforced by the principle that anything you want can be created through the proper use of your mental faculties. Gifted confirms that everyone has these special gifts, and whether you recognize it or not, you use them every day.

Some people are naturally good at creating the outcomes they desire, but most, like the main characters in *Gifted*, must learn to exercise great discipline. In order to get what you really want in life, you need to govern your mind. You see, there is a thought energy that flows to and through you. When that energy enters your mind, you have the ability to direct it. As you properly exercise your mental faculties and master your thoughts, you begin to create the good you desire.

Modern life is filled with examples of this type of creation. Everything we have on this planet began as an idea in someone's mind. Think of the clothing you wear, the phone you dial, the car you drive, even space exploration; every technological advancement and achievement known to mankind started as an idea in someone's mind.

We use the gift of imagination to originate, massage, and grow ideas until they can be seen in great detail. I am a firm believer that, if you see it in your mind, you can hold it in your hand. As the authors explore in this fictional story: thoughts become things. However, this message is not one of fiction. In fact, these ideas are universal and as applicable in real life as they are in this wonderful story. Whether we choose to admit it or not, the law works perfectly, every time, for every person.

As you read *Gifted*, notice the awareness, ideas and results that appear as its characters open their mind and consciously think in positive and productive ways.

Look for and focus on the good that exists all around you, while observing the difference it will make in your own life.

Remember, it all begins with a thought.

Bob Proctor, Bestselling Author of *You Were Born Rich*

ACKNOWLEDGEMENTS

They say it takes a village, and indeed, it does. And it's a very good thing that we love a collaborative effort. The uniting of many minds to create something wonderful and beautiful brings out the best of what man can accomplish. This book is no different. Here are the many thanks to the village and brilliant minds that made it all possible.

Bob Proctor, known as the master thinker, set us on a journey to enlightenment, knowledge, a new way of thinking and a brand new prosperous way of living. Without his passion and dedication to his love of teaching this material, we would not have even begun. There would have been no idea. The creative power would have been stifled, never allowed to flow freely. Thank you, Bob, for all you do, for all that you are, and for being "willing and able" to learn, create, and teach. Your sacrifices have changed not only our lives but who we are. We owe you a debt of gratitude which will never be repaid.

Sometimes you need that one person who opens your eyes to what you can do. That someone who sees in you, believes in you, when you can't see it or believe it yourself. Peggy McColl, a brilliant, *New York Times* Best Selling author, invested not only her time, but her expertise and her heart. She, in a most confident and persuasive manner, convinced us that not only could we write one book, but many books if that's what we choose to do. She stayed with us every step of the way showing us exactly what to do. She didn't scoff at our dream or tell us it would be difficult. Not once did she complain that we asked too much of her. Our most heartfelt thanks, Peggy, for without you, this book would never have been written.

No writer is successful without a stellar publisher. If nobody reads your work, it is destined to sit on a shelf, the ideas and stories bound forever within its covers. If you have the slightest desire to write, you must reach out to Judy O'Beirn of Hasmark Publishing. Judy's enthusiasm and support for our book reached beyond our expectation of a publisher. She knew exactly who needed to edit our work, and the alliances we needed to create to make our book a smash hit. Judy held our hand through the entire process, never letting go, always there. Without Judy's expertise, there would be no best seller. Thank you, Judy, for all you give to us. We can hardly wait to work with you on the sequel.

And last but not least, there is always one person who comes into your life, takes you under their wing, and opens doors for your success. That one person who seems to instinctively know who you need to meet, who needs to know about your project, who can help you with promotion and marketing, who can introduce you to the power hitter you need to make your dream a reality. Arash Vossoughi, instantly saw the vision we had for this book, knew exactly where to go with it, and moved swiftly to help. And it all happened so quickly and eloquently. Thank you, Arash, for your vision, your willingness to place your own reputation on the line for this book, and for the coaching, encouragement, and kick in the pants at just the right time to keep us moving forward.

Once you make a committed decision, the universe conspires to bring you everything you need to make your dream a reality. And that has certainly been the case with this book. Looking back to connect all the dots, we can see how God began the alignment of all that was necessary for our success, even before the idea for this book came to mind. And it can happen this way for you too. All you need is an idea and a committed decision. The rest will all fall into place and come into being.

To all of you, thank you for your help, for pursuing your own dreams and passions, and for being a part of our project. It would not have happened without each one of you. We tip our hats and bow our heads to you with love, gratitude and deep respect. Thank you.

CONTENTS

INTRODUCTION

BALCHAZAR'S PREAMBLE

Greetings! How lovely it is to see you. Thank you so much for picking up a copy of my book. Oh, dear, where are my manners? Permit me to introduce myself. I am Balchazar, the crow. Despite what you may think about this story, I am the center of this tale. Perhaps I should explain.

Unbeknownst to the humans in this book, they are about to embark on the journey of a lifetime. You might wonder how I know this. Well, I must confess, I am the one sending them on this most impressive series of adventures. Mystery, thrills, danger, intrigue, you will find it all as you turn the pages.

But wait, there is more, the thrills they are about to experience were created and carried out by a series of thoughts, once hidden deep inside their minds. How can this be, you ask? Private thoughts played out as actual physical adventures? Well, you see, these humans do not yet know, and possibly, neither do you, that there are laws that govern our universe. Laws that must be obeyed either consciously or unconsciously. Laws that never sleep. Laws that operate regardless of your knowledge or belief in them.

Have I piqued your interest? I hope so. As you must have realized by now, I am no ordinary crow. Over the years, I have familiarized myself with the universal laws, and now abide by them perfectly. I spend my days introducing unsuspecting people like you to the laws of the universe. And as you will see in this book, I also teach my students how to live harmoniously with the laws and how to create the life of their dreams.

I can see that you have questions. Please allow me to share an example. I presume you are familiar with gravity. Gravity is a physical law that affects each one of us. It does not matter if you believe in gravity or not, if you step off a diving board, you will fall and land in the water below. You cannot change it. But here is what is important, you can use the law of gravity to your advantage.

Instead of falling face first and slamming into the water, you can glide gracefully through its rippling barrier in the form of an athletic dive. In fact, while we crows are content with flying, you humans have quite an odd obsession of playing with gravity. You jump out of airplanes with parachutes, you strap skis to your feet and jump off mountains, you even launch yourselves dangerously off ramps on skateboards. My point is, you have learned how to work with the law of gravity in order to experience fun and enjoyment.

Like gravity, the laws of the universe are precise, and we can use them to our advantage. Werner von Braun, one of the fathers of space travel said, "The natural laws of the universe are so precise that we have no difficulty building a spaceship to fly to the moon and can time the landing with the precision of a fraction of a second."

You might be wondering how you can use the universal laws to create the life of your dreams. Well, in order to do this, God has given each of us six mental faculties, or gifts, if you will. Although each of us is in possession of all six gifts, some of us use them more than others, and sadly, we often use them in ways that are counter-productive to our happiness and success. Because, you see, these mental gifts can either create or destroy.

You may have heard the saying, "practice makes perfect." Well just as this applies to your gravity-defying activities, it also applies to the development of the mental faculties. The more we use these gifts, the more success we experience. You will clearly see in this book that when my students properly use their mental gifts, they are able to build the world, life and circumstances they desire.

So, what are these mental gifts? I'm so glad you asked. Here is a list, in no particular order: Memory, Perception, Intuition, Imagination, Reason and Will.

Throughout this story, you will read my imparting of wisdom, my instruction of the law, my guidance to use a particular mental gift. And frankly, you may see the required response or action before my students do. That is okay, just keep reading. And should you decide that you want to develop your own God given mental faculties, please go to **www.ReadGifted.com** for more information.

Okay, please turn the page, I will see you inside.

P.S. If you are curious, which I am sure you are, you can read an explanation of the six mental faculties at the end of this book. I promise, you will not be disappointed as you familiarize yourself with the faculties of your mind.

CHAPTER 1

THE LUNCH DROP

The lunch bell rang ending the most boring of classes, and a river of hungry students flowed out the double doors to the sun that was drenching the school yard. Katie stared at the screen of her phone while unwrapping a sandwich accompanied by a pudding cup and thought to herself, "This is the lunch of a six-year-old."

Charlotte, scrolling through social media on her phone, picked at her salad wishing for burgers and fries. Sidney tore into a tuna sandwich while picturing himself on a boat hauling in a big fish as the ocean sprayed his face. James and Emily carefully pulled pizza from a cardboard box that they ordered from an app, fifteen minutes before class let out.

"Why don't we eat at the mall?" Charlotte complained, barely looking up as she scanned for anything important she may have missed while enduring the last hour of World History. "This is just so juvenile to sit here at this picnic table. There are so many good places we could eat if we went to the mall. Come on you guys."

Emily, in her kindest way replied, "Charlotte, you say that every day. If you want to eat at the mall for lunch, you're free to go. But the rest of us don't have enough time between classes to go with you."

Sometimes Emily really pushed Charlotte's buttons. She didn't understand why anyone would want to eat lunch on campus, or care about being late to class. They were in high school, and as she scrolled through her social media account, she realized there was so much more happening outside the confines of the school yard. A world to be explored, people to meet, new things to experience. Charlotte felt so limited.

"I know, Emily!" snapped Charlotte as she finally looked up. "But aren't you tired of getting splinters from these worn out benches? And before you remind me again, I know I don't have a car!"

Emily looked to the sky, let out a sigh of disgust, and ending the conversation quickly mumbled, "We know, Charlotte. We all know."

The group silently turned to look at James, but before anyone could speak, James said defensively, "I'm not going to the mall. That's the last thing I want to do." James was the only one with a car and a license. The idea quickly died, and Charlotte went back to her salad. As she ate, her eyes drifted from her phone and she slowly scanned the students in the school yard, searching for anyone who could take her away for lunch.

As everyone took a deep breath and began to relax from the tension Charlotte created in yet another of her forceful rants, Peter arrived and walked straight up to Katie. Katie had just dropped her untouched pudding cup back into her lunch tote and prepared to take a selfie documenting today's unsatisfying lunch. Peter had a thing for Katie. To him, she was the most beautiful girl he knew, at school, in movies, in his entire life. He felt a slight leap inside his stomach every time he caught a glimpse of her. He wanted so badly to be with her, but Katie did not feel the same.

Peter crouched down, opening his mouth and eyes wide, to photo bomb her pic and then asked, "Hey, Katie, what's up?"

"Just eating lunch," she replied deleting the photo she just took. Katie was completely annoyed by Peter's feelings. As beautiful as she was, Katie definitely didn't see it. All she saw was flaws. She magnified them greatly in her imagination and believed everyone else saw the same. Her eyes were too big, cheekbones too small, face too round and no matter how many times she dyed her hair, it was never the right color. Every once in a while, she considered adding some blue to her hair, but ultimately, would never do it because of the unwanted attention it would attract to her.

"Do you want to go to the football game Friday night?" Peter blurted out.

Katie replied after putting her phone on the table and expelling a huge cleansing breath from her lungs, "No, not really." She found his question silly. Why didn't he see that she wasn't the least bit interested in him?

James was happy to extend an invitation to Peter. "We're all going to the game together. Do you want to come with us?"

In her mind Katie was silently hoping he would say no, but if he did go, she would at least have the cushion of the others around her and could avoid any awkward interaction with him. She quickly sent a group text to Charlotte and Emily with two words, "HELP ME!"

Emily responded, "harmless" with an angel emoji. Charlotte, was quick to follow up with two emojis, a diamond ring and a kiss. Katie was not amused, but all three girls giggled softly.

Although he was disappointed, Peter sat down next to Katie and began gnawing on a chicken leg left over from his dinner the night before. Yes, he would go to the game with the rest of the gang if it meant he could spend time with Katie.

Sidney was oblivious to Charlotte's complaining, Peter's courting of Katie, and Emily's keeping of the peace. He was still pretending he was fishing on a tuna boat on the high sea. Cold, pounding rain was impeding their progress and the mighty vessel was tossed about the waves. He looked skyward following the line of the main mast and discovered a lone crow perched at the top, completely unaffected by the wind or the dramatic back and forth sway of the mast. The crow let out a call that pierced the bubble of Sidney's imaginative world and brought him back to Earth where he noticed a black bird watching them from an oak tree high above their table.

"Wow! That's weird! Is that a raven? And what does he have in his mouth?" asked Sidney.

Emily knew it wasn't a raven, and was quick to correct. With lightning speed she searched for the bird on her phone. "That's not a raven. That bird is too small. See, it's a crow." She held up her phone and Sidney glanced at the screen, nodding in agreement.

Emily tapped a couple of times on the screen, then began to share what she considered to be interesting bits of information as her thumb quickly scrolled through a random site. "It says that crows are highly intelligent. They can recognize people and they share information to educate other crows in their communities. They let others know who they can trust and who they should be afraid of." She looked up from her phone. "It sounds like they're really quite fascinating creatures."

> **Balchazar:** *And this is my cue. Now it is time to introduce myself. I am going to teach my students that there is more to life than sandwiches, football games, phones and the mall. My students do not know how to think, or how what they think affects what happens in their lives. Most people believe they spend their day thinking, however, just because one has thoughts randomly rolling around in the mind does not mean one is thinking. Watch the excitement I am about to create.*

The crow flew down quickly from the branch of the oak tree and left a shiny object right in front of James before departing. Charlotte let out a shriek. She could feel the breeze created by the flapping wings as the crow flew by. The crow returned to the same branch in the oak tree and waited. "Sorry guys, I hate birds," said Charlotte. "They scare me."

Peter pulled the ear bud from his right ear. He looked at the shiny object in front of James and asked, "What is that?"

James had barely noticed the object; he was still stunned by the dive-bombing bird. He picked it up and slowly examined what appeared to be a coin. "I don't know. It might be valuable; it looks like it might be made of gold."

Emily grabbed the coin from James and flipped it from side

to side, checking out its intricate details. After a few minutes of staring she returned the coin to James, unpacked her laptop from her backpack and began to peck feverishly at the keyboard. While typing she questioned James, "Did you see the hole in the coin? Many countries in Asia and the Middle East use coins with holes in them. And did you notice the writing? That's not the Cyrillic alphabet."

However, before James could answer, Charlotte snatched the coin from him and softly bit it, hoping to see if it really was gold. Emily immediately knew what Charlotte was doing and said, "Biting is not a reliable test to determine if the coin is made of gold."

Not caring, Charlotte kept biting the coin, like she was nibbling on a cracker.

"It kind of resembles an old Indian coin," said James. "Sidney, do you remember last week in Geology, when Miss Tanner said we could get extra credit if we went to the antique exhibit at the museum?" Before Sidney could answer James continued, "I bet someone at the museum could tell us where this coin is from. I'm not convinced it's a coin though. Maybe it's a medal, or a prize from a competition, and the hole in the center was used to fasten it around the winner's neck."

"Maybe it's from an ancient decathlon or even Roman chariot races," added an excited Sidney. And Sidney was off in his imagination driving horses in a chariot race.

"Whoa, Whoa, Whoa, hold up there Sidney! It's only lunch time! Let's not get your imagination all hyped up this early in the day," mocked Peter. Sidney's over-active imagination often got him in trouble with his teachers. He was constantly getting called out for staring into space and drifting off during class. Peter was Sidney's lab partner in Chemistry this semester and was tired of paying the price of Sidney's lack of focus.

"Very funny," said a deflated Sidney. He knew Peter was popular and the only reason Peter chose him as a partner in Chemistry was because he excelled in science. Peter figured Sidney would do all the work getting easy A's for them both. But for some reason, whenever Sidney was in the lab and the burner was lit, his imagination took fire and he instantly saw himself as a mad scientist mixing formulas and causing mischief. He smiled to himself as he observed his imaginary lab inside his mind once again.

"Look! He's doing it again! He's off in another world! Sidney!" yelled Peter, "Come back to reality!" Peter started laughing as he made fun of Sidney, but inside his temper was rising. He was tired of Sidney's constant daydreaming messing up his plans.

"Okay, everybody calm down. We all know that no matter how much you yell, it's not going to change Sidney's hyper-active imagination," interrupted James. "Let's get back to the subject at hand. This coin, or medal, whatever it is. And the museum. Who wants to come to the museum with me after school?"

One by one everyone at the table said they would go, until only Peter was left. "Come on Pete, what do you say? Are you coming?" asked James.

"As long as I don't have to sit by him in the car!" Peter pointed to Sidney.

"Deal! I'll have Emily whip up a seating chart on her laptop before we leave," chimed James sarcastically, as he placed his hand on Sidney's shoulder and whispered in his ear, "Don't worry about Peter, I'll calm him down before we leave."

Sidney gave a weak smile and Charlotte rolled her eyes and joked, "Why don't we just have Peter ride in the trunk? That should solve the problem."

Peter feigned a fake look of hurt to Charlotte, but couldn't hold back from laughing. Katie and Emily giggled too and James spoke one last time with his hand still on Sidney's shoulder. "Then it's settled. We meet as soon as school is over. Don't be late." Then he eyed Katie, "Katie, that means you!"

"Whatever," sneered Katie. She stopped giggling and quickly picked up her books to leave. "I better hurry back to class so I'm not late," she quipped. No sooner had she left the table the bell rang, marking the end of their lunch break, and everyone joined her as she walked back to the building.

CHAPTER 2

ANCIENT COINS AND CURIOUS GIFTS

Peter was the first one out of class. He sprinted to the oak tree, hoping that Katie would get there before anyone else. Just thinking about a few short moments alone with her made his heart pound. Deep down Peter knew that Katie wanted nothing more than a friendship, but he pushed that feeling aside and began to visualize walking to class with her, hand in hand.

But today was not the day for Peter's dream to be realized. His thoughts were quickly interrupted as James and Emily approached, talking excitedly. As he watched them, his thoughts shifted to his best friend and his sister. "How can they be twins? They don't even look like they're related!" Peter muttered to himself.

Peter knew that fraternal twins do not look alike, but to him, siblings, let alone twins, should look somewhat similar. The only physical characteristic shared between the two was their dark brown hair, which was barely noticeable since James was now wearing his hair buzzed. James was a good six inches taller than Emily. And while his face was clear, Emily's was dotted with cute little freckles that made her look several years younger than her twin.

However, any physical differences between James and Emily were overshadowed by their uncanny ability to know exactly what the other was thinking, all the time! Peter thought this was the most amazing gift and loved to quiz his two friends and make sure their thoughts were in sync.

As they approached, Peter could tell they were talking about the coin. He yelled out to Emily sarcastically, "Hey Emily! Did you already read six books from the library on ancient coins?"

"Very funny," replied Emily, "And the answer is no, but I did manage to secretly use my phone to look at coins without getting caught during Algebra." Emily felt a little guilty for completely ignoring the lesson on absolute values, but knew Charlotte, the math genius, would help her if she had questions.

"I knew it!" Peter smirked. "Did you figure out where the coin came from?"

Before Emily could answer, she watched a distracted Sidney catch his shoe on a tree root, sending him shoulder first into Peter's chest. Sidney's phone flew through the air but Peter quickly reached out his hand and caught it the same way he would a fly ball in a baseball game. He looked at the screen and saw that Sidney had been watching a movie while he was walking.

Peter let his frustration of not being alone with Katie get the best of him, and took it out on Sidney, "Watch where you're going, Klutz! Why are you always off in another world?"

"Sorry, Peter," Sidney said, his eyes focused on the ground in embarrassment. He adjusted his horned rimmed glasses on his nose, reached out and grabbed his phone from Peter's hand, waiting for the focus of his friends to move onto someone else.

He was relieved when Charlotte arrived. "I'm here, who are we missing?"

Of course, Peter knew the answer, "Katie," he muttered softly. Peter felt a combination of discouragement and disappointment that Katie was the last to arrive. But here she came. He could spot her anywhere in a crowd. His heart immediately sank. Katie was talking to a guy, but he couldn't quite make out who it was.

"Oh no!" Peter groaned. It was Taylor, the captain of the

football team. Peter's face began to flush red with anger. "Why Taylor?" he asked himself. "Taylor can have any girl he wants. Why does he have to choose Katie?"

His internal dialogue was interrupted as Katie finished her conversation and joined the group. "What was that all about?" Peter asked a little too forcefully. As hard as he tried not to, he was letting his insecurities get the best of him. In an instant, he imagined Katie leaving the game Friday night, holding hands with Taylor, making his face redder by the minute.

His vivid, but negative, imagination was cut short when Katie answered, "He asked me out. He wants to take me to some new juice bar," she replied

"Are you going?" Peter was still turning red. He realized he was overstepping his bounds and revealing too much of his feelings for her. He quickly looked at his phone, hoping it would open and swallow him.

"I don't know, my parents are having some fancy dinner that same night, and they want me there. But I don't know why they want me there? I was thinking of doing something with Charlotte. Emily, what do you think? Do you want to join us?"

"Sure, but what are you going to do?"

"Don't worry," said Charlotte. "I'll come up with something so Katie doesn't have go to that boring dinner with her parents."

James was anxious to get to the museum. He didn't care what anyone was doing Wednesday night. He had his own agenda; the coin. "Who has the coin?" he asked.

"I do," replied Charlotte.

"Then let's go!" ordered James and the group headed to the parking lot and piled into his 2004 sedan. James inherited the car when his dad bought a new convertible. While he was grateful to have wheels, his eye was on the new ragtop. Now that was a car; his dad had gone all out when he purchased the new model. With no success, James asked his dad every day if he could drive it to school just once.

Tensions were running a little high, and no one spoke on the car ride to the museum. Emily had her nose in a book the entire drive. Peter was in the back seat behind Katie. He couldn't help but wonder why he'd never noticed how soft and shiny her hair is. Oh, how he wanted to reach out and touch it. But he refrained, knowing that would be weird, and draw way too much attention to his feelings.

With earbuds in, Charlotte heard only her favorite music, which is a bit too hard rock for everyone else. Katie was checking how many new likes she had on her latest posts.

Sidney was hungry, but instead of eating, he fired up his imagination. Dressed in a black tuxedo, he stepped out of a stretch limousine as the driver held the door for him. The walkway to the restaurant was roped off and flanked with beautiful women calling his name, all reaching out to touch him. He spotted a very tall blonde in a flowing red gown. As he approached her, he quickly removed and placed his glasses inside his breast pocket, offered the blonde beauty his arm, and escorted her into the steakhouse for what was sure to be a scrumptious dinner.

"Are you coming, Sidney?" asked James. He snapped back to reality to find they had arrived at the museum and he was the only one left in the car. He hurried out and avoided eye contact with Peter before he made another snide remark about his active imagination.

The museum was housed in a historic and sizeable brick building. The steps leading to the massive doors were flanked by a lion seated on each side. An oversized concrete railing provided a handhold for any who needed a little support climbing the steps. Emily was in awe of the building as she pondered all the information she would find inside. Charlotte and Katie weren't really paying much attention as they lagged behind.

Upon reaching the staircase, Charlotte jumped onto the rail, wrapped her arms around the neck of the lion and shouted to Katie, "Hey, take my picture with this lion!" Katie was happy to oblige. Of course, it didn't end there. Katie decided she needed a picture too. And finally, Charlotte stopped Sidney who was bringing up the rear. "Sidney, take a picture of me and Katie with this lion," she shouted. Without saying a word, Sidney took her phone, centered the shot and took the picture. He handed the phone back to Charlotte and leapt up the steps two at a time.

Inside the museum doors was a generic information booth

with a librarian like woman seated on a stool. She wore a plain white blouse with a bland museum-issued gray sweater that was draped across her shoulders. The glasses she wore were perched on the end of her nose and secured with a beaded strap. "Well here's something you don't see every day, teenagers in a museum. Can I help you kids find something?"

"Yes, please," answered James. "We're looking for someone who might help us identify a coin we found."

"A coin? Well, that sounds like something Mason could help you with. Take the elevator on your left to the third floor, turn right and you'll find our currencies of the world display, next to the ancient maps section. Ask for Mason Williams."

James thanked her and they took off for the elevator. Charlotte and Katie were so far behind that they entered the museum just in time to see the others disappear behind the elevator doors. When they arrived at the elevator they pressed the up button over and over, giggling and hoping it would speed up so they could catch up with the others.

Meanwhile, on the third floor, the elevator doors opened to reveal an ancient world of coins, paper money, medals, tokens, and maps. Sidney exited the elevator and immediately began to imagine himself at the US Treasury. He was wearing a green visor, had garters on his sleeves and a green apron with ink smears on it. The presses were rolling with page after page of freshly printed greenbacks flying off and nesting neatly into stacks.

James made the instructed right turn and walked to the tall man at the counter, "Hi, are you Mason?"

The young man quietly looked up from the artifact he was examining and placed his magnifying glass on the counter, "Yes, I'm Mason, can I help you?"

"Great to meet you. My name is James, this is my sister, Emily, and these are our friends. We found this coin. Well, we didn't actually find it. A crow dropped it right in front of me."

"A crow you say?" Mason asked.

"Yes, it was the strangest thing." James started to say.

"A black crow?" interrupted Mason.

"Yes, black," answered James. "Aren't all crows black?"

"Very interesting. Was there anything special about this crow?" asked Mason.

"Yes," responded a flustered James. "That's what I'm trying to tell you. We were eating lunch today and this bird..."

"The crow?" inserted Mason.

"Yes," snapped James, "A black crow landed right in front of me, dropped this coin, and immediately flew away." Although he was flustered at Mason's interruptions, James recounted the story without the slightest concern that Mason might consider him crazy.

After an awkward moment of silence, Mason spoke, "Yes, that is odd. But I believe I might be able to help you. May I examine the coin?" Mason extended his left palm to receive the coin from James. James began to dig in his pockets in search of it.

"Remember, James?" said Emily, "Charlotte has the coin." They both looked back to find Charlotte, but only saw Peter and Sidney, who was still printing money in his mind. Almost simultaneously the elevator chimed and its doors opened, revealing two giggling passengers, Charlotte and Katie.

"Charlotte! Over here!" yelled Peter, waving his hand, "James needs the coin."

Charlotte and Katie stepped out of the elevator and began to make the right turn to meet James and Emily at the counter. As she came around the corner, Katie stopped dead in her tracks. She stared at Mason, and was instantly in love. He was, tall, blonde, muscular and handsome, not at all like the boys at her high school, not at all like someone she would expect to be working inside a boring museum.

Mason was a graduate student. He worked at the museum as an intern while writing his doctoral thesis. He was highly intelligent, driven, and energetic. His genuine smile revealed his kind heart, but he had an aura of mystery about him. Katie couldn't put her finger on it, but there was something about him that created a feeling of intrigue. She was smitten. She couldn't move, frozen in time. Her eyes were focused, and her heart seemed to be beating outside her chest.

"Katie? Katie?" She snapped to when Peter jostled her. "Is something wrong?"

"No, no, nothing's wrong. Everything is very right," Katie replied in not more than a whisper. She immediately pushed her way past Charlotte, Peter and the rest of her friends, quickly running her fingers through her hair as she made her way to the counter. She no longer cared about the coin or what it meant. She intended to become very serious about things in the museum, especially its newest "attraction," Mason Williams.

When she arrived at the counter Katie introduced herself. As she shook Mason's hand she giggled flicking her hair over her shoulder.

Charlotte, pushed Katie aside and handed the coin to James, who then gave it to Mason. She immediately texted Katie. "Seriously? That was the most ridiculous come on I have ever seen!"

As her phone pinged Katie responded with three hearts and the words, "I love him!"

Charlotte looked at Katie, she was shocked. Here we go again she thought. Charlotte's phone vibrated and she picked it up to see the Shhh emoji with a finger over its lips.

Charlotte typed with disgust. "He's way too old for you!"

But when she looked up, Katie grabbed her hand and mouthed the word "please."

"Fine," whispered Charlotte. "But you owe me."

Katie squeezed her hand signaling she agreed. She leaned onto the counter to be as close to Mason as she could and certainly where he would notice her. She could not stop staring at him.

Charlotte rolled her eyes and looked around to see if anyone else was noticing Katie's embarrassing behavior.

Mason, like the rest of the group, was oblivious to Katie's best attempts to secure his attention. He rolled the coin from side to side with his fingers. He traced its engravings. After several minutes of his odd examination, the look on Mason's face turned from fascination to concern. "I've seen this coin before." Mason muttered under his breath as he stared in bewilderment at it. He raised his head and repeated slowly to James, "I've seen this coin before." He then began to have a conversation with himself, "Where did I... No! It can't be... It's not possible! Is it the same? I never considered he would work with others. It has to be him. It's not from school. It's not from the museum. But it just can't be. It must be. It looks identical."

Suddenly Mason stopped his conversation and rushed to the back of the room, where he began to recklessly rummage through his desk. He hastily pushed papers and curious looking artifacts aside, with some falling to the floor. He yanked open drawers and quickly slammed them shut, the entire time muttering under his breath "Where is it? I know it's here somewhere. Where did I put it?"

Without warning, he froze. His eyes focused on something buried inside one of the desk drawers. After what seemed like hours, Mason lowered both hands into the drawer, and retrieved a small wooden box no larger than his fist. Although the box appeared sturdy, he cradled it as if it were made of glass and would break at his touch. From a distance it appeared very simple, however, that was not the case. The lid had ornate, ancient-looking carvings, its corners were worn, but reinforced with brass and the front was adorned with a simple latch that had a well-worn patina which gave the appearance that the box hadn't been opened in years.

Everyone present was glued to Mason's every move. They stared intently as he conducted a meticulous examination of the box. Slowly raising it to his lips he blew a fine layer of dust from its top. Immediately Sidney imagined Mason as an archeologist handling a delicate treasure that had been hidden from the world for thousands of years.

However, Sidney was quickly brought back to reality as Mason touched a button and the latch clicked and lifted. Slowly, he opened the box. "What's in it?" whispered Charlotte, in a voice that no one heard but herself. And although he wasn't responding to her, Mason was now speaking in a hushed tone. They could see his lips moving but the sound was indistinguishable. The look on his face was a mixture of hope and disbelief.

His seriousness caused mixed reactions of curiosity and anticipation in the group. Charlotte grabbed Katie's hand again and was squeezing it hard enough to leave indentations from her fingernails. However, Katie was so focused on Mason that she didn't even notice the pressure on her hand. James was leaning up against the counter, an excited knot tightening in his stomach. Emily was desperately trying to read Mason's lips. Sidney's mouth was wide open in anticipation and Peter was quickly losing patience, aware that his frustration was once again turning his face red and fueling his temper.

Slowly Mason removed his right hand from the box and reached inside. He gripped something and when his fingers emerged they revealed a small, shiny object, but before anyone could catch a proper glimpse, the object reflected light from a nearby window. As the light hit the object, an extraordinary bright flash filled the room forcing everyone to shield their eyes.

The confusion caused by the flash of light awoke everyone from their trance. "What was that?" asked Katie.

"Maybe it was a power surge," James offered.

By this time Mason had returned to the counter. He picked up the coin that was lying in front of James. He then held up his right hand so the entire group could see what appeared to be a coin identical to theirs.

"This is amazing!" shrieked Emily. "He has a matching coin!"

"Let me see," chimed Peter.

Mason carefully examined the two coins. "These coins appear to be exactly the same in design and construction, only the symbols are different." But before he could continue, Charlotte let out a scream. Her eyes had drifted to the nearby window, where she noticed a black bird sitting on the ledge.

The bird cawed and Charlotte yelled, "That's the bird from lunch! The bird who gave us the coin! What's it doing here? Why's it following us?"

"Calm down, Charlotte!" snapped James. "It's just a bird. It's not going to hurt us."

"It's just a black bird," said Peter, as he instinctively stood in front of Katie acting as a shield between her and the bird. "Do you know how many black birds there are flying around? The chances of it being the same bird are astronomical."

"You don't know that!" yelled Charlotte. "I know what I saw. It's the same bird. I recognize it." Charlotte insisted.

"Whatever," Peter gave up any attempt to make her feel better.

Balchazar: *Indeed, Charlotte's observation is correct. They will all soon learn that it is I, Balchazar, the very same bird who* *gifted them their coin. Whether they like it or not, they have been chosen as my students, and will be seeing a lot of me in the near future.*

Mason stared calmly at the bird, and then began speaking to it softly. "Hello, old friend, I see the great teacher has chosen new students. You have led them to me for a reason. I'm forever in your debt. How can I help?"

"Hey!" screamed Charlotte. "He's talking to the bird. Why are you talking to that bird? Do you know this bird? You need to tell us what's going on, right now!"

"She's right!" agreed Katie. "I heard him. He's talking to the bird!"

Peter was staring at the bird. His intuition told him that Mason knew more than he was letting on; that he held the answers they wanted. "Mason, what do you know about this bird?" But his question was met with silence.

Charlotte was afraid the bird was going to come off the ledge and into the room where they stood. The window had no screen and was partially open. Peter was sensing there was much more than coincidence happening here, although he had no idea what it could be. Katie didn't care about any of it, she was plotting a way to get Mason to notice her. She pushed Peter aside so she could stand closer to Mason. Emily was surveying the situation, attempting to tune into the energy of curiosity and intrigue that filled the room. Sidney had gone to another world.

In Sidney's imagination, he was the psychiatrist in an asylum. His friends were all patients in this institution and he was the doctor studying their mental processes. He wore a white coat and carried a clipboard to note his observations. Mason was his subject. He wanted to hypnotize him and explore his mind. Maybe Mason had past lives that connected him to the coin and the bird. Maybe he had gone mad in his relentless study of history. Perhaps the reappearance of the bird took him to a world in which he was alone and there was no escape. Sidney's mad psychiatrist self had an evil laugh. Mwah, ha, ha, he laughed over and over in his mind.

They were all thinking the same thing, all but Sidney that is. "This is crazy!" They looked at each other awkwardly but no one dared speak, everyone was waiting for Mason. James could feel the curiosity escalating among his friends. Although he really wanted to hear about the coin, he knew that he had to quickly get the situation under control, or the chaos in the room would escalate. In an attempt to refocus everyone, he walked over to Mason, placed his hands on his shoulders, looked him in the eyes and said, "Mason, please. We need answers. What's the meaning of the coin? What does this bird have to do with anything? And why are you talking to it?"

All eyes turned to Mason and they waited for a response. Mason removed James' hands from his shoulders and walked back to the counter where he picked up both coins. He motioned for the group to follow him into the next room which contained a round table surrounded by large wooden chairs. It appeared the room was set up to hold small discussions while examining artifacts, as there was a magnifying glass on the table, bookcases full of books, and reference materials scattered about. "We can talk in here."

Mason closed the door behind them and started to speak. "What I have to share with you is definitely unusual, and you may not want to hear it or believe it. But please hear me out." He held up the coin he had retrieved from his box. "I found this coin when I was a kid. You can see, it looks like the coin you were gifted today. This coin came to me in circumstances similar to what you described. I found my coin buried in the back yard, standing next to it was a lone, black crow. I didn't believe it had any significance. I thought my dad had put it there for me to find during one of my archeological digs when I was playing. But he didn't. The discovery of this coin turned out to be the most important moment of my life. It led me on an adventure that brought me significant self-discovery and growth. I believe it will soon do the same with you."

"James, your coin," he continued, "has writing on it indicating the six divinely-given mental faculties that everyone possesses. He held up the coin and pointed to the symbols. "They read 'Intuition, Imagination, Will, Perception, Memory and Reason.' This coin dates back to Babylonian times. It's not a coin in terms of currency. It serves as a token or a reminder. The Babylonians understood the depth of the mind and the power each person holds in their thoughts. They knew any person could use these six faculties to create the life they want, that a person could "think" events into happening."

"Oh, come on! What are you talking about? You don't really expect us to believe that, do you?" asked Katie. Both James and Emily turned and gave her a dirty look with eyes that shut her up. Immediately she wished she hadn't opened her mouth. She wanted Mason to notice her, to want to be with her, she wanted time alone with him to get to know him. But now, she wanted to be invisible.

Mason responded with patience, "As a man thinketh in his heart, so is he. If you understand and remember this principle, everything you desire will come to you." No sooner did he finish that thought, his phone rang. "Hold on, I need to take this call, but I'll be back. I want to tell you about the crow. Just wait here, please." Mason quietly walked out of the room, closing the door behind him.

"What in the world is he talking about?" Emily asked James.

"I'm not sure. But it seems that this is no ordinary coin. It's quite fascinating actually," James replied. Emily had already pulled out her phone and was searching 'powers of the mind' and 'ancient Babylonians.'

"Well, I find this quite scary and creepy," Charlotte chimed almost in song.

Sidney, was in his own world. It seemed that every new object he saw caused his imagination to run wild. Standing in front of a small cabinet, he made a discovery. "Hey, you guys, come look at this."

"What is it?" Emily asked.

"There are six wrapped boxes, gifts, and they have our names on them." Sidney explained.

"What?" Katie asked as she jumped out of her seat and rushed around the table to meet Sidney at the cabinet.

Sidney pointed to the shelf where the boxes sat. There were indeed six meticulously wrapped boxes of varying size and shape on the center shelf of the cabinet. "They're beautiful," said Katie. "Look at the detail." Some were decorated with glitter, others had brightly colored creative designs, and all had exquisite ribbon tied around them. And as Sidney stated, each box bore a tag with one of their names. And in this cabinet were no other items at all, just the boxes.

Katie was stunned at the discovery. She stared into the cabinet asking herself all the obvious questions. "Where did these come from? How did our names get on them? How did they know we'd be at the museum today? Are we dreaming? I don't get it." she said out loud.

Charlotte joined Katie and Sidney at the cabinet. "Wow, those are the most beautiful boxes I've ever seen." The lighting inside the cabinet gave the gifts a unique aura and beauty, similar to the sparkle and shine experienced when looking at diamonds at a jewelry store. "Let's open them!"

"Wait a minute, is that really a good idea?" James asked. "We don't know if they're really for us, or…." His question dropped off as Charlotte had already opened the cabinet door and pulled out the gifts placing them on the table in the center of the room. For a moment they all sat in their chairs staring at the boxes. They continued to glisten just as they had in the cabinet, but now there was no light shining on them as before.

Charlotte was the first to pick up her gift. Her name was written in beautiful calligraphy. She felt special seeing her name in this script. The tag sparkled and glowed. It seemed magical. On the back of it was this phrase, "Breakthroughs are made by violating logic." As she read the sentence out loud she angrily said, "What does that mean?"

Balchazar: *What that means is that sometimes to solve a problem or get what one wants, one must do the illogical. Sometimes we talk ourselves out of taking the next appropriate step because it appears to be illogical. But the answer is always inside you. You have everything you need to achieve what you want. However, if you want to make a breakthrough, and achieve great things, violate logic.*

By the way, it is I who has provided these tremendous gifts. They are super powers. Pay attention as each opens their gift, see if you can determine which mental faculty is favored by the individual student, and then hold on! Things are about to get interesting!

The group was awestruck. Nobody knew what any of it meant. Curiosity was eating at Charlotte, she removed the ribbon and looked inside the box. She didn't say a word as she peered inside. She seemed even more confused than before removing the lid.

"What is it?" Emily wanted to know.

"Keys. It's a set of old keys," Charlotte replied. They were like skeleton keys, not the type of modern-day keys she was used to seeing. They were made of sterling silver and polished brightly. There were six keys on a simple black cord. "I don't get it, not even a little," said Charlotte. She carefully lifted the keys out of the box. As she did, something amazing happened. When she held the keys, she experienced a feeling of control. It was a calm and smooth control, not the forceful control she normally felt trying to assert herself by picking fights and creating arguments. She felt calm, collected and confident. She felt empowered. Charlotte quickly shook off the feeling and dropped the keys back into the box.

"Someone else open their box!" demanded Charlotte. They all looked at each other not wanting to be next. But Emily mustered the courage and removed the box with her name on the tag. Written on the back, in the same cursive style, was the phrase, "Everyone has a perfect memory."

"I see what you mean, Charlotte. This phrase doesn't mean anything to me. Why would it tell me everyone has a perfect memory?" Emily was confused. But something inside her compelled her to open the box, so she removed the lid. Inside was a writing quill. She lifted it from the box and pretended to write with it. Of course, there was no result. She just sat and stared, her mind trying to make sense of everything that was happening.

Charlotte took the lead. "Peter, open yours."

Peter picked up his box, gave it a little shake, and shifted it around in his hands looking at all the sides.

The phrase on the back of his tag read, "Nothing is impossible." He had no words, he uttered a dumbfounded, "Huh?" No one had an answer for him. They shook their heads. He untied the ribbon on the box and opened the lid to discover a locket. It was a beautiful silver locket.

Charlotte couldn't resist the urge to laugh. "Ha, you got a

necklace. Oh, you should definitely wear that. Katie, don't you agree he needs to accessorize? Go ahead. Put it on."

Peter tried to ignore her, but was embarrassed by his gift and Charlotte's harsh comment. There was an inscription on the outside of the locket, but it seemed to be in a foreign language, like Latin or Aramaic, or maybe it was Babylonian. He had no idea what it said. He tried to open it to reveal the photo he expected to see inside. But it wouldn't open. No amount of pressure helped. "Well, this is broken. I have no use for this. Katie, would you like to have it?" he asked.

"No, thank you. What would I do with a locket that won't open?" She didn't want a necklace from Peter anyway. The smallest opening she made for him could leave her vulnerable to his advances, and she would be certain that never happened.

By now the curiosity was so built up in Sidney's mind that he jumped at the opportunity to examine the box bearing his name. On the back of the gift tag he read, "If you can see it in your mind, you will hold it in your hand." He tore off the lid and pulled out a crystal orb. Nothing else, just the sphere which he cupped in the palm of his trembling hand. He stared into the orb. And for a split second he saw a flash inside the globe. "Did you see that?" he asked excitedly. "I saw a flash! Did you see that?"

But no one had seen anything. Sidney couldn't take his eyes off the ball. His mind was asking all sorts of scientific questions. Was it a light refraction? Was it a bolt of lightning? Was it an electrical current running through the ball? Then it happened again. There was a small, brief flash of light and Sidney saw it clearly this time. "Did you see that? It happened again! It was lightning, flashing in all directions! It only lasted for a second, but I saw it. I saw it perfectly." It didn't occur to him at all that he had also seen the flash in his mind.

Ignoring Sidney's question, Charlotte said, "James, you're up, open yours."

James wasn't sure that any of this was appropriate. Where was Mason? Why couldn't they have just discovered the facts about the coin and left the museum. But something inside him pushed him to the table and forced him to retrieve the gift addressed to him. The tag read, "Go as far as you can see. When you get there, you will see how you can go farther." Emily recognized that quote from Thomas Carlyle. Of course, she pointed it out.

What James pulled from the box with his name resembled a spyglass. When Peter saw how unique it was, he was jealous. James held the glass to his eye and saw nothing but black, not even a speck of light shone through the lens. "It seems to be broken," James said. "There's no light passing through it."

Peter believed he could solve the problem. "Are you sure? Turn the focus and see if that helps."

James did as Peter instructed, and indeed, the light came though just enough to make out a blurry image. He wasn't sure what he was looking at, or in which direction he had pointed the glass. He lowered it from his face, looked at the area in which he had pointed the spyglass, and then returned the glass to his face aligning it with his eye. For a split second he could make out the image. It was the cabinet that housed their gifts, but it didn't look the same. The old antique cabinet from which they had retrieved their presents, looked different through the lens of the spyglass. It now appeared to be made of gold. No sooner did he make the connection than the image was gone.

"Whoa!" exclaimed James rocking back in his chair. "This is insane. This can't be real. Has something happened to us?"

No one understood the comments. "James what is it?" Emily asked of her brother.

"When I looked the second time through the glass, I knew I was looking at the wood cabinet. But it didn't look the same as it does to the naked eye. It looked like it was made of gold. Something's not right. I don't know what it is, but that cabinet is definitely not made of gold."

Katie was the only one left. She didn't want to touch the box. She was incredibly uneasy, wanted to leave the museum, and secretly wished she had never come. But after a bit of cajoling she picked up the last box on the table. "Once you make a decision, the Universe conspires to make it happen," read the tag on her gift. Katie was in a bit of a fog. Decision? The universe conspires? That didn't sound good in her mind.

When the lid to the box was removed, Katie saw a small set

of scales. The scales teetered back and forth coming into balance. They were simple scales void of any markings at all. Katie dangled them from her thumb and two fingers watching them come into balance. She just stared. Nothing made any sense to her. Once the scales were balanced, she placed them on the table in front of her. Of course, because of the movement, they began to teeter again very quickly coming into balance. "You know you guys; I don't have a clue what's going on here. But I have no desire to stay in this museum. Something isn't right. Let's just go!"

Balchazar: *Careful, Katie. Thoughts are things. You will soon learn you have the power to create the results you want by carefully choosing the thoughts you think.*

Before Katie could finish her sentence, the scales began to teeter. How could that be? The scales were empty, there was nothing on either side to create any weight. She hadn't touched them. No one had, all she did was feel that something wasn't right, and then want to leave. But the scales teetered nonetheless.

The room began to rumble, and it felt like an earthquake beneath their feet. Charlotte screamed. Katie ran for the door. Emily followed. Lightning struck, once! Twice! And Boom! As Dorothy said, "Toto, I don't think we're in Kansas anymore."

CHAPTER 3

MISSION POSSIBLE

Before they could even ask what was happening, they found themselves inside a library. The scent of old books made the air musty and stale. The room had layer upon layer of wood, from the floor to the ceiling, and on every shelf in site. The shelves were lined with thousands of books stretching from floor to ceiling. Everything appeared to be in perfect order, as if each book had been meticulously placed. All four walls featured a rolling ladder which gave access to books located high above, just inches away from the coffered ceiling.

Emily was standing next to one such ladder, surrounded by some of the oldest first editions she had ever encountered: Shakespeare, Dickens, Emerson and Thoreau. Staring at the books, it was as if she'd been placed under a spell. Her brain was on overload as her eyes scanned the selection. She slowly stepped onto the ladder and began to climb, finally stopping and running her fingers across the spine of a compilation of works by Edgar Allan Poe.

Charlotte's squealing broke the silence, "What just happened?

Where are we? Look! What are we wearing? Somebody do something!"

Katie quickly scanned the room and was shocked by the Victorian-era clothing everyone was wearing. She concluded she must be dreaming. Realizing it was a dream, she relaxed and gazed at her billowing skirt. She ran her hands down her waist. The tight laces of her corset limited her ability to breathe in fully, but she didn't care, this clothing made her feel tiny. Katie quickly began to search for a mirror to admire herself more closely. As she moved, the stiff crinoline held out her skirt and caused it to sway back and forth in an exaggerated manner, as if she was dancing. For once she liked the way she looked.

Sidney's imagination immediately kicked into full gear. Finding himself dressed in period daywear, he pulled slightly at the wide collar. The sleeves of his frock coat were long and tight, unbuttoned to reveal the velvet waistcoat beneath. His trousers were so high waisted he believed them to be too large for his frame, but soon realized they were perfect in fit and length. The only thing that wasn't a perfect fit was the top hat perched on his head. It was too big, causing him to peer out from under its brim to see, like it was a visor. "I can't even be cool in my imagination," thought Sidney.

"Is everyone all right?" James questioned, quickly glancing at the group to ease his mind. They were together and in one piece. "Where are we?"

"No! We're not okay, can't you see that? What's the matter with you, James?" barked Charlotte. "You need to do something, and right now. This is not okay! Get us out of here!"

"Well, clearly we aren't at the museum," snapped Katie. "I knew I shouldn't have gone with you guys. Charlotte and I are going out tonight, so someone better figure out how to get us out of here," Katie glared at a visibly angry Peter. However, for some reason, her glare seemed to calm him.

"Wait, you mean this isn't a figment of my imagination?" questioned Sidney. "This is really happening? I thought I made this up? Where are we?" Sidney continued rambling and appeared more confused by the second. He performed a quick check of the many pockets he now had and exclaimed nervously, "My phone is gone! Where's my phone?"

His announcement caused the rest of the group to pat their pockets in search of their electronic devices. But the results were the same. No one in the group could find a phone. "What am I supposed to do without my phone?" yelled an upset Charlotte. "How are we going to get out of here?"

Emily didn't care about her clothing, her lack of a phone, the fact that she had no idea where she was, or how she arrived. She returned her focus to the books and was soon oblivious to the chaos below. After selecting a book from one of the top shelves and running her hands over its smooth leather cover, she opened it and flipped through its pages. All of a sudden, the quill she was gifted at the museum fell from the bindings of the book in her hands and floated softly to the floor. Staring in disbelief, she scurried down the ladder and yelled out to James, "Look! It's my quill from the museum."

Standing at the fireplace James yelled out at the same time, "Emily, look! My spyglass, it's here on the mantle." Thinking out loud, James voiced to the group, "I think I see what's going on here. Quick! Everyone, look for your gift from the museum because…"

"There's a connection, I know it." said Emily, finishing James' sentence.

James smiled at his sister's uncanny ability to read his mind, then tucked the spyglass into his deepest breast pocket. Peter needed to find his locket. Now he wished he had put it around his neck. Katie went in search of the scales. Sidney looked for his crystal ball, imagining that once found he could look in it and see the solution to their problem. In his mind, he was now in charge. He would find the answer they sought. He'd show everyone that he wasn't just a dreamer, he'd get them out of this place.

Katie found her scales on the bottom shelf of a sofa table. She was astonished. "James! I found my scales. There's still nothing on them, but they aren't balanced. I think there's something wrong with them. They're definitely broken."

James had no reply, but Emily spoke for him, "Katie, remember what happened just before we saw the lightning crash? The scales started out perfectly balanced, but when you put them on the table, they began to teeter. Are they teetering now?" Emily hopped off the ladder and picked up her quill from the floor. Soon, the memory of the chaotic events at the museum began to play in a loop over and over in her mind. Each time the loop repeated, the memory became more detailed. Although she hadn't made the connection, Emily was remembering while holding the quill in her hand.

"No, they're perfectly still," Katie stared at the scales, wondering if they would start moving again. She didn't want to touch them for fear of what might happen next.

"But somehow they did teeter just before the lightning," recounted Emily with the confidence of a scientist making a grand discovery. "And Sidney, did you say that you saw a flash of lightning in your crystal ball?"

"Yes," Sidney replied with great hesitation. He could see where Emily was going with this train of thought. He was about to be blamed for the predicament they faced.

"Sidney, find your crystal ball. Look in it. You might find a clue." Emily urged him on without any judgment. Sidney took to his search with all diligence, staying in the moment instead of picturing himself on a quest.

"James, do you see what I see? You're right. There's a connection between the gifts we received at the museum and our arrival at this library. I'm certain of it." With that final thought, Emily replaced the quill in a tiny book from the shelf and tucked it into a hidden pocket in her gown.

Balchazar: *I am very proud of my students, for they are dealing with this situation exceptionally well. Emily is indeed quite intelligent. She is correct in using her gift of memory to piece together events and correlations from the museum. However, even though her connections are accurate, they are incomplete.*

There is more to this transportation than Emily realizes. Soon enough she will learn how to use her memory. When she does, she will free her mind, her focus will expand, and connections will be made. But I do not want to spoil this for you. Let us return to the library and see where they take this.

"Okay, guys, this is getting creepier by the moment," said Charlotte. "I'm getting out of here. Follow me, I'll get us out of this mess. I'm sure the museum is just outside these double doors." Charlotte was convinced she had the right idea. She marched to the sliding double doors that confined them to the library. Reaching for the door handles she recognized the simple, black cord attached to the sterling silver keys she received at the museum. Quickly drawing back her hands, she pointed at the keys with her left hand, covering her gasping mouth with her right hand, "Oh my gosh, you guys, look! The keys I got at the museum are here in the lock of this door."

Katie came over and tried to open the doors, but they wouldn't budge. She forced with all her strength to turn the keys in the lock, but nothing happened. She tried again, jiggling the key with all her might. "Ugh. They're locked! We can't get out!" She whirled around in dramatic style causing her skirt to twist and turn about her.

"Peter, where's your locket?" James asked. He was taking inventory in his mind of all the gifts.

"I haven't found it yet," replied a worried Peter.

"Here's the crystal ball, but I don't see anything in it right now." Sidney had discovered the orb sitting alone on a silver tea tray strategically placed on the same sofa table where Katie found the scales. Sidney pocketed the ball.

"Everyone help Peter find his locket," James issued the order firmly but kindly. The entire group looked high and low. Charlotte dropped to the floor and looked under the furniture. She was unfamiliar with the workings of the crinolines under her gown and they popped up revealing the pantalets she wore beneath. She didn't even know enough to be embarrassed. However, a quick acting Katie dashed over and held them down to preserve Charlotte's modesty.

After several minutes of not being able to find the locket, the frustration level was high. "All right, let's be calm. Emily, do you remember anything else about the events leading to the lightning?" questioned James. "Do you have any idea where the locket could be? Does anyone have any idea?" James was sure if they thought hard enough someone would have the answer.

"No, I don't remember anything else," Emily was disappointed she didn't have an answer for her brother.

"In that case, one of two scenarios is at play here. First, the locket is not in this room, or second, the locket doesn't matter," James was trying to figure it all out.

"But it has to matter," chimed Katie. "Think about it. Why would the other gifts be here, but not the locket? Why would Peter's gift be the only one missing?"

"Good question," Peter's eyebrows creased together.

"Do you remember the quote you received with the locket?" asked James.

"Um, maybe, let me think… Oh yeah, something about nothing is impossible." Peter was pretty proud of himself bringing it to mind even though he couldn't remember the phrase word for word.

"Okay, maybe that's a clue. Peter's locket is missing and nothing is impossible." James was trying to put the pieces together. Maybe it meant nothing at all. But what else did they have to go on?

Emily's mind began to pick up where James' left off. "I see where you're going with this James. What if the answer to getting home is in the missing locket? And what if the message on the locket is what we need to figure out what's going on?"

"That's exactly what I'm thinking!" James was pleased to know his thoughts were in sync with his sister's.

But Charlotte wasn't having any of it. "Oh, come on! You guys are grasping at nothing here. I'm telling you if we can just get out these doors, we'll be back at the museum."

Katie returned to the sofa table to retrieve the scales. As her eyes fell on the scales, her mouth dropped open, she lowered herself to the bottom shelf and stared. "Look you guys. The scales are in balance. How did they do that?" Katie was stunned. She slowly, carefully picked up the scales watching for them to teeter, but they didn't move. She carefully placed them securely in the hidden pocket in her gown. She was beginning to think something magical was happening. Yet at the same time she was afraid to breathe.

They all ran to the double doors where Charlotte was waiting to lead them back to reality. She was convinced she had the answer. "How are we going to get out, Charlotte? The doors are locked," Katie reminded her.

Charlotte put her hand on the keys and felt a warm, soothing calmness move up her arm and fill her entire body. She'd been holding her breath in anticipation and with a huge exhale she turned the key in the lock and slid open the doors to reveal their exit. As she opened the doors, she felt a calmness, almost a power, that she'd never experienced in her life. She was confident as she stepped outside the library, fully expecting to see the museum. No one followed her.

"What do you see, Charlotte?" asked Emily.

Balchazar: *Now this is an interesting situation. Emily has just asked the newly calmed Charlotte what she sees, however, what she should be asking is "What do you feel?" My students will learn, hopefully sooner than later, that it is their thoughts, amplified by their accompanying feelings, that cause their results, both good and bad.*

"Well, it's definitely not the museum. I see a foyer, a huge staircase and people dressed like us. Hmmm, I don't get it. I thought for sure we'd be in the museum if we could just walk through those doors." Charlotte didn't know what to think of this. "James, this is all your fault. If you hadn't wanted to find out about that stupid coin."

"Let me see," barked Katie, and she pushed past Charlotte and stepped outside the library. "Whoa, this is bizarre. But look at all these fabulous outfits. Do you think this is for real? Did we really go back in time, or are these actors?"

The rest of them stepped out of the library and into the foyer. As they closed the doors leading to the library, a stocky, buxom woman came hurrying up to Charlotte and grabbed her by the arm. "There you are my dear. The string quartet is ready to play, but they can't start without you." As the hostess carted Charlotte off, she glanced at the group over her shoulder with a look of disbelief. No one went after Charlotte, and no one said a word.

They watched in stunned silence as Charlotte was handed a violin and they tuned their instruments. The quartet began to play and Charlotte's fingers danced on the instrument making the most beautiful music. She played with them as though she had been doing it all her life.

James voiced out loud what he was thinking inside, "I'm sure she's perfectly safe. They just want her to play in the orchestra. While Charlotte is occupied, we can split up and find the locket. If you find it, whistle and we'll get out of here."

Heads nodded in agreement. "We can do that," answered an excited Peter. "C'mon, let's find my locket!"

James and Emily stayed together and headed up the wide staircase to explore the mansion. Perhaps the locket was in a jewelry box in an upstairs bedroom.

"I don't like this, James," whispered Emily. "What if we get caught? What if they think we're stealing? This scares me."

"We have to do something. We've got to figure this out. Nothing's going to happen. We'll find the locket and be done with all of this." James was confident on the outside, but really unsure of what was to come on the inside. There was no guarantee that finding the locket would secure their way home.

Without a conscious thought, Peter began to act as if he was supposed to be there. He put on his best, most casual saunter, extended his arm to Katie and together they headed out into the foyer. Katie didn't really want to go with him, but what other choice did she have? There was only Sidney left, and she certainly wasn't going to hang with him. She looked back and realized that Sidney was no longer in the library. He hadn't gone upstairs with James and Emily. "Where did Sidney go?" she asked Peter, "He's not with us."

Peter chided, "I don't care where he is. He's probably under the desk, curled up in the fetal position daydreaming about the locket instead of trying to help us find it. Don't worry about him. He'll be fine."

"Haven't you noticed Peter, we're already in an imaginary world." Katie had no patience, but also no clue what she should do. Her only choice was to walk arm in arm with Peter. She decided to make the best of it.

They could hear the sounds of muffled voices, laughter, and music. There was a party going on. People were buzzing around like bees. Some were carrying trays of food, others had drinks, but everyone was wearing white gloves for serving. "Man, I just realized that I'm starving. I hope this party has some good food," moaned Peter. "If not, this is going to be really boring."

Peter and Katie synchronized their steps and walked across the foyer to yet another closed door. Katie lifted her hand for silence, placed her ear to the door, and listened briefly before turning the knob.

Katie heard muffled voices. Mustering all her courage, she turned the knob and pushed the door open. She didn't see anyone immediately, even though she could tell there was activity. Katie had opened the door to the kitchen. She stepped inside as though she was meant to be there. Peter closed the door behind them and a uniformed man came rushing up to shoo them out. "What are you doing in here? You'll be served in the garden or on the veranda. Out!"

"Please forgive me," Katie replied with a curtsey. "I need to find…. um, I was looking for…. I don't know how to say…."

"Oh, never mind then. I'll take you to the chamber pot. And you sir, OUT!" yelled the uniformed man.

The man escorted Katie to the bathroom while almost simultaneously pushing Peter out another door. Peter found himself at the side of the house. He popped a handful of tiny sandwiches in his mouth that he swiped from a tray on his way out of the kitchen. Soon he became concerned about his separation from Katie. However, the more he thought about it, the more he didn't care. He said to himself, "look at how great this place is," as he slowly walked away from the house.

A short distance away Peter could see a group of men and women laughing and playing croquet. The men were smoking cigars, and the women were gossiping about all sorts of things, making up stories just to be part of the conversation. Peter reached deep for courage and slowly began the short walk to join them.

Back inside the mansion, James and Emily opened the last bedroom door and slipped inside. "This is the last room to search. Let's be quick, but don't overlook anything." James was losing all hope of finding the locket in the house.

"James, this room looks like it belongs to the lady of the house." Emily was impressed with the ornate décor. "If we're going to find the locket, I bet it's in here."

James was seated at the dressing table systematically searching through each drawer.

Emily approached one of the two large armoires and carefully opened the doors to look inside. When she did, she was met with a scream. It frightened her and she screamed too. James jumped up from the dressing table.

"Sidney! What are you doing in there?" asked Emily, half whispering and half yelling at him.

"I was looking around and I heard footsteps. Rather than be caught in the room, I hid in this cabinet."

"Sidney, that was us you idiot! And you scream more like a girl than Emily!" James was concerned the hostess was alerted to their unwanted presence upstairs. "We've got to get out of here now," he urged them toward the door.

"But what about the locket?" asked Emily.

"I don't think it's here," said a disappointed James. There was a small velvet jewelry box on the dressing table. He opened it and saw several pieces in it, not one of which was the locket. "Hurry up, before we're caught."

James opened the door, saw no one and left the bedroom. As they headed down the stairs, there were a number of guests ascending, tipping their hats as they passed. James could feel his heart beating in his chest. "Man, that was too close for comfort."

With James on her right, and Sidney on her left, Emily walked through the foyer and straight out the front doors onto the veranda. She breathed a big sigh of relief to be outside. Sidney didn't have a clue. But what else was new? Sometimes Emily wondered if Sidney had any common sense at all.

The trio stood on the veranda surveying the grounds. The plantation was enormous and beautiful, with acres and acres of trees, shrubs, and flowering gardens. The weather was the perfect temperature with a warm, blue sky above.

Everywhere they looked they saw groups of people. There was

archery, croquet, music, and even a game of chess on a lawn table. Some were seated in conversation areas designated for sipping tea or brandy. There was talk and chatter everywhere. People were laughing and having fun. It should be easy to mingle, enjoy the party and find the locket.

"Okay, here we go," instructed James. "Just mingle, act as if we're supposed to be here, and we'll fit right in. There's a ton of people, so there's no way anyone can know every single person. Remember, we're looking for the locket so we don't have to be in one place for a long time. Just keep moving."

Emily was perfectly content to follow James. She wasn't convinced that this was the safest place, but she trusted her brother's judgment. They started down the steps of the veranda gazing from side to side, each one wondering where they should look first.

Meanwhile, Katie had returned from the bathroom and rejoined Peter. The two made their way to the group playing croquet. Without even thinking about it, Katie latched onto Peter's arm, holding it even tighter than before. She was letting her nerves get the best of her. She felt a little more secure at his side as they joined the cheerful onlookers. Peter had that jumping feeling in his stomach again. This was so much better than him imagining Katie holding his hand on the way to class. He wanted to puff out his chest and yell to the world that Katie was holding onto his arm.

The women watching the game were beautifully dressed in elaborate gowns. They raised parasols high above their heads to shield the noonday sun. Katie was fascinated by the fashion. She had already discovered the function of the pantalets and wondered how in the world these women bore the weight of all this tight-fitting clothing all day. In spite of it, she rather enjoyed the idea of hanging out with the debutants at the croquet game.

As they quickly scanned all the women present, they noticed that every woman there was wearing a locket of some type. "That's odd," thought Katie. "Peter," she whispered, "Do you see that everyone here is wearing a locket? How are we going to know which is yours?"

"If any of them are mine," Peter whispered back. Right now, Peter didn't care if they ever found the locket, as long as Katie was still next to him and holding tightly to his arm. He whispered, "How are we supposed to take the locket if we do find it?" This task seemed more impossible as time advanced.

"Oh well," thought Peter, not even waiting for Katie to respond. And he quickly threw his inhibitions out the window and walked right into the midst of the group and began to speak in what he assumed was appropriate language for whatever era of which they were now a part.

"Good day ladies and gentlemen. My name is Peter Westbrook and this is Katie, I mean Katherine, I mean Miss Wilding."

Katie immediately stiffened against the idea that these people would think she was with Peter. But there was nothing she could do about it; she was still too nervous to release his arm. She would not concern herself with it now, but would certainly let him know how she felt about it at her first opportunity.

Hats tipped and curtseys prevailed as the two newcomers were politely welcomed to the group. Conversation resumed among those present. They were discussing croquet, skill level, winners and losers. They placed friendly wagers and stopped every so often when they heard the sound of a mallet hitting a ball. Although Peter nodded his head in agreement, he wasn't listening. The only thing on his mind was finding his locket. And Katie of course.

At the other end of the grounds, James and Emily considered where to look for the locket. "You know, I'm not sure which way we should go first. This place is so big and there are so many people. How are we going to keep track of where we've searched?" James was attempting to come up with a methodology that would be precise and ensure the locket was found.

"I don't know, either. Everyone is moving around too much. If they'd just hold still this would be so much easier. I wish we could just freeze time. Even though she insisted they keep looking, Emily doubted they would find the locket.

"Why don't we start with that group of people at the archery competition? Then we can try the group seated around the chess set, and after that we can check out the crowd next to the stables," suggested James.

"Wait, James!" exclaimed Emily. "How could I have missed this? Where is your spyglass? Look through it and maybe you'll be able to see who is wearing the locket."

"Great idea, Emily," chimed Sidney. "And, there's no sense in going over to the archery competition, it's all men over there. I doubt they will be wearing the locket."

Sidney was right. James quickly removed the spyglass from his breast pocket where he had placed it earlier. As he looked through it he informed the group, "I'm not seeing the locket, but there's no need to go to the chess area either. I don't see a single woman over there."

"What are you talking about?" asked Emily. "We must be looking at two different chess games. The game I'm looking at has two handsome guys who are surrounded by beautiful women."

"Actually, there's only one group of people playing chess," corrected Sidney. "And there are definitely women in that group."

James verified with Emily and Sidney that they were indeed looking at the same group of people, then put the spyglass back to his eye. "No guys, you're wrong. There are no women at the chess game."

Sidney spoke softly, "So we see women at the chess game and you only see men?"

"Yes," said James. "Whether I look with my naked eye or through the spyglass, I see only men."

"Wait!" yelled Emily with an excited tone of discovery in her voice. "Look at the man playing chess. Am I crazy, or does that guy look like Mason from the museum?"

"No," said James. "He definitely does not look like Mason."

"Yes, Emily, he does!" shouted Sidney. "And look, perched on the chair next to him is a black bird. I bet it's that same bird that gave us the coin."

Emily grabbed Sidney's hand and squealed with excitement, "Quick, let's go talk to him. I bet he can help us find the locket."

Sidney stood motionless. He had never held a girl's hand before. What was this strange sensation that was now traveling through his nervous system? It was as if lightning was striking over and over underneath his skin. He pictured himself strolling next to a lake, hand in hand with Emily. He told jokes and she giggled as she cozied up next to him. But the coziness was washed away by the sound of James' voice.

"No," insisted James. "That's not what I see. It's a group of overweight men sitting around the chess table. I don't see anyone who looks like Mason."

"Why are we seeing different people?" questioned Emily.

"I don't know," replied a frustrated James. "But remember at the museum when the spyglass changed my view of the cabinet our gifts were in from wood to gold? There's something about this gift that allows me to see things differently than everyone else."

"This just doesn't make sense. I'm looking at these people with my own eyes." Emily doubted what James said he saw through the spyglass, "Let me see."

To Sidney's disappointment she released his hand and took the glass from James, raised it to her eye, and saw nothing but darkness. Not even one small speck of light came through. "This is weird. I can't see anything." Emily turned around in a circle trying to catch a glimpse of something, anything, but to no avail. Handing the glass to Sidney, she said, "Here, you try. Tell me what you see."

Sidney was now completely back to reality. He looked through the glass and saw nothing. "It would appear James, that you are the only one capable of seeing anything through this spyglass." And he returned the scope to James, the apparent rightful owner.

James placed the spyglass back in his pocket. "If I see men and you see someone who looks like Mason and a bunch of women, which is real? What are we really seeing?"

"There's only one way to find out," chimed Sidney. He started walking on a straight path to the chess game.

Balchazar: *You must be wondering, what is this strange instrument I have gifted James. Well, James is beginning to notice that whenever he looks through his spyglass, things change. But are these people and objects really changing form, or is it his perception of these people and objects that is actually changing? Often, it is the way we look at something that determines what we see. Might I suggest you give serious consideration to the way you see things as we continue our story.*

Meanwhile, the guests at the croquet game found Peter to be quite charming. "Here my good man, you must join in the game," insisted a tall, handsome man who had just finished his turn. It was obvious to Peter and Katie, from the attention he was receiving, that this man was someone of importance, and a person with whom people wanted to be seen. "Someone hand this kind gentleman a mallet."

Now that Peter had been roped into playing croquet, Katie had fully released his arm and was on her own. Due to the friendliness of the group, she began weaving her way through the crowd, searching for the locket. She couldn't even remember what the locket looked like, but was certain she would know it when she saw it. As she pushed her way between the packed women, she smiled and mouthed the words, "excuse me," acknowledging her rude behavior.

There were two possibilities she could see for Peter's locket. Now she needed a ruse to get him out of the game. "Oh, Peter, my dear..." she called. "May I speak with you please... darling?"

Peter smiled and handed his mallet to a nearby onlooker. "Please my friend, take over my place in the game. It would appear that m'lady requires my attention. And believe me, I do not want to give her cause to be unhappy with me." The gentleman onlooker chuckled understanding the consequences of an unhappy woman. Peter made his way to Katie who pulled him aside, reached up, and whispered into his ear.

"See that woman right there in the blue gown?" whispered Katie.

"Don't look!" She snapped, pulling Peter's face back so he was looking at her.

"Sorry? I thought you wanted me to look," said a confused Peter.

"Of course, I want you to look," said Katie. "But not now. I don't want her to think we're talking about her."

"Oh!" said Peter as he stared deeply into Katie's eyes. "I get it. I'm sorry."

"It's okay," said Katie. "I don't think she saw you, she's too busy checking out the man who invited you to play the game. Anyway, I think she's wearing your locket. But I'm not sure. It's between her and the woman with the pink parasol and the fingerless gloves.

She might have it too."

"What's a parasol?" asked Peter.

"It's an umbrella. Don't you know anything? I don't have time to explain all this to you," snapped Katie.

But before she could finish her little rant Peter grabbed her by the shoulders and said "Katie, that's awesome. Good work. But here's the question. How are we going to get it off if one of them has it?"

"I don't know. It's your locket. That's your problem, not mine." Katie turned away and began to scan the grounds. She was lost in excitement over all the beautiful gowns and all the handsome young men in attendance. She was ready to ditch Peter and find a real man.

At the same time Katie was ready to be done with Peter, James, Emily, and Sidney reluctantly approached the guests seated around the chess table. Emily and Sidney watched the ladies giggling and flirting with Mason. Sidney wondered how Mason did it. All these beautiful women were completely focused on him. Sidney had never had a girlfriend, and barely even spoke to girls. Emily, Charlotte and Katie were his only female friends. In his mind Sidney made a mental note. "I've got to ask him how to do that!"

"Oh, Mason, do go on. Please tell us again about your adventures abroad," gushed the woman. Emily stood at full attention. Clear as day, she heard the woman call the man Mason. She recognized Mason's voice when he recounted his time in Europe with the Queen's footmen.

"Did you hear that James? Sidney? Did you hear it? That's Mason! I heard that woman call him by name."

Sidney shook his head, "I didn't hear it, but I see him! And I can see the bird too. It's definitely Mason. He's in a white chair with a high back, and the bird, that same bird that has been following us today, is right there on the chair with him."

After listening to Emily and Sidney, James knew there was only one thing to do. He confidently walked over to insert himself into the group. "Mason, so good to see you here, can you help us please? We're a bit confused. We really have no idea what happened or how we got here. But clearly you will have the answers we need."

As the people parted to create space for James, the seated gentleman rose with a puzzled look.

"I'm sorry my good man. You must have me confused with someone else." And he was right. He wasn't Mason at all. This gentleman, although reasonably good looking, was short and heavy set, just as James had seen.

"Please excuse me," said a confused James. "I won't take any more of your time."

As he walked away, a stunned Emily stood with her mouth wide open, "Sidney, what just happened?"

Paralyzed by shock he finally responded, "When James walked up to the man and everyone moved out of his way, everything changed. Mason turned into someone else and all those girls turned into guys!"

"Something strange is happening here," voiced a very concerned Emily. "Let's go find the others and get out of here!" No one spoke, but everyone agreed, and James began to lead them back to the mansion.

Back inside the mansion, Charlotte was feeling isolated and abandoned having played with the quartet for what seemed like hours, with no clue as to where her friends had gone. So, when the suggestion was made that the musicians take a break, she graciously thanked them. Checking to make sure her keys were still inside the hidden pocket of her dress, Charlotte literally ran out the front doors to the veranda in search of her friends. She could feel her heart racing as she prayed that they hadn't left without her. Gradually she reasoned with herself and repeated, "They wouldn't leave me. They wouldn't leave me. They wouldn't leave me." Still she wouldn't believe it until she found them.

At the croquet game, Katie positioned herself away from the ladies who were watching and stood alone where she could be seen by the men in the game. Peter was trying to get a close look at the locket worn by the woman in the blue gown. He didn't think it was his locket, so he maneuvered his way over to the woman with the pink parasol. Yes! This one looked very familiar. Peter was almost certain it was his locket.

Now, all he needed was a plan to retrieve it. But how was he going to come up with that? He stood next to the woman in pink, smiling at her, rocking back and forth on his heels, trying to think of an idea of how to get the locket. Nothing was coming to him, and the longer he stood there, the more anxious he became. Plus, he could tell the woman with the pink parasol was starting to get uncomfortable with the way he stared at her. She finally moved away from him and sought the security and comfort of friends closer to the mansion having tea. She chose a cup, poured the tea, and selected several petit fours to accompany it.

Peter joined Katie who was once again annoyed by his presence, "Can't you just leave me alone, Peter?"

"No, I can't. You're right. The woman in pink has my locket. But I have no idea how to get it from her. I think we need to find the others. James will know what to do. The only idea I have is to walk up to her and rip it off her neck! And all that will do is call attention to us, which we definitely don't want."

"Oh, all right," Katie said with disgust. "Where is the woman in pink?"

"She went over to the house. Let's head that way."

Peter took advantage of the moment and courageously reached out and put Katie's arm through his once again as they headed back to the house. She didn't resist. He was loving every minute of this beautiful summer afternoon.

As they were crossing in front of the stairs to the veranda, out ran Charlotte who plowed right into them. "Oh my gosh you guys, I'm so glad to see you. I thought you left without me."

"No, Charlotte. We still don't have the locket. But we know where it is," Katie replied.

"Where? Let's get it and go, before the quartet is looking for me again."

"It's not that easy. It's hanging from the neck of that woman over there in the pink." Peter indicated the location of the woman in pink with the nod of his head.

As Charlotte turned her head to look, Peter grabbed her face and snapped, "Don't look at her Charlotte! We don't want her to know that we're onto her!"

Katie rolled her eyes at Peter and slowly turned away from the two. Peter and Charlotte gazed in the general direction of the woman in pink. Once he made eye contact, Peter could not stop staring at her. Not only was she beautiful, but he knew he had to get the locket from her. She turned to face them and both Peter and Charlotte quickly averted their eyes to avoid detection. "You're right," said Charlotte. "This isn't going to be easy."

"Suddenly, Peter's eyes broke away from the girl in pink just long enough to see James, Emily and Sidney walking their way. "Hey Peter," yelled Emily. "You guys aren't going to believe what just happened. Sidney and I saw Mason and that bird, without a doubt. We even heard him speaking. But by the time we could get to where he was sitting, he was gone. He disappeared. He turned into someone else."

Peter looked to James for confirmation, but he couldn't give it. He recounted what had just happened to them. "Something really strange is going on. Have you guys found the locket?"

"Why yes, we did, kind sir," said Peter, speaking in his Victorian-era tone. "Oh yes indeed, it's right behind us, dangling from the neck of that beautiful lady. See, the one in the pink gown carrying the parasol."

"Why are you talking like that?" James laughed.

"I'm just trying to talk like all the people here." And the best friends both burst out laughing.

After James had pulled himself together he asked Peter, "How are we going to get it? What's your plan... kind sir?" They both giggled again.

"All right," interrupted Katie. "Enough messing around with your lame accents. The fact is, we have no idea how we're going to get the locket off her neck. It's an impossible task. Peter's bright idea is to walk up to her and rip it off."

Balchazar: *Oh, my friends, can you see that Katie is having a difficult time believing in herself? She has incorrectly stated that the task at hand is impossible. It is imperative that everyone knows nothing is ever impossible! For every problem there is a solution. And the solution is always inside you. Fortunately, Katie is not alone, and her friends don't share her feelings of impossibility. Please, do continue reading.*

"We have to figure this out guys, there has to be a way," said James. His friends could tell he was slipping into his "analyze all the options" mode. "Think!" James said, "Everyone think."

"You know what?" said a frustrated Katie, "I don't even care anymore. I've had enough of this. I just want to get that locket and get out of here."

Balchazar: *Katie is about to take the first essential step toward success. Take action…take massive action.*

It didn't take much for Katie's mind to step into action, and her feet moved just as fast. She wasn't even sure how it happened. As she was walking, she noticed that the clasp of the locket was caught on the parasol of the lady in the pink dress. "I've got an idea; I know how to get the locket."

When she reached the woman Katie asked her a simple question, "May I help you release your locket? I noticed that it's caught on your parasol."

The woman in pink responded with nothing but a smile, and then turned around so Katie could clearly see the clasp and the parasol. Katie reached up and released the clasp holding one end of the locket's chain in each hand. No sooner had she placed both hands on the locket, the woman in pink dissolved into thin air, leaving Katie standing with the locket in her hands. A terrified and traumatized Katie screamed out and whirled around to look at her friends, who stared dumbfounded at what just happened. Others screamed, and chaos ensued.

"Let's get out of here!" Emily begged. Katie dropped the locket into Peter's open hand. Peter stuffed the locket into his pocket so he wouldn't lose it, and the gang rushed off to find safety.

They ran in an undetermined direction. The fight or flight mode was operating in full gear. Peter's intuition guided them to the stables. "We'll be safe here and we can figure out what to do next." The sweet smell of alfalfa filled the air in the stables.

Charlotte took in a huge lung full of air and choked on the scent of manure. Through the coughing she told the group, "I don't know what just happened out there, but this can't be real! This is freaking me out, what are we going to do?"

Sidney was hysterical, "Katie you melted a lady! You killed her! We're murderers! We're all going to jail. I thought I was just dreaming all this up in my mind, but I'm not. That lady really melted!" Pacing in circles, Sidney couldn't escape the bizarre and frightening series of events that had happened. Hyperventilating and whining, he was trying to make sense of it all. "What's real? What isn't? Was Mason really there? I saw him with my own eyes! Emily, you heard his voice! He's here. Where did he go? Why did that woman melt? Why is this happening to us?"

"Calm down, Sidney. Get a hold of yourself. No one is going to jail," said James in the most reassuring voice he could manage.

But his best efforts had no effect on Sidney. "You don't know that James. Someone is going to get in trouble for this," Sidney was inconsolable.

Balchazar: *It should be very obvious to you that Sidney needs to bring order to his mind. You cannot find a solution when your mind is not at ease. Order is heaven's first law.*

"Sidney, look at me," coached Emily. Taking his hands in hers she continued, "We'll figure it out. But we can't do it while you're having a come apart. Just breathe. Look into my eyes. Be calm. Breathe with me."

The slow steady rhythmic exercise of breathing in and out with Emily was just the thing Sidney needed to calm his mind. Slowly he mustered enough control to remain quiet. Without thinking, Sidney reached into his pocket, took hold of the crystal ball and squeezed it as though it was a stress ball. Even though it didn't give in his hands, he felt a warmth on his palms that calmed him.

Peter was the only one not out of breath from the quick sprint to the stables, "This is just too unreal. Let's figure out how to get out of here. I don't know how much more of this I can take."

"None of this makes any sense." James was attempting to organize his thoughts in his most pragmatic way. Although remaining cool, calm and collected on the outside, this was extremely challenging, even for James.

Charlotte reached deep into her mind for a solution. "Let's start at the beginning. Somebody tell me what happened." Charlotte felt certain that if she had all the facts, the picture would come together, and she would know exactly what to do.

Sidney was thinking calm, soothing thoughts allowing his imagination to carry him far away to a tropical island. He was lying on a beach being fanned by a beautiful tan girl in a bikini. But as he looked more closely, the girl was Emily, the first girl to hold his hand. The smile on his face indicated he wasn't paying a speck of attention to the conversation.

"Sidney! Are you listening?" Charlotte wanted to know. However, she knew the answer before she asked.

Sidney came to, he glanced at Emily, then into the crystal ball. He saw the same ocean waves he just visualized in his imagination. How can that be? "Guys, did you see that?"

"See what?" Charlotte wanted to know.

"I was daydreaming about being on a beach with a beautiful girl and when I opened my eyes I could see the beach in my crystal ball. What does that mean? How can that be?" Sidney was really curious now. There had to be an explanation for this phenomenon.

Charlotte was on it, "Do it again, Sidney. Imagine you're on the beach. Let's see if you can make it happen again."

In his mind Sidney went back to the tropical beach and imagined it exactly as before but without thinking of Emily. He was walking with the warm sun kissing his body and the sand squishing between his toes. The image was perfectly clear in every detail.

"There it is!" Charlotte exclaimed. "I can see it, Sidney. I can see the beach in the crystal ball. Wow! What does this mean?"

"Clearly there must be powers in these gifts," was the conclusion that James drew.

Balchazar: *Yes, indeed, James, yes, indeed. There is power, but the power does not rest in the physical gifts you have received. Rather, the gifts are merely a symbol for you to familiarize yourselves with the powers you hold within. Do you see it in their thoughts and feelings? Do you hear it in their words? Do you see it in their actions? Do you see it in yourself? If not, keep looking, it is soon to be discovered.*

"Now, just a minute," Emily chimed in. "We know from the museum and the library that there's some connection between our gifts. Sidney saw the lightning in his crystal just before we found ourselves in the mansion library."

"And my scales teetered!" shouted Katie. It was making sense to her too. Katie removed the scales from her hidden pocket. They were still in balance.

"Shhhh!" Peter hissed, putting his index finger to his lips, "I hear voices. I can't tell what they're saying but I think someone is looking for us."

"Are you sure?" Charlotte wanted confirmation.

"There is no doubt, I KNOW." Peter was angry that Charlotte would question him.

"We've got to get out of here!" Katie was in tears. "We're trapped there's no place to go." Katie began to pace and hold her throat. She was certain they were coming for her.

"It's ok, come over here. There's a door at the end of the barn." Charlotte could visualize their escape. They all moved to the door but found it locked.

"We're trapped. They're going to find us. Oh no, oh no, no!" Katie's anxiety was escalating.

"I'm sure we can safely escape if we can just get through this door," said Charlotte.

"Use your keys. Maybe they unlock more than just the library." Emily was hoping it worked.

Without hesitation, Charlotte retrieved her keys from the hidden pocket inside her gown, selected one at random and thought, "Please let it work. Please let it work. Please let it work." She placed it in the lock. It seemed to fit. She turned the key, she heard the tumblers fall, tried the knob, and opened the door. Everyone rushed the door pushing Charlotte through to the other side.

Sidney, the last one to enter slammed the door behind him. "We're not out yet. We're still trapped," he yelled.

"Wait a minute. What if we aren't?" said Emily. "James, things look different through your spyglass. You saw things that no one else could see when we were on the grounds, remember?" asked Emily. "What does the spyglass see in here?"

James retrieved the glass, held it to his eye and began to look around the room. He saw saddles, bridles, grooming brushes, and blankets. There were bits and spurs. He saw nothing unusual or different until he reached the back wall. "Oh, look guys, there's a door on the back wall. We can get out that way," exclaimed James.

"James, there isn't a door on the back wall," Charlotte said.

"There is! You just can't see it." James walked quickly to the back wall, moved some trunks out of the way and pointed to where he saw the door. "Put your key right here where you see this knot in the wood, Charlotte."

Although hesitant, Charlotte complied. What did she have to lose, all the while repeating in her mind, "Please take us out of here, please take us out of here."

As she pressed the key up against the knot, Katie could no longer be silent. "What's the matter with you guys? There's no door, there's no lock, we're not going to get out this way!"

As Katie spoke, Sidney saw the lightning flash in the crystal illuminating his imaginary beach. "Oh, hurry Charlotte, there's lightning in the crystal!"

Katie instinctively looked at the scales. They had begun to teeter. Charlotte pressed the key into the knot. The key melted into the wood like it was made of warm butter, and slowly the wall began to open like a door. The lightning struck, the scales teetered out of balance and Wham! Bam! Gone! They were out of the tack room.

CHAPTER 4

THE ILLOGICAL ISLAND

In a matter of seconds, the door created in the wall of the tack room opened to a tropical paradise. As they stumbled into their new environment there was no time for their eyes to adjust to the bright sunlight, causing hands and arms to quickly serve as make-shift visors and shields for protection. While their eyes began to slowly adjust, one by one, their other senses awakened to their new surroundings. The rhythmic sound of waves rolling gently onto the beach created a much-welcomed calming effect after the drama from just moments ago. The air was humid and as they opened their mouths to breathe, they were met with the slight taste of salt. They were now standing on a wide-open beach with sand that stretched for miles. Slowly, they began to wander. As they walked along the pearl white beach, it was as if their bare feet were being massaged by the soft sand.

Even before their eyes had fully adjusted, it was obvious they were on a tropical island. To their right was the most beautiful, crystal blue sea. To the left was a definite line of palm trees and thick vegetation. High above the trees were the tallest and greenest mountains they'd ever seen. What a beautiful place, and what a relief to be free from whomever was about to enter the stables at the garden party.

No longer beautifully adorned in the period dress of the Victorian age, each found themselves prepared for a day in the outdoors. They felt much more comfortable in their cargo shorts and tee shirts. Each of them was also equipped with a backpack, except for Sidney. To his horror, he found a lightly colored fanny pack around his waist. Once again, he lamented why he always had to be so uncool.

"This place is gorgeous!" Charlotte said. "It's so warm and calm, maybe even a little romantic if the right person was here." Charlotte was feeling completely relaxed, and relieved that her magic keys facilitated their escape. She stretched out in the sand and thought "Who would I choose to be stranded on a deserted island with? Peter, James or Sidney?" After a short process of elimination, she decided on James. "Sidney…NO! Peter, well it's obvious he's in love with Katie, so I guess I would choose James. I don't think Emily would mind. He's smart, he's decent looking." She giggled out loud at the silly conversation she was having inside her head, and said to no one in particular. "If only I had a swim suit right now, just look how clear the ocean is. I wonder where we are. We must be somewhere in the Carribbean, don't you think?"

While listening to Charlotte, Katie's thoughts soon got the best of her and she quickly realized how grateful she was to not be wearing a swim suit. How embarrassing that would be! She felt the sun drenching her skin and ran into the water thinking, "I want to be a mermaid, swimming with the dolphins and the seals, making friends with underwater creatures."

James lowered the backpack off his shoulder and unzipped the main compartment. Inside he found his spyglass and a pair of hiking boots, "Hey you guys, look in your backpacks. I've got hiking boots and my spyglass."

"Same here, boots and my locket, which I'm going to put around my neck, again, before I lose it." Peter took the added precaution without consideration to any other circumstances. He wanted to know where the locket was at all times. And by having it around his own neck it was easy to reach up and confirm its presence at any moment.

"Same with me, James, except my quill is alone. The book it was in is gone."

"I've got my keys!" Charlotte proclaimed with a touch of snobbery in her voice, "And these are the cutest boots. Katie you are going to love these." She saw herself as the savior of the group reaffirming her notion that if they would just do things her way everything would work out fine.

Katie reached into her backpack, found the same boots and her scales. "Look, the scales are in balance. I wish I knew what brought all this about. The scales are in balance and then they're not and then we're gone with the lightning. Does any of this make sense to you guys? It's really bugging me that I can't figure it out." By simple deduction based on recent events, Katie's instincts told her there was significance and power in her gift if she could just understand it and learn to use it. She determined right then and there she'd figure it out.

Sidney was so excited, "You guys, this is exactly what I imagined in my head and then saw in my glass ball! I think I created this." Sidney was captivated by his newly found talent. Skipping around on the beach, he did fail to mention to his friends that the only thing missing was Emily in a bikini, fanning him with palm fronds. He didn't care though, he would keep that to himself. But he had another idea. He pulled the glass orb from his fanny pack, closed his eyes and imagined a sandcastle. He let his vivid imagination run wild. It was tall and rectangular. It had towering turrets, a moat and a draw bridge. All the stones from which the castle was built were stacked neatly and symmetrically to form walls. There was even a damsel in distress locked in the highest tower of his imaginary castle. So, of course, there must be a knight in shining armor scaling the castle walls to save her, that would be Sidney.

Sidney loved the image of the castle he created in his imagination. Slowly cracking one eye open, just enough to peer into the crystal orb, he could vaguely see the sandcastle. It was there, just like he thought it would be. All the castle details he saw in his mind were present within the crystal ball. He could see the damsel, the knight, the tiny little stones. Upon seeing the castle in his crystal, he was compelled to build it. He didn't even stop to talk to the others, he moved forward with his plans. He found the perfect place on the beach where the sand was deep. This was where he would erect his dream.

> **Balchazar:** *Yes, you can see that Sidney is catching on that there is power within his imagination. He is learning that if he sees it, feels it, and believes it, he can actually make it happen. Just like in the case of a simple sandcastle, we must all learn this valuable lesson: If you can see it in your mind, you will hold it in your hand.*

Sidney had no idea how he would build such an elaborate structure. But he didn't care. He was going to give it his best try. He opened his fanny pack to stow his crystal ball for safety, and he couldn't believe what he saw. Inside his pack were the tools for him to build his castle, along with a pair of hiking boots. How did they all fit in there?

Carefully and methodically, Sidney began to pull each implement from his fanny pack. First, was a hand shovel, the kind that was typically used in gardening. Next, he pulled a plastic bucket from inside the pack. How were these things even fitting inside his small fanny pack? There were pallet knives, paint stirrers for smoothing, straws for blowing away minute bits of sand and additional buckets for hauling water. The tools just kept coming out of the fanny pack, like clowns piling out of a clown car. Sidney was beyond excited. He could hardly stay in his own skin. He began digging and running back and forth between the ocean and his building site. Sidney saw his castle as a reality.

> **Balchazar:** *Once you make a decision, the universe conspires to give you everything you need. Sidney did not have to know how he would build the castle, all the necessary tools were given to him easily, allowing him to create in reality the picture he formed in his imagination.*

The others looked on, chuckling at Sidney's apparent innocence. Katie had returned from the water, pretending she was a mermaid, and was inclined to help him but stopped short when Sidney admonished her to go away.

Instead she walked back to the water and strolled along the beach. "Oh, this is so relaxing," Katie said to herself. "The sun is so bright and so warm, I wish I had sunglasses, and sunscreen would be a good idea too," she thought. It never occurred to her to look in her backpack, which she had left sitting on the sand with the others. She continued her stroll as the clouds on the horizon began to move toward the beach. Maybe a storm was coming? Katie didn't care. She was enjoying her time alone in her own private paradise. Besides, these were the same fluffy clouds she and Emily used to stare at as little girls. They'd lie on the trampoline in her back yard and describe the pictures they found in the clouds.

Peter was fiddling with the locket around his already tanned neck, rolling it back and forth along the chain. Suddenly he got a feeling that they needed to leave the beach. As fast as it came he doubted it, telling himself it wasn't a very strong feeling, he could ignore it. He couldn't see anything going on that made him uneasy. Yes, he could see dark storm clouds in the distance, but they didn't mean anything. Everyone was having such a great time relaxing on the beach.

Charlotte and Emily joined Katie and the three began picking up sand dollars that lined the beach. Peter and James were enjoying the sun when James said out loud, "I wish we had a football."

"Yeah," responded Peter. "I bet the girls would even play with us. Hey James, what do you think my chances are with Katie?"

James abandoned all compassion and blurted his response with a chuckle, "None! You have NO chance with Katie."

"C'mon James, tell me how you really feel?" Peter laughed. "It's okay, I'm up for the challenge."

"Okay," said James. "I think I will refer to this challenge as Everest."

"I like that," replied Peter. "Definitely difficult, but not impossible."

The two friends laughed. "So what about you? Who do you like?" questioned Peter.

"You know," responded James coyly. "Let's just worry about Everest right now."

"Okay buddy. Operation Everest is now in full force!"

The boys laughed, and James noticed that the girls had traveled quite a distance down the beach. They were laughing, dancing and having a blast trying to hang on to the shells they had picked up.

"What are you doing out there?" James couldn't generate enough volume to be heard over the rolling waves. Thinking he would be able to see them better if he took a look through his spyglass, he reached for his backpack. Upon opening it, there was a football. Forgetting all about the girls, James was excited by the discovery. "Hey, Peter, look! There's a football in my bag. Let's play!" He made a perfect toss to Peter.

Everyone was having a great time, thoroughly enjoying the sun, sand and the ocean. The peace and calm was a welcomed break. Sidney had company from time to time while creating his sandcastle. The girls came and went from the football game. Each of them discovered other items in their backpacks as the hours passed. There was water and food provided at the exact moment they expressed hunger and thirst. Katie found the sunglasses she wished for, and Charlotte's backpack provided the necessary sunscreen. They were grateful for the magical backpacks. It seemed anything and everything they wanted or needed appeared just because they thought about it.

Despite the fun, Peter kept his eye on the sky, noticing that the clouds were moving closer to the beach. His subtle feeling of uneasiness was now a steady knot resting in his stomach. He felt that something was about to transpire, and couldn't help but wonder what they should be doing, not only to protect themselves, but to get back to the museum. "You know, I've been watching the clouds come in over the ocean, and I think we better find a place to get out of the weather."

James disagreed. "What are you talking about? There's no weather coming. Those are harmless clouds."

Peter was uncertain. His gut was telling him that action was required, and that they were running out of time. "Go ahead James, look at the clouds through your spyglass and tell me what you see, because I think you're wrong. If you don't see anything and I'm wrong, I'll drop it once and for all."

James complied. Returning to his backpack and retrieving the spyglass, he took a look at the horizon. What he saw was terrifying. "Oh no! Peter you're right. We've got to find a place to hide. Those clouds are black, and there's major lightning and wind. This is not good. Find the girls and let's get moving."

Balchazar: *You see Peter has increased his awareness of the truth that lies in his intuition. Not yet with a complete understanding of what he is experiencing, Peter cautiously refers to his gift as a "feeling in his gut." This is quite all right for a student at his level. However, he stunts his growth by frequently brushing off his feelings. As Peter improves at following the feelings he recognizes from his intuition he will exercise and develop his gift. Listen to that still small voice in your head, practice makes perfect.*

The golden sky turned gloomy as the bright sun hid itself behind dark storm clouds, causing the temperature to drop and the rain to fall. The girls ran to the boys. Katie was especially glad she wasn't in a bathing suit as Charlotte complained of her wet clothes. James persuaded an unwilling and now frustrated Sidney to abandon his unfinished masterpiece. Everyone was willing to comply with Peter's suggestion to head for cover in the lush vegetation just a short distance from the sandcastle.

Emily held her backpack over her head as they rushed to shelter. They stood under the canopy of the broad leaves of tropical banana, palm and coconut trees. Sidney opened his fanny pack and retrieved a rain poncho. He slipped it on and flipped the hood over his head. That felt much better. Katie was shivering in the cold and followed Sidney's lead discovering a raincoat in her backpack.

Peter knew instinctively that although they were okay for now, this was not going to last. The speed of the wind was increasing and the rain was getting heavier and heavier. "I don't think we're going to be safe here. I don't see a break in the clouds, and we don't know how long this will last. We need to find someplace safer than this."

"Where do you suggest we go? We don't even know where

we are? Do you want us to wander around aimlessly until we find someplace better?" Emily didn't understand Peter's thinking. She wanted more logical ideas before she left the safety of the trees.

"I can't explain it. I just know we need to move. So, you can come with me or you can stay here. But I'm telling you, we need to stay together and we need to get moving. I think if we go toward the mountains we'll find a safer place." Peter truly didn't understand what was going on inside him. But he knew that his intuition about the storm was correct. He wasn't going to waste any more time. Gathering up his belongings, he left the shelter of the trees and headed toward the mountains.

Charlotte believed in Peter and fell in step behind him. Although Katie had no desire to follow Peter, she didn't want to be separated, so she complied. Sidney was scared, he didn't know what to do. Stay or go were the only two options. It seemed to him that if things got worse they could always return to the shelter of the vegetation. He decided to go with Peter.

James looked at Emily and nodded, "There's safety in numbers. We have to stay together, Emily. We've managed to figure out everything up to this point. Maybe our gifts will keep us safe. Let's go." And without waiting for a response, James took her hand and followed the gang.

The group worked their way back and forth between the trees, creating a small path to the foothills. The sounds they heard from deep inside the forest were frightening. Screaming primates, shrieking birds, and they even thought they heard the roar of a lion. They hoped the last one was just the storm causing their ears to play tricks on them. The rain increased, and so did the wind, causing Katie to bend at the waist to block the gusts and pelting rain that seemed to keep blowing her off course.

Finally, it appeared that they had arrived at a path that would lead them to the mountains. The wind was so loud that Peter had to shout to be heard.

"This trail is really beaten down, like people or animals travel this way often. Maybe if we follow this path we'll find a safe place to get out of the storm." The path took off in two different directions and Peter was uncertain which way to go. Faced with the choice, someone had to decide. "Right or left guys. Which do you think?"

"It looks to me that if we go to the right, the path leads up the mountain. If we go to the left the path heads away from the mountain." James' observation provided no more clarity, only more confusion and uncertainty. But going to the right seemed to make the most sense. Moving up the mountain, getting to higher ground, seemed the safest and most logical.

Peter made a choice. He was taking the path which led to the left, and appeared to go down the mountain. He was met with argument. "That's the worst thing we can do. That path probably goes back to the beach where we'll be completely exposed again. Standing in the trees is safer than going that way!" Katie wasn't interested in following Peter to disaster.

"Look Peter, if we go to the right, it clearly leads up the mountain. We should be safer at higher ground." James tried to reason with Peter, and even though he was doing his best to hide his fear, he was unable to disguise his frustration.

"No, I know that's not right. We need to go left." Peter was never more certain of anything in his entire life.

"I'll go with you, Peter. I don't know why, but I believe your feeling is correct." Charlotte was mustering all her courage, and the two stepped out onto the path leading to the left. James, Emily, Sidney and Katie turned to the right.

James was overwhelmed and uneasy with the idea of separating. "Please you guys, this way!" he begged. "I'm scared that if we separate something really bad is going to happen, someone could get hurt. We have to stay together. Please, I'm begging you. Come with us."

But Peter was adamant. He wasn't going to be swayed. Charlotte hesitated for a moment. "James, why don't you come with us? We can all stay together. If we find out the path leads back to the beach, we'll turn around."

"With what I saw in the spyglass, we may not have time for that. We're going this way. Now come on! Stop being ridiculous, you're making a stupid choice!" James was shouting, his anger taking over.

Balchazar: *Peter is learning to listen to and trust his intuition. He has remained steadfast in his faith and belief, and will continue taking action, doing the next indicated thing until finally he reaches his goal.*

Normally Peter would have an ugly retort for James. But instead he was perfectly calm, a first for him and his flash temper. Without even responding to James or to Charlotte, he turned to the left and disappeared around the corner. Charlotte had tears in her eyes, but she relented and went with Peter. She believed that if anything happened to him on the path she would be there to help him.

"I have a really bad feeling about this, James," said Emily. The truth was, James had the same bad feeling. Maybe he would never see Peter again.

"Come on Emily, let's go." And the remaining four headed to the right, on the path they believed would lead them up the mountain. No sooner did they depart, a huge bolt of lightning flashed across the sky into the clearing and struck a nearby tree with a terrible crack. Sidney was hyperventilating again, or possibly just breathing hard because he was sprinting up the path.

The intensity of the rain continued to increase, and the gang could see water running down the path as gravity drew it to lower ground. The dirt covering the trail quickly became a river of mud, making it difficult to stay upright and to move forward. The girls and Sidney were slipping in the mud and James was exhausted from helping them up, over and over again. They clung to tree branches when the wind impeded their progress and several times made a human chain to climb up the steep hills they encountered. "I'm afraid if we don't find shelter soon, we're really going be in trouble," worried James.

"Oh, like we're not in trouble now! What's your solution, James? What do you want us to do? You were so sure this was the right way," Katie barked. And with that release of her anger, Katie turned around a bend and came face to face with the end of the road, literally. There was no place else to go. They were standing in front of the side of the mountain. Sheer rock. The only choice was to turn back. Katie burst into tears and secretly wished for her mother. Sidney turned to his imagination to remove himself from his dismal reality. He created a soothing image of himself back on the sunny and calm beach finishing his sandcastle.

They were doomed. Emily looked to her brother for guidance although she was doubtful since his choice had already proven unfruitful.

"I'm really sorry. I thought this would be the right way." James' apology was sincere.

"Well it wasn't! You always think you're right! You think you're the smartest, that you're better than the rest of us! Well, you're not!" Katie screamed through the hysteria of her tears. She was soaked to the skin, cold, scared and regretful. She was about to give up.

"We have no choice but to turn around and head back. We'll go the way Peter suggested and hopefully we'll find him and Charlotte." And saying nothing more, James retreated back down the treacherous, muddy path. Katie seemed to feel better the louder she cried, but no one could hear her, the storm was too intense. It drowned out everything. Not even the animals could be heard. They were probably all safe in their secret hiding places. Instinct would tell them what to do and where to go.

Meanwhile, Peter and Charlotte moved quickly along their chosen path. It was easily navigated and they covered a lot of ground in a short period of time. The sounds of the forest and the intensity of the wind and rain spurred them on. It wasn't long before Peter saw it. "Charlotte look! Right up there, just beyond that ledge."

"What are you talking about? I don't see anything."

Peter didn't care. Safety was in his sights. He took her by the hand veered off the path slightly, climbed a hill and pulled himself up the ledge. Once on the ledge, he got down on his belly, reached both hands over to grab Charlotte, and called, "One, two, three!" He pulled with all his might. Charlotte pulled herself with all her strength and used her legs for added leverage to get up and over the ledge. Now covered with mud, they ran into the safety of a cave. Charlotte breathed a huge sigh of relief. They were out of the storm. It couldn't touch them now. Peter had been right all along. She was grateful she'd followed him.

"We might be in here for a while, maybe we can build a fire and dry off." Peter had a plan. He began to gather sticks and dried vegetation that were strewn about the ground of the cave. He instructed Charlotte to bring as many rocks as she could find, and before long they had all the materials to make a fire. But how to start it? Peter tried striking two rocks together over and over and over again, but couldn't generate one single spark.

"I want fire. I want fire. I want fire." Charlotte kept repeating in her mind. She could feel the warmth it would generate and the feeling of her dry clothes. Holding that picture in her mind, Charlotte got an idea. She reached in her backpack and held the sterling silver keys in her cold hands, remembering the two previous times that the keys had opened doors for her. The calm and the warmth from the keys traveled up her hands and arms just as they had when she held them before. She relaxed with the calm that came from holding them. "Fire, nice warm fire, with sparks dancing like fireflies, and flames shooting high in the air, spreading warmth throughout the cave."

The more she thought about the fire she wanted, the more detail came to Charlotte's mind. She focused on the image of the fire in her mind. Mentally she felt the warmth, she saw the glow, and she became comfortable.

Peter had nearly given up trying to start the fire, and in frustration threw down the rocks. "I wish I had my phone!" he yelled. "I thought for sure I was doing this the right way, but I must be doing something wrong. I need to look it up."

"Don't give up, Peter. I know you can do it. You can create the spark to start the fire." Charlotte encouraged him. She didn't know why she believed in him. Perhaps it was because he knew instinctively which path to take. But even more so, she knew there was nothing to lose.

Peter picked up the rocks, took a deep breath, and let it out. He struck them together, once, twice, and finally on the third try, the spark flew. It landed on the kindling and the dried grasses they found in the cave and began to smolder. Peter gently blew on the grass and before he knew it the wood caught and the fire burned. Charlotte and Peter hugged each other as they jumped up and down with joy. They were going to be all right.

James, Emily, Sidney and Katie were making their way back down the mountain. Emily was so cold her hands and feet felt numb. Katie was blown about by the wind so much that she had repeatedly cut her face and hands on the nearby trees and rocks. She was hurt, scared and exhausted. Sidney was oblivious. In his mind, he was climbing Mt. Everest, determined to make it to the top.

The group made it back to the fork in the path and without hesitating continued on, following Peter and Charlotte's footsteps. James secretly hoped they would find the others, however his mind was overtaken by worst-case-scenario thoughts. He challenged himself to stop thinking about all the harmful and bad things that could happen. He made a conscious effort to think only that they were someplace safe and that soon they would all be reunited.

Charlotte sat on the cave floor, in front of the fire, with Peter cradling her in his arms. Between the fire and the warmth of their two bodies they had become dry and quite comfortable. As Charlotte gazed at the dancing flames she could feel Peter's strong hands rubbing her arms for warmth. The more she stared at the red and orange fire the more her thoughts drifted, to strange, yet comfortable thoughts about her and Peter. Thoughts of the two of them holding hands at school, eating lunch alone at the mall, studying together, and then kissing. At the thought of that kiss, Charlotte jumped up.

"What's wrong?" asked a startled Peter.

"Nothing!" snapped Charlotte. "Nothing's wrong. I was just getting a little too warm by the fire." Charlotte was sick in her stomach. Why did she just have those thoughts about Peter? She didn't like Peter that way. She knew Peter liked Katie. And as much as Katie wouldn't admit it, Charlotte knew Katie enjoyed all the extra attention she received from him. Charlotte coached herself mentally as she walked around the cave, "Don't worry, that was nothing. You were almost asleep in front of the fire. It's been a long and crazy day. Those were random thoughts. It didn't mean anything. You are not in love with the guy who likes your best friend."

Peter stood up and walked to the opening of the cave. He didn't know what he was watching for, but he knew he needed to watch.

It was difficult to see through the rain and the bending of the trees in the wind. Still he stood watch. "Charlotte, look!"

"What? What is it?" Charlotte was relieved to be jolted from the ridiculous conversation going on inside her head.

"It's James! I can see him coming up the path. We need to signal them to let them know where we are." Peter left the safety of the cave and headed out to the storm, yelling at James and waving his arms.

Peter managed to finally catch Emily's attention. She stopped her brother saying, "Look James. Up on that ledge. It's Peter!"

"Sidney, you climb up to the top of the ledge. We'll help you. And when you get there, help me get the girls up." James hurried, pushing Sidney along.

Peter was already on his belly again, ready to help Sidney up the ledge. Sidney wasn't very strong, and James pushed him up with all his strength. "Come on, Sidney. You can do it." James was trying to offer words of encouragement, but his tone wasn't at all motivating.

Finally, with one last coordinated effort, Sidney was over the ledge, kicking mud and debris in James' face. Getting the girls up was much easier. And finally, James, tired from all the pushing, pulled himself up onto the ledge. They ran to the safety of the cave, never questioning where Peter was taking them.

The girls all hugged each other, happy and grateful to be reunited. Charlotte led them to the fire where they could warm up and dry their clothing. They relaxed in the safety of the cave and were relieved to be back together. James didn't want to admit to Peter that he was wrong, and no one said a word about it.

The storm showed no signs of easing up. It was just as fierce as it was hours ago when they first entered the cave. Peter was starting to think that there must be something else they should be doing. But he was the only one.

Katie sat with her chin resting on her knees, tucked beneath her jaw, her arms cradling them to hold them in place. Suddenly she let go and stood up on her knees. "Did you guys hear that?" No one heard a thing. "There it is again." Still they heard nothing. "I definitely hear something. It's coming from deep inside the cave. Maybe we aren't as safe as we think. It feels like we're being watched. Don't you guys feel it? Is it just me?"

James asked, "What does it sound like?"

"Wings, flapping wings?" Katie replied, "And I can hear breathing, creepy breathing." Anxiety began to build inside Katie.

"I hear it too," Charlotte confirmed.

"It's probably just bats," James tried to reassure them. But the girls weren't having it.

"It sounds like it's coming closer." Katie was on her feet now. She was ready to dash out of the cave and back into the storm. And then it appeared, and it wasn't a bat at all. Katie could see the huge eyes glowing from the depths of the cave. "It's there, and it's huge. And it's coming for us!" She was shouting as the creature moved closer and closer.

Peter's hand unconsciously reached up toward his neck for the locket. Charlotte did the same holding her keys. She was chanting through the fear. She could start to feel the calmness from her keys spreading through her body.

James pulled his spyglass from his backpack and looked into the deep darkness of the cave. "I see the eyes, Katie, but they're small, like little bitty eyes. Whatever it is, it isn't going to hurt us."

"No James! I'm staring at them right now. They're huge!" Katie was almost hysterical again.

"Stop!" yelled Peter in a reprimanding voice. "You guys have to believe." Touching his locket had brought the clarity and calmness to his mind he needed to share. "The card that came with my locket said to act as if nothing is impossible. I thought it would be impossible to find my locket when it was lost, but we found it. It's the same thing here. If James says this creature won't hurt us we need to believe him and know that NOTHING is impossible, that this will work out."

James took his glass to the opening of the cave and looked out. There was no storm. The sun was bright, not a cloud in the sky, the wind was calm and the rainforest was at peace. In the distance, he could see a treehouse. It was magnificent, and there seemed to be activity there. He lowered the glass not believing what he saw, and looked out with his naked eyes. The storm raged just as before. So, he looked through the spyglass once more, and confirmed. Indeed, the storm had quieted, the sky was clear, and the treehouse stood in the distance.

The creature was moving ever closer. Katie could make out more than just the large glowing eyes. It was green and scaly. It seemed to have wings, even though it was walking slowly toward them, and it dragged a long tail behind. Katie was not convinced by Peter's words and was now hiding behind him, practically pushing him toward the creature.

A calmness had come over Charlotte, which caused her to think about the card that came with her keys, "If nothing is impossible, then there's a way out. The tag on my gift said something about violating logic. So perhaps if we're to get out of this, we need to somehow violate logic."

Balchazar: *Oh…here we go, now, I like where Charlotte is going with this. First, she has not forgotten the lesson that nothing is impossible. Next, she is heeding my advice to violate logic. It is often difficult to grasp what it means to violate logic. Well, let me tell you, it is very simple. When you violate logic, you avoid the norm. You refuse to follow the crowd. You are the one who takes the road less traveled.*

Katie had no other option than to start believing, "Great! Then tell me what logic are we supposed to violate? And hurry up and decide because I can't wait here anymore. I'll take my chances in the storm."

"That's it!" exclaimed Charlotte. "We take our chances in the storm." She ran out of the cave and into the rain. When she stepped outside, the storm stopped. The wind died, the clouds cleared, the ground dried, and the birds sang.

Charlotte whirled around holding her arms open as if to say, "See I told you." She headed to the ledge to find a path away from the cave. The others followed, but the creature had caught up to them. As the creature came out of the cave, he opened the expanse of his wings, took flight and in his talons picked up Sidney in one foot and James in the other. It all happened so fast they didn't realize what just transpired until Emily screamed.

"James! James!" The creature had her brother and there was nothing she could do. She was reaching into the air as high as she could, running after him until she reached the ledge. She could go no further. Her heart was broken, and fearing the worst, she dropped to the ground, covered her face in her hands and sobbed. "He's dead! He's dead!" She couldn't stop, she was overcome with despair.

Somehow, without explanation, Charlotte was still calm. "We'll find them Emily. I don't think this is necessarily bad. We did the illogical. We stepped out into the storm and it stopped. Let's do the illogical and go find them. It'll be okay."

Balchazar: *There is a universal law known as the law of polarity. It states that nothing is good or bad, it just is. Humans make things good or bad by attaching their own emotions to a situation, just like Emily has attached fear and grief of the loss of her brother. But things are not always what they seem, in fact, they usually are not.*

Emily looked at Charlotte with a blank stare. She couldn't make sense of what Charlotte was suggesting, let alone believe they could find James and rescue him. But Charlotte seemed so sure and confident.

Peter believed that Charlotte was right, "I agree with you Charlotte. At the very least, there's no purpose in staying here. Let's go." They gathered their backpacks and headed out. Emily blindly followed without a single thought. They found a way off the ledge and back onto the path and headed in the direction the green monster flew.

They had walked along the path without direction for about 30 minutes. What could they do? The creature had disappeared not too long after taking off. They really didn't know where they were going. All of a sudden, the shrill sound of a bird calling could be heard in the distance. "There's that sound again." Katie heard it, stopped in her tracks and listened more intently. "I can hear the wings flapping, and that eerie call, it's from that creature."

"It's coming this way again!" Everything in Katie's body tensed in preparation for the arrival of the creature. They all looked to the sky, and with fire shooting from his nostrils, the creature appeared, swooping down on them, this time snatching Katie and Emily. Their screams could be heard for quite a distance until they were too far away to be seen or heard.

"He took off in the same direction," Peter observed. "Maybe he'll be coming back for us too." Peter was beginning to give up all hope of surviving. He wondered, how does one prepare for the end?

Charlotte tucked her keys into her backpack. "I still believe that we do the illogical. I don't know how this will end, but I do know this, nothing is impossible, and we need to do the illogical thing." She took off in front of him singing a made-up song with lyrics chiming, "Nothing is impossible. Do the illogical."

Peter followed her, "I have an idea, Charlotte. When the creature comes back for us, the only way to save ourselves is to hide under the trees. The creature won't be able to fly through the trees, and we can probably outmaneuver him that way."

"But Peter, that's the logical thing to do." Charlotte was conflicted. She wanted to do what Peter suggested. That made sense to her. But she was focused. It had proven effective to do what seemed wouldn't work at all. Was this the right time to do the illogical?

It wasn't long before the creature returned, breathing fire, wings flapping, and eerie screaming. Peter grabbed Charlotte and began pulling her into the trees. Charlotte resisted, pulling against Peter. And even though she was scared to death, she knew what she had to do.

"Stop it Charlotte! Come on!"

"No! Let me go!" Charlotte finally pulled away from Peter, and ran back onto the path, away from the trees, giving the creature a full view of her.

"Charlotte! Charlotte!" Peter wanted to go out onto the path to get her, but instead stayed put in the trees. He dropped to the ground and stayed as low as he could. The creature blew fire across the trees, forcing Peter back onto the open path. Peter was now exposed. The creature easily grabbed him and Charlotte, and off they flew.

Charlotte was so scared she held her breath and closed her eyes. All she heard was the rhythmic flapping of the wings. It didn't take long for her to realize that she wasn't being hurt by the talons. She was actually quite secure. She opened her eyes, looked over at Peter and saw he was okay too. In fact, he actually smiled at her. Could Peter be having fun? No that can't be.

They looked to the horizon and saw the treehouse that James had described. They were headed toward it. Closer and closer they flew, and it wasn't long before they could see their friends. "Look, Charlotte! I see James! I can't believe it. He's ok!"

"And there's Emily, Katie and Sidney!" Charlotte was relieved. Had this creature really collected them all and brought them here? As they approached the treehouse, Charlotte wondered how they would land without getting hurt.

The creature circled a few times, and on one pass, gently dropped Charlotte onto the floor of the treehouse. She was unharmed. Katie and Emily ran over to welcome her. They picked her up off the floor, brushed her off, and hugged her. At that point the creature passed again, dropping Peter to the floor.

As Peter was released from the talons, the creature began to shrink. His scaly green skin morphed from green to black, and scales changed to feathers. His big round head became more elongated and a long beak protruded from the place he originally breathed fire. The long-pointed tail withdrew toward his body and fanned out into tail feathers. When the metamorphosis was complete, the crow landed on the railing of the treehouse.

"What just happened? And how did we survive?" Katie was the first to try and piece everything together. "So, we were just kidnapped by this griffin-like creature, who brings us to a treehouse where no one lives, drops us without hurting us, and then turns into the crow we saw at the museum?"

"What makes you think it's the same crow?" questioned Charlotte, who couldn't make sense of anything.

As the group began to argue, they were interrupted by a familiar voice. "Now that you're all here, I want to welcome you." It was Mason's voice. Everyone turned to the center of the treehouse and saw Mason seated in the same high-backed rattan chair from the veranda at the southern mansion. Holding a helmet in one hand, and a backpack in the other, Mason was dressed in the gear of a fighter pilot.

"I suppose you're wondering what's been going on," he said with a mischievous smile on his face. "I'm sorry that I left you at the museum. I really wanted to explain some things to you, but when I got back to the room you had already transported. I think someone else had other plans for you." He looked over at the bird who snapped his beak and cawed loudly. "However, now that my friend Balchazar has brought you to me, I'm sure you're ready for answers."

Mason reached into his backpack and produced the coin James had given him at the museum and asked, "Do you remember when we were talking about this coin? Let's continue that conversation. The gifts you acquired at the museum are merely symbols of the powers you already possess within you. You may have already discovered that as you traverse these alternate worlds, your gifts are becoming more and more real to you. You are slowly learning how to use them to your advantage. It's normal to focus on the physical conditions you're experiencing. However, in the case of Peter, James and Charlotte, you just witnessed what can happen when you pay attention to what and how you feel."

He continued to speak as he stood up and moved toward Balchazar. "You have to realize there's power in your awareness. Be vigilant and stand guard at the portal of your mind to ensure that your thinking is proper. Remember, what you see in your mind, you will hold in your hand."

He finished and everyone had questions, but at that moment, no one could even form words. Katie was trying to process the ambiguity in Mason's statements. They knew this was a puzzle they had to put together, but how?

Mason put his helmet on and then his backpack as he walked to the edge of the treehouse, Balchazar began to morph once again into the griffin-like creature. Flapping his huge wings, Balchazar waited for Mason to climb onto his back.

"Wait!" yelled Katie. "You can't go. We need to know what to do! Please tell us what to do!"

Mason turned, "Katie, your answers will come as you need them. The desire you hold inside ensures it. Just like seeds that are planted in soil, there must be a period of growth. Be patient.

Continue on your way. You're on the correct path."

Balchazar took flight with Mason on his back. The entire group stood in awe.

Katie finally broke the silence, "This is so confusing. There's no way we can figure this out without more information. How do we know any of this is real?" Katie was genuine in her need for answers. But she didn't understand that she herself was blocking the answer from coming to her because of improper thinking. She didn't know the answer she needed was already inside her.

Sidney could sense a vibration in the air. The lightning was flashing in his mind. He reached into his fanny pack to retrieve the crystal only to confirm that it was flashing there as well. "Katie, it seems to me what you just said triggered the lightning. Where are your scales?"

Katie retrieved her scales, they were in balance when she pulled them from her backpack. But as soon as she set them on the floor, they began to teeter. The lightning flashed all around them more intensely than before. Perhaps it was because they were high above the ground in a treehouse. Nonetheless, the lightning flashed, the thunder roared, the scales teetered out of balance and they were off.

CHAPTER 5

THE INTERFERENCE PUZZLE

Before they even opened their eyes, they knew by the lack of heat and humidity they were no longer on the tropical island. Instead, they were staring at a seven-foot-tall, massive holly bush hedge. Although beautiful with its red berries, the leaves were adorned with the sharp, stickered points that could be painful to touch. The hedge projected into the distance in both directions for as far as the eye could see.

James couldn't help but admire it and contemplate its purpose. "Look at all the berries on this hedge. I wonder who took the time to plant this, what is it for? Is it a barrier? Is it protecting something? Man, it's tall!"

Katie abruptly chimed in, interrupting James' questioning, "I really hate to burst your bubble, but while you think it's wonderful, it just makes me think of Christmas. And you all know how much I dread Christmas." As she spoke, the hedge transformed from a holly bush to boxwood shrubbery, neatly and precisely trimmed.

"Whoa! Did you see that? The bushes just changed. All of the holly is gone." Katie was stunned, but curious. Her marvelous mind swirled in a thousand directions attempting to decipher what had just happened. The words she just spoke flashed across her mind. Was it coincidence, or was there actually something to her thinking?

> **Balchazar:** *Katie is about to learn an important lesson. That is to think about what you WANT, not what you DO NOT want. When your focus is on what you want, you get what you want. Likewise, if you focus on what you do not want, you quickly get exactly what you do not want. Such is the basis of the law of attraction. What you think and focus on, you receive.*

In her mind, Katie returned to the museum, concentrating on the scales she received, and the adventures they had experienced. What were the thoughts she had while opening her gift? She relived the times when the scales were teetering out of balance and Sidney saw the lightning in his crystal ball. "Does what I say or think have anything to do with what has been happening? It must!"

Her mind continued to race, "James can see things differently when he looks through his spyglass. Sidney sees everything he imagines inside his crystal ball. Charlotte's keys open doors where there are no locks. Peter's intuition takes us where we need to be. But how do I fit in this scenario? How do I make my gift work to my advantage?"

Katie escaped to the deepest recesses of her mind, trying to put all the puzzle pieces together. She knew there was something to figure out, and now she was desperate for that lesson to come to light.

While Katie was deep in thought, the rest of the group was discussing this new place and their fascination with the boxwood, exploring, and looking for anything that would clue them in as to why they were standing in front of it. Emily was the first to see the sign. They approached it with anticipation. As they drew close, she read it out loud:

The Interference Puzzle:

Make a committed decision. Move toward the goal.
Use your will to focus on the goal, to the exclusion of all else.

Balchazar: *Now it is time for my students to learn that nothing happens until you first make a committed decision. Once a decision is made, you will move toward your goal, for the universe conspires to make it happen. But remember, you must not become distracted, for distraction stalls.*

Emily couldn't hold her excitement in any longer. "Do you see this? This is a puzzle. I love puzzles; this is going to be so much fun."

"That's great Emily, but we're standing in front of a giant bush. "How do we get in?" inquired James.

She looked at the hedge, "I want to work the puzzle, and I'm going inside."

As though Emily had commanded it, an archway appeared.

"Wow!" exclaimed Peter, "You girls have super powers! Katie told the hedge to change and Emily created a door. How did you do that?"

"Well Peter, all I can say is that you better be careful, or you'll be going through this hedge as a toad!" chuckled Emily.

Everyone laughed and Emily turned to the group, "You're coming with me, right?"

They all nodded in agreement and walked through the arch. As they entered, all eyes moved to a meticulous map drawn on faded parchment paper and fastened to a wooden frame.

Sidney examined the drawing and noted that it had missing sections, edges that were curled, torn and stained. It was difficult to read, and the longer he stared, the quicker his mind began to wander. Now, he was looking at a pirate's map. There were ships, islands, seas and, of course, sea monsters. In the center was a giant X, marking the location of a bountiful treasure. But as he began to hear pirate voices making threats to walk the plank, he was jolted back to reality by Emily shouting.

"Look at this map. It's a drawing of a maze; routes, corners, turns, dead ends, it's all here. I think we're supposed to navigate to the end, and this map shows us exactly the way to go."

"This map looks pretty complex, but the one thing I don't see is an exit," voiced a concerned James.

"Yes, but that's got to be part of the puzzle," said Emily.

Reminding them that the map was attached to a frame, Charlotte asked what she thought was obvious, "How are we supposed to follow a map we can't take with us? There's no way we can memorize this."

"We don't have to memorize it," explained James as he turned to his twin, "Emily, take out your quill and copy it."

Emily was impressed, "Good idea."

"This should be easy," said Peter.

Emily took out her quill along with a small notebook she found in the backpack. After several seconds of drawing on the paper, the page was still blank. There was no ink coming out of her quill.

"I don't know why I thought this would work. Quills don't have an internal supply of ink, and I have no ink well. I'm drawing, but nothing is showing up on the paper, nothing!" Emily was disappointed that her gift didn't seem to work.

"Now what do we do?" Katie looked at Peter.

"Let me think," said Peter.

"I know, everyone look inside your bag for something to write with, a pen, pencil, chalk, anything."

They all opened their backpacks, except for Sidney, who trying to hide from the group, unzipped his geeky fanny pack. No one had anything in their bag that could be used for writing.

"Now what?" asked Katie, again, this time with more frustration.

"Wait a minute. Emily, I can see your drawing." For some reason, when James looked through his spyglass he could read the seemingly invisible ink from Emily's quill. "Keep drawing!" he ordered.

Emily still couldn't see what she had drawn on the page. But at James' insistence, she continued writing, drawing and making her notes. To everyone's surprise, James could clearly see the details on each page as Emily quickly copied. Not wanting to miss any details, the group began to offer suggestions and particulars they believed Emily should transcribe. They had no idea if Emily was including them or not, but they believed she was.

Page after page she drew until the entire notebook was filled with the invisible drawings that duplicated the map posted to the sign.

Emily was eager to start the puzzle, but she had doubts. What if something happened once they got inside the maze, or if James couldn't see the writing in her notebook? She knew there was no way she would ever remember the turns and directions she had just copied. But, there wasn't much she could do about it, so she pushed her doubts aside and said to the group, "I'm finished, let's go!"

After studying the map, Peter headed off in the direction he believed to be best. He didn't seem to care if anyone followed him or not.

The others dashed in after him as if they were starting a race. When they caught up, Peter was already at the first crossroads. "Which way do we go, Emily? Do we turn right or left? Righty-tighty or lefty-loosey?" asked Peter.

Fear gripped Emily, she had already forgotten. She drew this part of the maze long ago. Without even thinking that the pages of her notebook were empty, she pulled it from her backpack and flipped to the first page. Rhyming out loud to herself, "Right-tighty, lefty-loosey. Oh! Oh! Oh! I remember. We go left! Lefty-loosey." Emily was extremely proud of herself. The page was still blank, but she remembered the first turn was left. "See! This is fun! I remembered the way! We can do this!"

Balchazar: *It is important to remember that everyone has a perfect memory. I know it is hard to believe, but the key is to develop it, just like you would other muscles in your body. Do not allow yourself to believe your memory is not perfect. Take action and exercise it, develop your own perfect memory.*

They turned to the left and continued on their trek. Katie was bringing up the rear, running her fingertips along the boxwood as she traveled. She was still trying to figure out in her mind the connection between her thoughts, words and the scales, but it wasn't coming together. The group disappeared from sight, and Katie barely noticed.

With her closed notebook and quill in hand, Emily navigated the group. "Look at us," said Sidney, "We're like little lab mice darting back and forth looking for a treat at the end of the maze."

"Do NOT imagine that we are lab mice!" yelled Peter. "I do not want to turn into a mouse!"

Sidney didn't know how to react, so he just stood, frozen, until Peter started laughing. Once he did, so did the rest of the group. "C'mon Sidney, get it? When you imagined the sandcastle it appeared in your glass ball and then you built it. It's funny. It was a joke."

Sidney laughed a little and thought to himself, "I think I like Peter in this maze." He quickly imagined himself as the lab assistant looking over a glass enclosed case with five mice scurrying through it. "I guess I won't have to turn Peter into a lab rat. He already is one in my mind." Sidney relaxed and laughed.

Noticing that Katie wasn't with them, Charlotte asked, "Where's Katie?"

Looking around, they saw no signs of her. Emily was the first to notice a little white mouse rush to Charlotte's foot and nibble on her shoelace. Charlotte screamed and franticly kicked her shoe, flinging the innocent little mouse onto the soft grass.

The mouse was momentarily stunned. As it began to lift its head, bristly white hairs elongated to dark curly locks. Beady, pink eyes darkened to the soft eyes of a sleeping beauty, and tiny, stubby legs stretched to the toned, muscular arms and legs of a gymnast. As they stared, they realized to their horror, that it was Katie transforming before their very eyes.

Charlotte ran to Katie's aid apologizing profusely, "I'm so sorry Katie. I didn't know that was you. I would have never kicked you off my shoe had I known. Are you okay?"

Dazed and confused, Katie asked, "What just happened?"

Fearful of repeating the incident, Peter chose to remain silent. Instead he glared at Sidney with clenched fists. The disapproving stare caused Sidney to turn beet red. He knew it had been his thoughts that transformed an unsuspecting Katie to a tiny white mouse. But fortunately, no one but Peter put that puzzle piece together, and for now he remained quiet about it.

"There's something very strange about this maze," cautioned James. "Let's stay close to each other and look out for anything that's out of the norm."

"Umm, James," replied Charlotte. "We were just transported from an island to this maze, which unexpectedly changed into a different type of bush and then mysteriously created a door for us to enter. EVERYTHING about this place is out of the norm!"

"You're right," said a slightly embarrassed James.

"We get it," added Emily. "None of us knows what to expect here, so let's be on the lookout and give each other a heads up of anything we think might be an issue."

"Point taken," said Peter. "How about we start moving again, I have a feeling that we need to get out of this maze as soon as we can."

Everyone agreed, and after confirming Katie's well-being, Emily once again took the lead.

Peter was in protection mode. He ignored the fearful thoughts swirling in his mind and walked over to Katie and grabbed her by the hand. "Stay close to me Katie, I won't let anything happen to you."

Katie was still stunned by what had happened. Normally she would protest to Peter holding her hand, but now, his touch brought a welcomed calmness and security that she desperately needed. Katie merely nodded her approval, not saying a word.

"I'm certain this is the way we're supposed to go, but it's a dead end," Emily announced nervously to the group. She stopped and rested her hands on her hips, "Did I make a wrong turn? Are we supposed to go back?" She questioned the others as she flipped through the blank pages of her notebook, hopeful something would appear on the empty pages. "James, look in my notebook and tell me where we're supposed to go."

"Emily, what are you talking about?" asked a confused James. He walked past her, straight through the shrubbery that was blocking their way.

Emily could hear James' voice but couldn't see him.

Charlotte had an epiphany. Suddenly it all made sense. "What am I thinking?" she questioned herself, already knowing the answer. She reached into her pocket and took hold of her keys. As she did she felt a gentle warmth and confidence travel up her arm, "This is a distraction, an illusion. I'm going to walk straight through the hedge just like James did."

Feeling more herself and more confident Katie voiced proudly, "I think I get this. I know I have to think the right thing. I don't exactly know what the right thing is. But I know if James can walk through the bush we can too." She took out her scales and saw they were in perfect balance. "Yes! See, look at my balanced scales. I know this will work."

Gazing into his crystal ball, Sidney imagined everyone walking through the hedge, and the appearance of the image inside the ball was magical.

"Okay, here I go!" Charlotte called out excitedly. She walked to the hedge, reached out and felt it. It was dense. Her confidence waivered and she hesitated. However, before she could think, James reached through the bush and took her hand.

"There is no hedge, Charlotte," James declared.

"There is, James, I can feel it."

"Can you feel my hand?" he asked her.

"Yes."

"Then come on. Trust me, there is no hedge."

Charlotte gripped James' hand with such force he felt like his fingers would snap. "Relax!" he cautioned. "I'm not going to let go. Remember, there is no hedge. Just take one step forward, you'll see."

With her free hand Charlotte clutched her keys. Once again, confidence flowed through her arm. She closed her eyes for protection, released her keys and positioned her free arm in front of her face for the same reason. Taking a giant breath, she held it and stepped into the hedge. As James gently drew her to him she felt nothing.

Charlotte was thrilled with her achievement and laughed out loud while hugging James. He was shocked and didn't know how to respond when Charlotte gave him a little kiss on the check. So he did nothing, but inside, his thoughts were flying faster than a jet engine. Finally, he broke free from them and told himself not to read into it, "Charlotte was just excited. She's just a friend. Move on."

"Emily, you're right! This is the way. There's no hedge! Come on you guys!" Charlotte jumped up and down. The others followed, each walking through the nonexistent shrubbery. Emily was relieved and reassured at the same time. Why did she doubt her memory? She was right the entire time.

Katie repeated to herself, "There is no hedge. There is no hedge. Everyone is right in front of me. There is no hedge." She stepped to the bush and glanced at her scales. They were perfectly balanced. She closed her eyes, moved forward and joined her friends.

Balchazar: *Humans are taught to live through their senses. They are conditioned to believe only after they see to confirm that belief. Humans say, seeing is believing. I say to you it is the other way around. Believing is seeing.*

Charlotte ran ahead of the others. She no longer believed a map of the maze was necessary. Thinking she solved the puzzle, Charlotte suggested they walk through all the bushes and quickly come out on the other side. However, when she tested her theory, she soon learned this was not the case. She plowed face first into the hedge she tried to walk through, the force of which caused her to fall on her backside. Everyone had a good laugh and praised her for trying.

But James was confused, Charlotte had just kissed him and now he didn't know the appropriate reaction. He rushed to her side, knelt down, pulled a couple of leaves from her hair, grabbed her hand and helped her off the ground. "Are you okay?" he asked in a concerned tone.

"I'm fine," Charlotte said as she giggled. "All I did was fall, calm down James." Charlotte didn't understand why James was so concerned, but didn't dwell on it. She let go of his hand, brushed herself off, and said to Emily, "Lead the way."

James stood confused staring at Charlotte. "I'll talk to Peter about this," he thought. "He has much more experience with girls than I do."

Emily resumed her leadership position and easily guided the gang. Each time they came to a crossroad it was clear to her which way to go via her perfect memory. She was finding it easier and easier to recall as she relaxed. It seemed that as long as she kept her mind calm, her memory took over. She flipped through the empty pages of the notebook, nothing had changed. She was unable to see anything she'd copied. Still, she wasn't confident enough to let go of the book, so she kept her grip tight.

"Look, is that a drink station? I hope so, I'm so thirsty," said Emily. "I need a soda, with ice, lots of ice." Emily had already seated herself on the nearest red vinyl barstool.

Charlotte joined her, "I'll have a diet and Katie will have the same." She tapped her hand on the bell that rested on the counter. *Bing-Bing.*

An octopus dressed in red and white stripes shot up from beneath the counter. Charlotte screamed and backed off her stool. The octopus stood before them with a huge smile on his face. With one tentacle he wiped off the counter, with another he moved the bell, and at the same time, one dashed out, wrapped around Charlotte, and pulled her back onto the stool.

"Don't be nervous young lady. My name is Gerry, and I'm here to help. How may I be of service?" He gave an ever-so-slight bow.

Charlotte relaxed; there was something very calming about Gerry. Feeling the same, the rest of the group sat on the remaining barstools. It didn't take long before they were laughing at Gerry's jokes while he prepared their beverages.

Sidney was hungry; he wished he was eating his favorite meal. He piped up, "Hey Gerry, I'm kind of hungry. Can I order some food?"

"Indeed, you may. But, I don't have a menu. Please, don't limit yourself to a menu. You may ask for whatever you like. What do you want? Give it careful consideration."

Balchazar: *As Gerry has so eloquently suggested, we need not be limited by our own beliefs. Anything you want can be yours. So, think, really think. What would you actually like to do? What would you love to have? What do you desire more than anything? Let your imagination be your guide. My students must learn that the truth is simple; you can have what you really want.*

Sidney closed his eyes to imagine exactly what he wanted. He was thinking of his favorite food. He wanted tacos, with guacamole and sour cream, loaded with tomatoes, cheese and hot sauce…not too spicy and not too mild, just right.

Gerry noted Sidney's order in his memory, there were no pens or notebooks in any of his tentacles. He then moved on to the others, who promptly gave their selections.

"I'll have a steak sandwich please, with coleslaw," said James.

Peter was next, "Spaghetti and meatballs for me."

"I'd like a burger and fries, which I never get to have," giggled Charlotte.

"Tofu and noodles, please," came the request from Emily.

"Tofu and noodles? That's what you really want?" asked Gerry. He knew better. She wasn't going to get that one past him as her true desire.

"Well, I guess not," she answered, turning slightly pink in her face from embarrassment. "What I'd really like is a huge, hot fudge sundae with sprinkles and whipped cream, and extra cherries. And then I'm going to spoon it into my drink and make a float. Yum! That's what I want."

"Oh, stepping out of the health food routine are we Emily?" snickered Katie. "I'd like salmon, please, crusted with Cajun seasoning, fingerling potatoes and a small green salad."

After each order was placed, Gerry stretched six of his tentacles above his head. There was no moving about, no fussing or arranging, and no visible cooking. He didn't leave the counter or look away, he simply reached sky high. When he brought his tentacles back into view, each was holding a perfectly plated dish prepared to the exact specifications of his guests.

Except for the sound of silverware scraping against their plates and the pleasing mumbling that affirmed the deliciousness of their food, no one spoke while they ate. No one except for Gerry, he talked the entire time. All the while busying himself by refilling their drinks and knitting what appeared to be several pairs of bright orange mittens with his spare tentacles.

Finally, Peter spoke up, indicating it was time to go. They said their good byes to Gerry. He refused to let them leave before opening their backpacks, and Sidney's fanny pack, to insert their favorite candy bars, which he knew without asking. "You'll want it for a snack later. Now go on, you still have a long road ahead of you. But remember, don't let your thoughts limit you. Decide what you want and go for it. It doesn't matter if you don't know how you'll do it. Just decide, and the rest will happen in time."

"That was awesome!" cried James as they walked down a long, straight path.

Peter agreed, "That was the best spaghetti and meatballs I've ever had!"

"Gerry was so sweet and nice," said Katie.

"I know," said Charlotte, "I miss him already."

"I'm stuffed!" said Sidney.

They burst into laughter. But they were soon interrupted by Emily as they turned a sharp corner. "Guys, I think we solved the puzzle. This is the end!"

Emily was standing in front of another arch, which appeared to be the exit to the maze. Everyone was thrilled to follow Emily through the door. High fives were exchanged and the mood was jovial.

After their brief celebration, Katie asked, "If this is the end, what do we do now?"

Emily searched her memory and came to the conclusion that where they were standing had to be one of the missing pieces of the puzzle map. She was unable to tell them where to go.

Peter had a feeling. He acted on it and spoke up, "I think we need to move forward in a straight line. Our path is directly in front of us."

No one else had a better suggestion, so they began walking, moving forward. Peter and James were leading. They continued their conversation about Gerry and the amazing food they devoured. The girls giggled as Katie revealed her infatuation with Mason to Emily. Charlotte rolled her eyes, once again reminding Katie that he's too old for her. Lagging behind the group was Sidney, all alone, a more comfortable place for him, off in his imagination, rather than conversing with the others.

Suddenly, the earth began to shake and rumble, "Earthquake!" yelled Katie.

To their utter amazement, the ground began to split beneath their feet, opening a bottomless chasm. To save Peter from falling into the abyss, James grabbed him by the collar and pulled him to safety.

"Thanks!" slurred a shocked and breathless Peter.

Like so many other times in the maze, they couldn't see a way around the newly formed gap, which spread as far as they could see.

"Now what?" yelled Charlotte. "Peter, you said this was the way to go! I can't believe we have to turn around and go back." She spun around, and began walking alone, in the direction of the maze they just exited.

Before anyone could stop her, the ground shook once again. Looking over the deep canyon they saw six weathered doors rise slowly from the depths of the earth.

"Wait Charlotte! Come back!" yelled Katie. "Look, there are doors."

James took out his spyglass. He believed it would reveal how to cross the deep ravine. Oddly, through the glass, he saw there was no ledge, no cliff, and no newly-formed hole in the earth. Instead, the soft and squishy grass they were standing on provided a continuous path to the six doors.

"What do you see?" asked Emily.

"I see a clear path to the doors," answered James. "I don't see a canyon."

"What?" exclaimed Charlotte. "How? I think your spyglass is broken!"

James ignored Charlotte; he was confused by her actions earlier in the maze, and now it was wearing on him. "So what if she kissed me," he thought, "I'm tired of her negativity." He bent down and felt the ground below him. Where the others saw his hand touching nothing, James felt the solid ground in front of him. He went for it. Without seeking anyone's approval he put one foot in front of the other and began walking toward the doors.

It appeared to the group that James was stepping off the ledge to what would certainly be his death. Emily screamed in shock. But he didn't fall. They watched in awe. To them, James was walking on air. Believing what he saw in his spyglass, he knew he was on solid ground and arrived at the doors in a matter of seconds.

Still ignoring the shouts and screams from his friends, he turned around and yelled out to Emily, "It's an illusion. The ground is there. Feel it yourself and come across."

Emily knelt down and began to run her hand over the canyon, but unlike James, she did not believe, and she did not feel solid ground. Her mind flipped on like a super computer. In it, she searched the map she had drawn. "Is this a continuation of the puzzle? There has to be a clue somewhere on that map. Think Emily, think."

She remembered the instructions from the first sign, it said, *Make a committed decision. Move toward the goal. Use your will to focus on the goal, to the exclusion of all else.*

"Make a committed decision, that's the key to this puzzle!" Emily whispered to herself. "I have to decide and I have to focus," Emily did just that. She decided there was a hidden path in front of her, and that she could walk to James. As her belief began to swell inside, she knelt on the ground once again. She moved her hand across what appeared to be air, but this time felt solid earth. She squealed excitedly and jumped up. Not allowing any time for doubt or fear to creep in, she imagined herself already across the canyon and standing excitedly at the doors. She shook off her nerves, put one foot in front of the other, and quickly made her way across the canyon.

"You did it, Em! I knew you could do it!" shouted James.

Emily's confidence was at a record high after making it to the doors. Fully aware of the solution, and how to make it across, she yelled out. "Katie, here's what you have to do. Decide that you are going to do this. Believe you can do it. You'll be able to feel the ground once you have made the decision and believe, and then all you have to do is step forward."

Katie walked up to the ledge. She knelt down hoping to feel solid earth. Instead, she screamed, "This is so deep; I can't even see the bottom!" She immediately stood up and yelled to Emily, "I can't feel the ground." She looked to Peter, started to cry and said, "I can't do this!"

Peter took Katie's hand and held it gently in his two hands. He was more comfortable doing this with her. "It's okay. You can do this Katie." He struggled not knowing what to say for encourage-ment, then an idea flashed through his mind. "Katie," he said more forcefully, "You're a gymnast. You do brave things every day. You can do two backflips with a half twist while you're standing on a mat. I've seen you do a front layout from the gymnastic horse. If you can do that, then you can walk across this canyon. I know you can. Just think. How can you make this work for you?"

Peter was quite proud of his encouraging words. He didn't know where they came from, but felt it was exactly what Katie needed to hear.

Katie understood what Peter was saying. She tapped into the confidence she exhibits on the gym floor, "How can I be comfortable walking on air?" she asked herself. After several moments of deep thinking it hit her, "I can be comfortable walking on air if I imagine that I'm walking across a balance beam."

Katie reached into her bag and found her scales. They were teetering. But as she imagined herself walking across a balance beam to the other side, the scales gently slowed and became balanced.

Katie stood at the ledge; the beam was real in her mind and in front of her. She pictured herself walking across it to the other side. She felt the exhilaration of competition. She turned to Peter and acknowledged him the way she would a judge. Then she leapt onto the beam, arms outstretched for balance and walked across in perfect form.

She hugged Emily and James and yelled out to Charlotte, "It's your turn. You can do this. It's not hard. Just figure it out in your mind."

Charlotte stepped up to the ledge but retreated fearfully as she heard the sound of an engine revving into action. She turned and saw a motorcycle.

Sidney had let his imagination take control and he stood about a hundred yards away from the canyon, his feet were resting on the ground, supporting his bike. His hands turned the handlebars and revved the deafening engine. He tightened his helmet and pulled down the visor to protect his eyes. He hit the gear with his foot and the bike jumped into motion. He raced toward the canyon, building up speed. He reached the imaginary jump he created, and the bike launched perfectly in the air. He soared past Charlotte and Peter, both staring with gaping mouths as he spanned the canyon and landed roughly on the other side, barely missing Katie.

"How did he do that?" asked a confused Charlotte.

"Imagination," said Peter. "As much as I hate to admit it, that nerd can do anything he wants with his imagination."

Charlotte felt empowered after watching the others cross the chasm. "This doesn't have to be complicated," she decided. "I'm going to imagine myself walking across a bridge." She made the decision and a wooden, plank bridge appeared. The rickety jungle bridge was suspended over the canyon and included hand rails made of rope.

Charlotte took her first step onto the shaky bridge and said, "Okay guys, here I come." She moved slowly, clinging to the rope, as the bridge swayed from side to side. Traveling slowly, she found her groove and continued her crossing. She stepped gently, methodically choosing each foot and hand placement. She had precision focus. Unexpectedly, the plank she stepped on gave way. She screamed and watched it fall into the bottomless abyss.

Shaken, Charlotte stood still.

The soft, compassionate side of James overpowered the frustration he had earlier for Charlotte. He ran to the opposite side of the bridge and yelled, "It's okay Charlotte. Keep coming. The bridge is fine!"

She made eye contact with James, then it hit her, "I need my keys. I need to feel the calm of my keys." But she was too terrified to let go of the rope. So, she improvised. In her mind, she imagined she was holding her keys, and gradually began to feel the welcomed calm they always bring. The more she concentrated, the better she felt.

After just two steps, a fierce wind swept the bridge from side to side causing her to lose her footing. Now on her knees, Charlotte stared at the vast expanse beneath her. Fear now controlled her mind. "I'm going to die!" she thought.

Then she heard James yelling, "Ignore the wind Charlotte. Focus on me. You're almost here. Just a little more."

He was standing at the end of the bridge, but Charlotte was paralyzed, unable to move one inch.

"Look at me!" yelled James. "Charlotte, Look at me!"

Finally, she looked. Her eyes locked with his.

"Stand up! Put one foot in front of the other!" he instructed.

Charlotte knew there was only one way she was going to get off this bridge. She released one hand from the rope, reached into her pocket and grabbed her keys. Immediately, she felt calmness and relaxation in her mind and her limbs. No longer frozen with fear, she began slowly to stand. The calmness in her mind allowed her to think. "Focus," she said to herself. "Focus. James is right there. Just go to James. Nothing else matters. Just walk to James."

She ignored the wind and placed one foot in front of the other until James reached out and grabbed her. He hugged her and this time, without thinking, he gave her a kiss on the check. "You did it, Charlotte! That was amazing!"

"I did it," she thought. "Yes, I did it!" Charlotte was ecstatic.

James released Charlotte as Emily and Sidney approached. They both embraced her in a bear hug. But all Charlotte could think about was that peck on the check. "Why did he do that? What does it mean? How do I feel about that?" She didn't have time to process her thoughts. James was now yelling at Peter and all attention was on him.

"Come on Peter," James shouted. "It's your turn."

Peter was on his knees. Even though he couldn't feel any earth beneath his hands, his intuition told him that what James saw in his spyglass was real. There is a path here. All I have to do is move forward. Move forward and the path will appear.

Peter stood up and moved toward the very edge of the ledge. In his heart he believed the path was in front of him. He trusted his intuition and he also trusted his best friend. He believed he could do this. He stepped out and his foot hit solid ground. He laughed nervously as he told himself everything was okay. He focused on his belief and continued to walk forward, seconds later he was with the rest of his friends.

Balchazar: *As was nicely demonstrated by our young friends, no matter what your challenge, everyone must find their own way. You have to find it yourself. No one can do it for you.*

As they all talked loudly and excitedly, they were interrupted as they felt the earth trembling again. They turned and watched as the chasm they had each crossed closed.

"Is this for real?" yelled Charlotte. "All I had to do was hold out for five more minutes and I wouldn't have had to cross that jungle bridge that almost sent me to my death!"

Still shocked by the closing of the giant canyon no one said a word. But then a sudden thought raced into Emily's overactive mind, "No Charlotte, I think it's just the opposite. As part of the puzzle, each one of us had to figure out our own way to get across the canyon. Once we were successful, the puzzle was complete and it closed."

Smiling, and speaking before Charlotte could interject another negative theory, James turned to Emily, "You took the words right out of my mouth."

Peter was right behind James, "Yeah, yeah, yeah, but now that we're here, what do we do? Have you noticed that none of these doors has a doorknob?"

"What?" shrieked Katie. "What good is a door, without a doorknob?"

After searching her memory for a short moment Emily responded, "Remember when we were in the stables, before we went to the beach? We couldn't see a door in the wall, but James saw it with his spyglass, and he had Charlotte unlock it with her keys."

"Yes, I get it," said Peter enthusiastically. "This has to be the same thing. James..."

But as he looked to his best friend, he saw that he had already pulled out his spyglass and was examining each door closely.

Charlotte pulled the keys out of her pocket. "I've got my keys James, where do I need to put them?"

But James was silent, still examining the doors with the aid of his spyglass. "There are no doorknobs on these doors and there are no key holes."

"That can't be right, keep looking," said Katie.

"No," he said again. "There's no way to open these doors. Hold on, there's a message."

"What does it say?" asked Sidney.

"I bet it's another puzzle," shared Emily.

"Why doesn't everyone just shut up and let James talk!" yelled Charlotte.

James removed the spyglass from his eye and looked back at his friends. "The message looks similar to what we saw when we first went through the arch. It's on parchment paper, but it's more faded than what we saw before, I think I can still read it." He closed one eye and brought the spyglass to his other. They could feel his concentration and were filled with impatience as they watched his lips move without sound.

Finally, he spoke, "I think I have it."

"What does it say?" breathed Katie.

"No one is ready for a thing, until they believe they can acquire it. The state of mind must be belief, not mere hope or wish."

"What?" yelled Charlotte. She was frustrated and disappointed beyond words. Tears flooded her eyes, "Why can't it just tell us how to make the doorknobs appear? We're never going to get home!"

"No, Charlotte, it's okay," Emily replied excitedly. "This is still part of the puzzle. We can figure it out."

But Charlotte didn't want to hear anything else about puzzles. She turned around to leave and walked straight into a man standing behind her. She looked up and gasped. It was Mason. He was dressed in scuba equipment, complete with flippers, goggles and an oxygen tank in his hand.

"What are you doing here? Have you come to confuse us even more?" Charlotte's face turned red. She was embarrassed at her outburst, but didn't back down. "And why are you dressed like that?"

"I hate to tell you this, but I don't have a bag of doorknobs with me. However, I must share how impressed I am with your completion of the puzzle. Charlotte, it's obvious that you're upset and have a lot on your mind. Tell me, what did you discover while completing the puzzle?"

Charlotte was surprised at the direct question from Mason. Still reticent, she folded her arms across her chest, gave him her best angry glare, and refused to answer.

Not wanting to aggravate the situation, Mason calmly answered his own question. "Charlotte, I don't blame you for being angry. Perhaps when you put some distance between you and the bridge, you will see that your will and your focus served you well when you crossed."

"That's a different way to look at a near-death experience," laughed Peter.

Mason now turned to address Peter, "Did you know how you were going to cross the chasm when you first saw it?"

"No, I didn't have a clue."

"Sometimes you have to change your perspective. When you change how you see a thing, the thing you see changes, just like it did for you at the chasm."

Mason saw nothing but confused looks, so he continued, "James saw solid ground, Charlotte, a jungle bridge, Katie a balance beam, Sidney a motorcycle, all different solutions, but all yielding the same result. There is no right or wrong answer, just whatever works for you. Each of you had to engage your imagination, your focus, your will, your belief and your faith."

"I'm sorry, but I have to leave now. You've had a busy day today, but your journey is not yet complete. Remember what you learned in the maze. In time, you'll see how everything fits together. And that's when the real magic happens!"

He stepped into his flippers, secured the goggles on his head, inserted his mouthpiece, adjusted his oxygen tank, gave them a quick thumbs up then snapped his fingers, disappearing into thin air.

"Wow!" said Sidney. "The next time we see him I'm definitely asking him to teach me how to do that!"

"Seriously!" said an exasperated Katie. "He's gone again. What does he mean our journey is not complete? I wish he'd stick around for once and tell us what's going on!"

But before anyone could think about what Katie just said, Sidney felt something vibrating. He unzipped his fanny pack and saw lightning striking inside his crystal ball. "Guys, it's happening again. I see lightning. I think we're about to be moved."

Katie unzipped her backpack. She could see her scales teetering, still inside the bag. "Oh no! Here we go again!"

And as quickly as Mason snapped his fingers they were gone.

CHAPTER 6

FROSTING, CONCRETE AND QUICKSAND

The room was pitch black. No one could see a thing. They were seated on the floor and the group was as silent as it was dark. Slowly, Sidney began reaching out his arms to feel for anything around him.

"Hey!" yelled Charlotte, "Who just hit me in the face?"

"Sorry, that was me," answered Sidney. "I'm pretty sure we're not at the maze anymore. I can't see a thing, but man it smells really good in here. Do I smell...bread?"

"None of us can see!" interrupted Katie. "It's pitch black in here." Katie was annoyed by Sidney's statement of the obvious. Until he spoke she hadn't noticed the warm soothing scent. "But you're right, it does smell good."

Peter asked, "Is everyone here? Emily? James? Are you here?"

"Yes," they both answered in unison.

Emily reached out her arm and asked, "Who am I touching?"

"It's me," replied Katie. "Here, Emily, hold my hand. Everyone reach out and grab hands. Let's try and get a feel for where we are, then maybe we can orient ourselves in the dark."

As they used their arms to find each other, the girls apologized for their misplaced hands and awkward jabs. Peter knew instantly when he clasped hands with the person to his right that it was Katie. He recognized the softness and size of her hand. He remembered his daydream standing at the oak tree walking to class with Katie, holding her hand. The thought of this made his insides tingle. Maybe there really was something to all this stuff about his thoughts.

James wondered if he might be next to Charlotte, but knew immediately he had Peter's hand on his right and Sidney's on his left. He decided to mess with Peter and started to tickle his hand, however, Peter knew it was James and smacked him. The two boys stopped laughing and Peter spoke up, "Now what?"

James laughed. "I don't know, but here we go again. If we could just get some light in here, maybe we could figure out where we are and what we're supposed to do. I really wish I had my phone, if so, we would all have plenty of light."

Suddenly Charlotte yelled out excitedly, "Someone's glowing! Who is it?"

"Where?" asked Sidney. "I don't see it."

"I don't know? Somewhere right in front of me," and she reached out her foot to see if she could touch whoever it was.

"Hey!" said Peter. "Who just kicked me?"

"It's Peter! Peter, keep talking. Look to the sound of Peter's voice."

"There is definitely light coming from you Peter, what is that?" asked Emily.

"I don't know." Peter attempted to look at his body and then started to feel it to see if he could find whatever it was the others saw glowing. Suddenly he felt heat. It was coming from the locket that was hanging around his neck. He reached down his shirt to grab it. As he brought it out from under his shirt the light was there, and now brighter. "You guys! It's my locket. I can't believe it. It's glowing, and it's warm too. What does this mean? I wonder if it's finally going to open for me."

As Peter examined the locket he could tell the light was coming from inside, but no matter how hard he pried, he still couldn't open it, "I can't open it! I don't know what's wrong with this thing."

"Peter, it's okay," reassured Katie. "Your locket is glowing and giving us light. I can kind of see where everyone is now. Why don't you shine it around so we can see where we are."

Peter removed the locket from his neck and caught hold of the chain just in time to keep it from falling. "That's strange. I almost dropped the locket, but I swear it was going to fall up instead of down."

Ignoring what he had just said, Emily interrupted, "Peter, I have an idea. Shine the locket on the floor; it's the closest thing to us. Maybe we can get a clue."

He moved the locket around. The floor was strange. It wasn't any type of material he was familiar with, not carpet, not tile, not wood, not concrete. It appeared to be laid out in a grid, and it was white. As he moved the locket around, he saw what looked to be a large vent connected to a pipe, and next to that a bulb. "Um... guys, this is going to sound a little strange, but I swear there's a lightbulb screwed into this floor."

"A lightbulb?" said Charlotte. "That's ridiculous! Shine your light over by me."

Peter started to crawl over to Charlotte, but then, Sidney yelled, "No. Peter, come over here. There's something next to me that feels like a lightbulb."

Peter changed directions and headed over to Sidney. Sure enough, as he shined his light both he and Sidney saw the lightbulb screwed into the floor. "How odd," thought Peter. "I've never seen lightbulbs screwed into a floor."

After a moment of silence Emily spoke up, "Peter, what's your gut telling you right now?"

"You don't want to know," he replied.

"Yes, I do, because I think mine might be telling me the same thing."

"What?" said Charlotte. "What's going on? Are we in trouble? Are we in danger?"

"I think," said Peter, "We might be sitting on a ceiling."

"What!" yelled Charlotte. "That's impossible. If we were on the ceiling we would be upside down and all the blood would have already rushed to our heads by now. Not to mention we would have fallen to the floor."

Peter held the locket above his head, hoping he would see that he was wrong. But the dim light didn't illuminate any other details. "I wish this locket was brighter." As soon as he said the words, the light inside the locket turned from a soft glow to that of a bright flashlight.

It took a few seconds for everyone's eyes to adjust to the increased brightness now shining from the locket, but when they did, it was clear they were sitting on a ceiling. Below them were stacked boxes, bags, wooden counter tops, small appliances and stainless-steel walls.

"What is this place?" asked Sidney.

Emily was the first to respond, "I think we're inside a…"

"Kitchen!" yelled James. "We're in a kitchen. That's why it smells like bread. This must be a bakery." James was a bit excited by his deduction of their location. "But why are we on the ceiling? How did we get upside down? And how is it that I don't feel like I'm upside down? None of this is making any sense."

"Sidney!" yelled Peter. "Did you do this? This seems like just the sort of thing that you would be imagining just to mess with us!"

Sidney was put out of kilter by Peter's tone. His nerves got the best of him when he answered Peter's accusation. Sidney thought Peter wouldn't believe him no matter the truth. "No! No, this has nothing to do with me. I was just thinking about Mason and wondering how this is all happening to us."

"I don't believe you!" said Peter. "Let me see your crystal ball. I want to see if there's any type of a bakery in there."

"There's not, I swear!" Sidney reached for his waist and felt his crystal ball inside his fanny pack. Not wanting to remind everyone that he was the only one with a fanny pack, he quietly removed the ball and handed it over to Peter. "See, it's totally blank. I'm not imagining anything right now."

"Well maybe that's the problem," interrupted James. "You probably need to be imagining some way for us to get right side up. I'm going to get my spyglass out to see if I can see anything that might help."

"That's a great idea," said Emily. "Everyone get your gifts out and see if you can find any clues that will help us get off the ceiling! Now that's a sentence I never thought I'd say." Emily mumbled under her breath.

Each of them began rummaging through their pockets and bags to see if their gifts from the museum had arrived with them. "My bag is empty!" yelled Katie. "I don't have my scales. The only thing in my backpack is the candy bar Gerry gave me and a rope, and I don't even know how that got in there. I don't need a rope."

"Wait!" said Sidney. "We can use that rope."

"For what?" asked Charlotte.

"He's right," said Peter. "I can tie it around this vent and use it to climb down to the floor. Pass me the rope. Hurry!"

Peter wrapped the rope around the exposed ventilation pipe several times. Then he tried his hardest to remember his knot tying skills from his short-lived days as a boy scout. Finally, he was finished. He tugged on the rope. It seemed secure. "I think it's ready. I guess I can go first."

Everyone watched intently as Peter secured the rope. Emily was the first to notice that the light coming from inside Peter's locket was gradually giving off more light. "Peter, your locket is getting brighter. Look, the entire room is lit up now."

"What's that stuff on the floor?" asked Katie.

"It looks like snow," replied Sidney.

"It is snow. It's snowing!" said James. "Look. But it's just in one spot."

Charlotte was exasperated with the whole scene. "It can't snow inside. Have you guys lost your mind?"

As they tried to see where the snow was coming from, Emily shrieked. "It's coming from the vent that you just tied the rope around, Peter."

"What?" said a startled Peter.

Sidney scooted over to the vent, reached down and stuck his hand under it to collect some snow. "Well, I don't think its snow. I don't know what it is, but it's not cold," he said as he examined the white stuff in his hand.

"Let me see!" said Charlotte. She reached over and Sidney dumped the white substance into her hand. She put it up to her nose, smelled it, stuck her pinky in it, and then tasted it. Charlotte started laughing, "It's flour! We're in a bakery and it is snowing flour from the vent. Here, try it." she said as she reached her hand out to Emily.

"What happened?" questioned Peter. "I swear there was no flour coming out of that vent when I started tying the rope around it."

"There wasn't," said Emily. "It must have started after you tied your knots. But why? It makes no sense."

"We're upside down on a ceiling," said a frustrated James, who was examining the room through the lens of his spyglass. "Nothing about this place makes sense."

"James, what do you see?" asked Peter.

"Well, if you can believe it, through the lens of my spyglass, we are all sitting on the floor, not the ceiling. And the pile of snow on the ground is really a giant stack of pillows."

"Does that mean that we're really not on the ceiling?" asked Sidney.

"I think it means that we need to look at the situation we're in from a different perspective," answered James.

Balchazar: *James has the right idea. Watch.*

"How so?" questioned Sidney.

"Well, let me think for a minute."

After a few minutes Emily broke the silence, "James, you look a little strange when you're thinking."

Everyone laughed and Katie asked the question again, "What do you think this means, James?"

"Okay, let me walk you through my thoughts here. We think we're on the ceiling. However, none of us feels light headed or has blood rushing to our heads, so that tells me maybe this is some sort of illusion. For some reason, we see ourselves on the ceiling, but the spyglass shows me that we're all on the floor. If I think back, this glass usually shows me some alternate view. Remember when we were in the maze and I could see things no one else could?"

Everyone nodded but no one could make any sense of what James was saying.

"Maybe it has something to do with what we're thinking," said Sidney. "When we were on the beach I thought really hard about how much I wanted to build a sandcastle, and then in just a couple of minutes, everything I needed to build one appeared. Maybe it's the same with this. Maybe we just need to think the right things about being on the floor and it will happen."

Katie started to say something, but before she could get the first word out Peter interrupted her. "Katie, stop! I know what you're going to say, but don't. I have a good feeling about this. I think Sidney has the right idea. We should all take a few minutes and think about being on the floor."

"Let's do it!" said James. He could tell Katie was upset, and knew an argument was coming if he didn't act fast. "Close your eyes, do whatever you need to do to put yourself in the right frame of mind. Think about being on the floor. See yourself standing on the floor. Believe that you are already on the floor."

It hadn't been more than 30 seconds and the sound of Sidney laughing brought everyone out of their "thinking zone." As they looked around they saw Sidney lying on the floor below them. He was in the flour, making a snow angel and laughing.

"I did it you guys. I imagined myself on the floor making snow angels in the flour and now here I am. It works. Come on. Hurry up."

It took a couple of minutes for everyone to get focused again, but as they did James suddenly stood up and walked across the ceiling to the wall. He then lifted one foot from the ceiling and placed it on the wall. He followed it with his other foot and he began walking seamlessly down the wall, as if he was standing on the floor. Once he got to the floor he did the same thing with his feet and there he was, on the floor. He walked over to Sidney and extended his hand to help him out of the flour. "Come on," James said excitedly, "Let's go explore."

After a few more minutes of focused concentration, the next person they heard was Emily. She was on the floor, on top of a huge pile of fluffy pillows, giggling. "James! These are the pillows you saw through your spyglass." She jumped up and ran after Sidney and James who were walking into the next room.

Charlotte, looking at Peter and Katie, was visibly frustrated. "Do either of you have any suggestions on how we should do this?"

"It doesn't seem to be complicated, Char," said Peter. "I think we should just imagine ourselves standing on the floor."

"Those pillows look really fun!" replied Katie.

"I agree," said Charlotte. She grabbed Katie's hand and mustered her determination. "Let's do this. Concentrate really hard."

"Okay, just close your eyes and imagine both of us on the pillows." Katie held out her hand to Peter, "Are you coming with us?"

Peter was so shocked he could hardly speak. He grabbed Katie's hand and muttered an indistinguishable, "uh huh." Immediately he regretted everything he just did. The clumsy way he grabbed Katie's hand, and his lame attempt at a response. But then it hit him. Katie reached out to hold his hand. Peter was so excited he could scream.

The sound of the girls talking brought his focus back to the task at hand. He realized he needed to stop thinking about Katie and start thinking about the pillows. But what if he didn't make it down with them? Even though he was so sure he had the answer, now that he had to take action himself, he doubted his intuition.

Peter worked hard to bring order to his mind. He cleared out all thoughts, and with laser focus imagined himself on the pillows, still holding Katie's hand.

Charlotte had a plan, "I'm going to count one, two, three, jump. And then we all jump and hopefully we should land on the pillows."

Katie couldn't make sense of that idea. "If we jump, won't we just land again on the ceiling?"

"Just try it with me Katie; what do we have to lose?" Charlotte knew beyond any doubt that a simple jump would land the three of them in the center of the pillows just as they wanted. She didn't know how she knew. She just knew. She had the introspective confidence of knowing in spite of the seeming reality. "One, two, three, jump!"

The next thing Peter heard was the sound of Katie and Charlotte giggling, while prodding him in the chest.

"Open your eyes," said Katie. "We made it."

Peter opened his eyes. He was lying on a huge stack of pillows. Both Katie and Charlotte were hovering over him with pillows in hand, still laughing. "Wow!" he exclaimed. "We really made it. This is amazing!"

Charlotte smacked Peter in the face with a pillow, and then ran as she and Katie laughed. He was now alone. "Oh well," he thought.

"I still held Katie's hand!"

"Now what?" he yelled to the group.

James was the first to respond, "This place is awesome. If you go through that door you can see all the different food displays. Oh man, it all looks so good. I know it hasn't been that long since Gerry fed us, but I'm starving."

"Well, let's take advantage of where we are," said Emily. "Let's eat!"

Just then, Sidney walked in holding a tray of pastries, pies, cakes and, James' favorite, donuts.

"Ask and you shall receive. Is anyone else hungry?" questioned Sidney. "This place is empty and there's a ton of food. I don't think they'll mind if we eat some."

Everyone rushed over and grabbed something delicious from Sidney's overloaded tray. Charlotte picked an éclair, while Emily took a cupcake. James grabbed the only chocolate donut. Peter went straight for the strawberry torte and Katie picked at the flakey layers of a tiny chocolate filled croissant. Unlike the others, her decision was based on which treat she thought would have the least number of calories.

Aside from exclamations of how yummy the baked goods were, no one spoke while eating. Once they finished, Sidney went back for a slice of lemon meringue pie.

Katie broke the silence. "I hate to bring up bad news, but I just want to remind everyone that I still don't have my scales. I don't know where they are."

"Okay," said James. "Does everyone else have their gifts?"

"My quill is right here," Emily raised it in the air.

"I have my keys," answered Charlotte. "They've been in my pocket the entire time."

All eyes were now on James again. "So, Katie's scales are the only thing missing? Okay, we can handle this. Let's all split up and look for them."

"They have to be easier to find than my locket," said Peter.

"At least we know that no one will be wearing them," laughed Emily.

They separated and began looking for the scales. Sidney rummaged through the cabinets. Katie was behind him searching the wire rack shelves that lined the back wall of the bakery.

Katie screamed. Spatulas began flying off the shelves and she ducked to avoid being struck in the head. "What's going on?" she shrieked.

But no one, not even Sidney heard her. They were all concentrating on their individual search for the scales. As Katie looked around attempting to decipher the circumstances, she failed to make the connection that each time Sidney opened a cabinet door another spatula soared past her head.

On the other side of the kitchen, Charlotte was systematically opening the giant walk-in refrigerators and freezers encompassing one entire wall. Emily stared at the ovens, wondering how the doors were opening and closing on their own. She was unaware that each time Charlotte opened and closed a refrigerator door, the same thing happened to one of the oven doors.

Despite all the opening and closing of doors, the scales were nowhere to be found inside the refrigerators, freezers or ovens.

Frustrated, James pulled out his spyglass to scan the room. Through it, he saw a large conduit of light that began at Peter's locket and ended on a lone shelf in the corner of the kitchen. "I think I know where the scales are!" he yelled, still looking through the spyglass.

"Where?" asked Katie.

"Well, when I look through my spyglass, Peter's locket seems to be pointing the way," James followed the light from Peter's locket to the indicated spot on the shelf.

"My locket! How?"

"There's a bright light coming from it, and it ends right here on this shelf." James lifted his hands to pull Katie's scales from the top shelf.

"My scales!" yelled Katie. She reached out to grab them and noticed they weren't balanced.

As they stared at the scales, Peter heard a humming noise that was growing louder by the second. "What's that noise?"

They began to look around the room until Sidney yelled, "It's this giant mixer. Did someone start it, or is it mixing on its own?"

Everyone walked to the mixer. It was the largest mixer they'd ever seen. As Sidney stared at it, he imagined himself in a white baker's coat and hat. He was the head baker in an enormous kitchen, leaning over a mixer, adding ingredients, until his cinnamon flavored dough was mixed properly. He ordered his assistant bakers to remove the dough and tie perfectly shaped knots.

While they created cinnamon rolls, he moved onto the cake section of his kitchen, where his decorating experts were creating the most amazing triple-layer birthday cake. Sidney dipped his finger in the frosting and tasted it. "Delicious, but this blue isn't dark enough." The imaginary bakers immediately began mixing more blue food coloring into the yummy frosting.

Next, he walked over to the ovens, where they were pulling out freshly baked chocolate-chip cookies. He held his hand out and was served a cookie. It was hot, but as a master-level baker who'd burned himself repeatedly throughout his career, Sidney's fingers were numb to the heat. The cookie broke apart perfectly, with just the right amount of gooey chocolate clinging as he placed a bite in his mouth. He savored the flavor of the cookie. He knew he had the best bakery in the city. Everything he touched turned to delicious tasting gold.

Sidney was jolted from his imagination as the motor of the mixer kicked into a higher gear. It sped up and created an even louder noise.

"I think something's wrong with this mixer," Emily's eyebrows creased together. "Why is it operating on its own in the first place? I don't like this."

Abruptly, a loud clunking noise came from the ceiling. It was as if giant iron gears were grinding against each other. When they looked up, the ceiling was rotating to the right. After the ceiling turned 180 degrees, it came to a grinding halt. Now that the noise had stopped, there was no longer a ceiling above them. The rotation had caused it to disappear. They were now staring at a cloudy blue sky.

Before anyone could say a word, they heard the same noise again, only louder and closer. The floor they were standing on, along with about six feet of the bottom half of the room, began to move. The rotation was the same as the ceiling, only in the opposite direction. It turned 180 degrees to the left, and then slammed to a stop, causing everyone to stumble and catch their balance.

The bakery floor they were standing on just seconds before was now dirt. Instead of kitchen islands and countertops, there were make-shift tables covered with blue prints. Where shelves filled with baking gadgets and supplies once stood, there were now tools and heavy equipment strewn about. "Did we just move to a construction zone?" asked Charlotte.

But before anyone could answer, the same grinding noise sounded and the remaining middle section of the room rotated. When it stopped it was full of beams, scaffolding and iron that stretched from the floor to high in the sky.

The oversized mixer they had all been staring at was now a very large concrete mixing truck. They stared at the rotating drum and the chute through which the concrete would eventually flow.

"What. Just. Happened?" Emily put a hand to her forehead.

Everyone was silent, dumbfounded. Finally, Sidney spoke up, "If I had to describe what just happened to us, I'd say it's like we're in the middle of a giant Rubik's cube. Everything around us switched and now it's all different. We went from the bakery to a construction site."

"I don't understand why we'd suddenly shift to a construction site." James scratched his head. "Everything was going just fine. We were all able to get down from the ceiling. We found Katie's scales."

"Something strange happened with the giant mixer at the bakery," replied Peter. "It started on its own; we were all staring at it. Then it picked up speed. I feel like it's responsible for bringing us here."

"I know why we're here," whispered Charlotte.

"Why? Did you do something?" Katie wanted to know.

"Yes," replied Charlotte. "It's the strangest thing, and I can hardly believe it myself. After I ate my éclair, I took a cupcake from the tray. I had one bite of it before we came to look at the mixer. As we were staring at the mixer I was thinking about the icing on the cupcake. I didn't like it. I thought it was too hard. Like concrete! I thought the cupcake frosting was like concrete.

For a second, I thought about the mixer being full of pink concrete that they poured on the cupcakes." She paused for a moment and no one said a word. "There's no explanation for this, except that I thought it."

Balchazar: *Your mind has the power to accept or reject any idea that is placed into it. You must very carefully guard the portal of your mind. Do not think of what you do not want, for you will create more of it. Think only of what you do want, and you will create more of it.*

Peter walked over to the mixer, "Well, Charlotte, let's see how strong your thoughts and theory are. Anyone want to take a guess as to what color the concrete is inside?" He opened the door to the truck and found the lever. He released it and swiftly returned to the others. The drum on the truck switched directions and a thick river of pink concrete began to flow down the chute.

"Charlotte, this is incredible," cried Emily. "Your thoughts did this!"

"I mean, it's all so hard to believe," replied Charlotte. "Although, I guess it shouldn't be hard to believe. I got myself down from the ceiling and onto the bed of pillows. And now this…It's just… Something I've never thought about before. I guess I've always thought that things just happen to me. But maybe all this stuff isn't random?"

"I know," said James. "This is kind of a game changer. If we know that what we think can really happen, there's a lot more attention we need to be paying to what we think about."

"I hate to interrupt," said Katie. "But that pink concrete is "flowing out of that mixer fast, and it has us cornered."

Sure enough, after everyone was shocked to see the pink concrete, they failed to notice that they were standing against a pile of steel beams, and the only way for them to get out was to walk through the concrete that was being poured in front of them.

"Oh my gosh!" said Emily. "We need to get out of here. That concrete is piling up high."

"What are we going to do?" Sidney wrung his hands together.

"I think the only option is to walk through it," replied Peter. "Does anyone have a better idea?"

"Let me look through my spyglass and see if it shows another way out," said James. He pulled it out of his bag and surveyed the area carefully.

"Do you see anything?" asked Katie.

"Yes, when I look at the concrete I see sand, pink sand. I think that's a sign that it's okay for us to walk through it."

"Peter, how do you feel about that?" asked Emily.

"I think that sounds fine. James' spyglass hasn't let us down yet."

"Then let's get out of here before this concrete gets any higher," said an anxious Charlotte.

They stepped into the pink concrete and instantly sunk well past their ankles. It was nearly impossible to lift their feet from the stiff mixture. Peter managed to get one foot out, but his shoe and sock were missing.

"I don't think this was such a good idea," whined Sidney. "Are you sure it wasn't quicksand that you saw in your spyglass, James? It's like were going to sink and be buried ali…"

"Sidney Stop!" yelled James. "Don't say anymore! Do you realize what you could be doing by thinking that?"

"What's wrong with him talking about quicksand?" asked Katie. "He's just making a comparison."

"Katie! Don't you remember how we ended up here in the first place?" yelled Charlotte. "My thoughts on pink concrete!"

Tensions were rising. The familiar grinding noise they heard inside the bakery was now coming from above. They looked up and saw the cloud-filled sky rotating. After moving 180 degrees it stopped, placing them below a scorching yellow sun with vultures flying overhead in a circular formation.

Before they could even talk about what was happening, they began rotating in the opposite direction. When they stopped, there was nothing around them but sand. Nothing. Not a single tree, branch, leaf, or rock. Nothing but sand!

Instantly, the last piece of their Rubik's cube started rotating and finally their move was complete. They were in the middle of the desert, with nothing around them but sand, sun, wind and vultures.

"I'm so sorry guys," yelled Sidney. "Can anyone move? Is it really quicksand?"

They all tried to extricate themselves from the sand, but no one had any luck. The more they moved, the more they seemed to sink.

"We're only in this up to our calves," said Peter. "Everyone stay calm. We have time to find a way out."

"You want me to stay calm while I'm SINKING IN QUICKSAND!" yelled Charlotte. "Forget it! We need to get out of here, NOW!"

Balchazar: *One of life's most challenging lessons to learn is to respond, not react. When one responds, one remains in control. When one reacts, one relinquishes control.*

James spoke up, "Peter's right. We have to be calm. Getting upset isn't going to help. Let's all think. There has to be something we can do to get out of here."

Finally, Emily spoke, "I remember something I read. I don't remember where, but it said something like we need to change the way we look at things, once we do that, everything will change."

"Why are you saying that Emily?" asked a confused Charlotte. "What do you mean?"

"I'm not sure what it means, it just came to my mind, so I thought I needed to share it. I felt like it was important."

"Okay Emily," said Peter. "How can we change the way we're looking at this?"

"That's the million-dollar question," answered Katie. "But I'm not sure any of us has an answer. Right now, we're looking at this as a bad situation, one that could potentially be deadly, painful, all kinds of bad! We're all nervous. None of us wants to sink in this quicksand. We're all trying to think of something that will free us. So, I guess what Emily could be saying is that we should start looking at this from the opposite perspective?"

"Yes, that's a great start, and that's what she said," replied Peter. "But tell me, how do we stop ourselves from being nervous and scared when we are sinking in quicksand?"

"We just have to do it!" yelled Sidney. "We don't have a choice. We have to take control of our minds and our thinking. When I'm using my imagination, I can block out everything that's going on around me. I focus on whatever I choose. If we're going to get out of this mess, we need to ignore everything that's around us physically, and think of something completely different."

"Okay, let's try it," said James. "Everyone close your eyes and focus on something good. Don't give any thought to what's happening to us right now."

It was probably about a minute before Emily said, "I can't do this. I can't get the quicksand and the inevitable doom out of my mind!"

"Oh great!" said Katie.

"There's a way," said Charlotte softly.

"What did you say?" asked Emily.

"I said, there's a way. I know how we can get out of this."

"How?" Peter was attempting to push sand from his now covered waist.

"Remember when we were on the island and were running from that giant bird creature? I think we need to do the same thing here. We have to do the unexpected. We have to let the bird catch us and take us away."

"Charlotte," Peter was looking down at his covered waist, "I think the sun has gotten to your brain. The only birds around here are the vultures that keep circling us. They're just waiting for our demise, then they're coming to get us. And I'm not about to let that happen."

"No wait," cried Emily. "Charlotte, I get what you're saying. And you're right. We have to do the illogical. In this case, we have to let the quicksand take us. And we have to know and believe this is all going to work out."

Balchazar: *Now they are on the right track. Believe, have faith. Do not allow your external circumstances to control your thoughts. You have everything you need inside you.*

"Has everyone here lost their mind?" Peter's face was getting red. He couldn't contain himself any longer. The stress and the fear had overtaken him.

"I haven't lost anything, Peter. And you need to pay attention to what we're saying if you want to get out of this mess," snapped Emily. "Calm yourself and start listening to what your intuition is telling you. We don't have all day to figure this out." The sand was closing in.

Peter opened his mouth to argue with her but turned his head at the last moment and caught a very stern look from Katie. His mood immediately changed. "Okay," he said. "Give me a minute to pull myself together."

James said, "I agree. I think the way we violate logic is by doing nothing. We let ourselves sink into the quicksand."

His comment was met by silence. James scanned the group and saw nothing but the blank stares of frightened faces silently questioning his sanity. "I know it seems crazy, but think about it. Escape is the logical thing to do right now. We can violate logic by not trying to escape!"

The silence continued.

Finally, Peter spoke, "I was afraid you were going to say that, but you're right. Even though it sounds ridiculous, my intuition agrees with it."

"Maybe," said Sidney. "We don't need to focus on what happens when we slip INTO the quicksand, but what happens as we slip THROUGH the quicksand. Why don't we look at the quicksand like it's a gateway to another place, and once we pass THROUGH it we're released."

"I agree," said James.

"Well, you're definitely not asking us to do something easy!" said Charlotte. "But, if I can make pink cement with my thoughts, I can definitely make quicksand into something that's not scary."

"I'm in," said Emily. "It's so crazy that it has to work."

"Is this my only choice?" asked Katie. "I guess I will sink with you and see where it takes us. You better not be wrong."

Peter was now holding his arms above his head because the sand was to his chest. He voiced the question on everyone's mind, "Where do we want to go? Are we all going to focus on the same thing?"

James took over, "Think about someplace you really want to go. My thoughts aren't going to be as strong about wanting to go to the mall as Katie's will be. No offense Katie."

"None taken, not everyone is a born shopper," she replied.

"Do you think we'll all end up at different locations?" asked Sidney. "Or do you think the person with the strongest thoughts will take everyone to the same place?"

Charlotte answered, "My thoughts took everyone from the bakery to the construction site, and Sidney, your thoughts brought us all to the desert."

"Why don't we all hold hands as we slip through the quicksand?" suggested Peter. "That's what Katie, Charlotte and I did at the bakery, and it could be enough to keep us together."

"That works for me," said Emily. "Grab hands and start thinking about where you want to go. We're running out of time."

"And may the strongest mind win," said Charlotte with a nervous laugh, sounding more like she was asking a question than making a statement.

They reached out and clasped hands. Fortunately, Peter was next to Katie. He clasped her hand tight, not wanting to think that it might be the last time he holds it. He gave one last encouraging word as the sand passed his chin, "For what it's worth, I feel really good about this. Think strong!"

With that they fell into silence. Each one of them concentrating harder than ever. Charlotte went to her happy place. She was at the symphony, listening to a flawless performance of a beautiful piece of music. Sidney ended up at the zoo, watching over the penguins inside the arctic exhibit. Katie, of course, found herself at the mall. This time she was shopping for the perfect outfit to wear on her first date with Mason. Emily visited a library, where she began searching for books on the human mind and the power of thought. Peter dined alone with Katie. James was packing his parachute in preparation for a skydive. Nothing brings him a rush like thrill seeking, and skydiving is top on his list.

With everyone focused on their thoughts, they seemed to sink the last foot at an accelerated rate. They remained as calm as they could, and kept their eyes closed and their hands clasped. Deep down in their thoughts, each hoped their location would be the chosen one. One by one they quietly slipped under the sand, until there was no evidence they'd been there at all.

Peter opened his mouth to tell Katie he loved her, but instead of tasting sand, he felt the force of a wind tunnel. The air was moving at a ferocious speed. He opened his eyes and saw Katie screaming, but not a sound could be heard. They were in a freefall 13,000 feet above the ground. Each one of them had the same shocked reaction, and they were all terrified. Except for James.

Katie knew James' thought had taken control, and she was not happy about it. But now was not the time to bemoan that detail. That could be dealt with once they reached the ground. And it would be dealt with. However, right now, her mission was survival. The only person who had been skydiving was James, and everyone was looking to him for guidance.

James' eyes were full of the same shock as the rest of the group, however, unlike everyone else, his shock turned to excitement, rather than fear. James has studied skydiving for years by reading and watching videos online. Finally, he earned enough money and talked his parents into letting him go. After his first dive he was in love, and immediately wanted to do it again. His excitement was so infectious that his dad went with him the second time, but not the third.

Although his goal is to be a licensed skydiver, he has only completed half of the required tandem jumps. But none of this matters right now. He was in the middle of a freefall and must act fast.

His eyes darted around as he began to assess the situation. He could see they were still holding hands and that everyone was wearing a dive suit with an attached parachute. His friends looked scared, but everyone was conscious and alert. He was holding Emily's hand on one side and Peter's hand on the other. He gave each a quick squeeze to let them know it was going to be okay. Then made eye contact with the others in an attempt to convey the same.

Emily knew her brother loved to skydive and that all she had to do was watch him. If she did what he did, everything would be okay. She began to envision a perfect landing and held the image of everyone else doing the same.

Even though James repeatedly invited him to go, Peter had not gone skydiving. But from everything James had told him, Peter knew at a certain point they were going to have to throw out their chute, which would trigger a series of events to slow them down and allow them to land in a controlled manner. Although he listened with fascination when James talked about skydiving, Peter sincerely wished he would have taken James up on his offer and joined him in the sky.

Sidney had done a good job calming his mind. He did not consider himself a daredevil, but was very grateful for his overactive imagination. In his mind, he was not skydiving. He was a bird, an eagle, soaring effortlessly through the air, scouring the landscape below for his next meal.

Charlotte started out a mess, but quickly pulled herself together. She knew if she was going to survive she had to get herself under control, fast! She had seen the effects of her thinking and she immediately started imagining herself on the ground, safe and sound. Her mind was filled with these thoughts as she watched James for further instruction. Charlotte remembered the calming sensation that came to her each time she held her keys. And while she couldn't touch them now, she let herself feel the same calmness and serenity as if the keys were in her hands.

Katie was holding onto Peter's hand so tightly he actually thought it might be broken. Her grip on Peter's and Charlotte's hands helped to calm her. The anger she'd felt toward James had subsided, and now she was focused on breathing. She kept her eyes tightly shut, only taking quick peeks every few seconds. She didn't want to see what was coming.

It was time to start the deployment process for the parachutes. All eyes were on James. He let go of Peter and Emily and waved his hands in the air, signaling for everyone to do the same. The group followed. Katie was startled by the release of Peter's hand. He shook and flexed it attempting to bring it back to life, relieved to know that nothing was broken.

James reached his hand back and grabbed the cord to release the pilot chute. He motioned for everyone to do the same. When everyone had put their hands on the cord he held up five fingers on his left hand. He did a countdown with his fingers, four, three, two, one, then he ripped his cord and everyone followed. All six pilot chutes caught in the air and inflated. A series of reactions quickly took place that ended with everyone's parachute fully open.

A feeling of relief came over them. They had gone from around 120 miles per hour to about 17 in a very short time. James now motioned for everyone to grab the two toggles that are used to steer. He yelled for them to play around and get a feel for them. He wasn't worried about the landing, below them was a giant green meadow, he couldn't have asked for a better site and conditions. He knew the landing would be a little rough for everyone, and he hoped they wouldn't get hurt.

James touched down first. He quickly released his parachute and turned to watch Peter make a very nice landing himself. He stumbled forward, but didn't fall. Sidney was next. He hit the ground and rolled into a ball. James and Peter ran over and helped him untangle from his parachute.

Next was Emily. She was running in mid-air, and practically landed on her tiptoes. She was all grins. James was proud of his sister's perfect form. She was a natural.

Katie and Charlotte were coming in too close together, they smacked into each other, causing Katie to slide on her knees. Charlotte ungracefully landed on top of her. By the time everyone made it to them, the two girls were lying on the ground laughing.

"We did it!" said Charlotte. "I can't believe I just skydived."

"That was so much fun!" said Katie. "James, you're going to have to take me with you the next time you go."

The group sat on the grass, laughing and talking about the exhilarating experience they just had. Katie had completely forgotten how angry she had been at James for choosing to skydive as his escape. They questioned each other about what they had been thinking and laughed about how different their experience would have been if they had ended up at the mall or the library.

As the conversation slowed, Emily asked, "So now what?"

"Good question," replied Peter. "But I have to confess, it feels good to be sitting here without any stress or problems."

They all agreed. Katie opened her backpack, pulled out her scales and set them firmly on the grass. "I have my scales; does everyone else have their gift?"

One by one they took their gifts out and sat them on the grass. As they looked at them, Emily asked "What is that inside your crystal ball, Sidney? I can see a shadow."

As they got closer to check it out, Peter spoke, "It looks like a person, and it's getting bigger, like he's walking toward us." They stared at the ball and could tell it was a man, and he was definitely getting closer. His features were coming into focus. It was a race car driver. He pulled off his helmet and ran his fingers through his blond hair.

Sidney shouted, "It's Mason!"

A twig snapped behind them and Katie looked up and screamed. Mason was there, dressed in his racecar suit, holding his helmet. Katie's confidence was boosted after her successful skydive. She was ready to do something about her attraction to Mason.

"Don't be alarmed," he said.

Everyone turned around and saw Mason.

"Mason, how nice to see you," said Peter. "You seem to have a habit of always showing up just after we experience a major crisis."

Mason chuckled, "From what I've seen, you guys are doing a fine job of getting out of any crisis that comes your way. Charlotte, your idea to violate logic and sink into the quicksand was spot on, congratulations. It appears that you are beginning to understand the power your seemingly simple thoughts have. Would you agree?"

"Most definitely," said Charlotte. "However, I wouldn't believe it if I hadn't experienced it myself. But after getting off the ceiling and the pink concrete, and skydiving, there's no doubt in my mind that if I can think it, I can make it happen."

"You are so right," replied a beaming Mason. "The six of you have discovered a valuable lesson at a very young age. A connection that most people never make at all, even after a lifetime of proof. That's why Balchazar chose you as his students. He knew your minds would be open to his lessons, helping you create the life of your dreams. However, you still have a lot to learn. You've only scratched the surface with the knowledge you now have. As you can see, you know enough to get yourselves in trouble, but also, enough to get yourselves out of it. Remember the power of your thoughts. Focus on the gifts you've received and appreciate how you can use them."

"What's next?" asked James.

"Your journey has just begun," said Mason. "And the best is yet to come. Decide what you want. See it in your mind. Hold it there. Believe it will happen. Then let it happen. More adventures will find you as you do this. Your awareness will increase, and you'll witness the power of your mental faculties."

Mason turned to walk away.

Katie yelled, "Don't go yet! I want to go with you."

He turned and looked at her with a big smile, "Your gifts, study your gifts. It'll all become clear. I'll be seeing you sooner than you think."

With these parting words, he left. They stared at him until he disappeared, fading into the tall grass.

Katie was upset that Mason ignored her request to go with him. After a moment of stewing she complained out loud, "What does he mean by all of this? How are we supposed to know what to do with those vague instructions? Yes, we know our thoughts have power, but give us some direction!"

Suddenly, lightning shot across the sky. Sidney gasped. He grabbed his crystal ball and yelled, "Lightning is striking in my crystal ball. Katie, your scales!"

"I know! They're teetering. Brace yourselves everyone."

And in a snap, they were gone, leaving behind nothing but six open parachutes blowing softly in the grass.

CHAPTER 7

GIANT BELIEF

The air was chilly and the night was quiet. Although it was dark, a giant moon and a million stars hung brightly in the sky softly illuminating the ground below. As Peter's eyes adjusted, he realized he was standing in grass that towered over his six-foot-tall body. He was alone. He reached his hands out to part the grass and cautiously began to walk through the thick blades. He yelled out the names of his friends, leaving an adequate pause between each person's name, "James…Katie…Emily…Charlotte…Sidney? Where are you guys? Is anybody out there?" There was no response.

Finally, he heard the faint sound of James' voice, "I'm here, but I have no idea where here is!"

Peter tried to follow his best friend's voice, but then he heard Katie. "James? Is that you? Where are you?"

"Katie! Yes! It's me. But I have no idea where I am. I'm surrounded by grass. I can't see anything but the sky above me. Are you alone?"

"I'm alone," she responded. "Keep yelling and we can walk in the direction of our voices."

Katie wondered silently how she managed such logic. This was a first for her. Normally, being alone in a situation like this would consume her with doubt and panic, but for some reason, not tonight.

Both Peter and Katie could hear Sidney, "I can hear you guys. I think you're close. I have my crystal ball in my hand, but I can't see anything, it's too dark."

As Sidney looked up to the sky, his imagination kicked into overdrive. He was now a famous explorer on a ship navigating the seas with Columbus and Magellan. He stood at the helm and studied maps of the stars. Holding a sextant to the sky, Sidney used the constellations to guide his crew across the sea. They were on a mission to discover unknown and distant lands. But before any discovery could be made, a quick shout from Emily brought him back to the dry grass that currently surrounded him. He thought to himself silently, "If only I had my phone, GPS would pinpoint my location in a matter of seconds."

Emily was close enough to hear Sidney and the others. "If only I had a megaphone. Then everyone would be able to hear and find me." She tilted her head back and yelled up to the sky, "I don't see anything except for stars and the moon!" She wished desperately there was a defining feature or landmark she could see.

"That's all any of us can see!" yelled a frustrated Katie. "I see something to my right that looks kind of like a wall. It might be pine trees. Maybe we're by a forest?" Suddenly, Katie had a bad feeling inside. She didn't like the darkness and she wished for her dad. Her dad was strong and smart. He'd know exactly what to do in this situation. As thoughts of her dad continued to race through her mind, she realized she wasn't as grown up as she thought she was.

Emily yelled back, "If I jump high enough I think I can see the same line of trees. Katie, I think you're in front of me. Let's play Marco Polo so I can come to you. Don't move, just yell!"

Emily and Katie called back and forth as Emily followed the sound of Katie's voice. She was confident in every step she took. She knew she would find her friend.

As Emily pushed her way through the tall grass, her mind began to focus on her twin brother, James. She could feel him contemplating his next steps, and she felt his uneasiness. Her mind drifted back to the outdoor party at the mansion. She recalled their search for the locket and the feeling that nothing is impossible. "Nothing is impossible. Nothing is impossible. Nothing is impossible." She repeated this in her mind over and over, hoping James would pick up on it.

Soon, her thoughts shifted and she began a conversation with James, in her mind. This wasn't uncommon for the two. As twins they shared what Peter referred to as a "special power," which was the ability to read each other's minds. "James," she thought, "Remember outside at the mansion. Nothing is impossible. Everything worked out for us. Nothing is impossible. You can figure this out. What do you see? What do you feel? We're all here. You're not alone."

Although it was quiet and she was focused, she didn't immediately feel a response from him. As James tried to calm himself he opened his backpack and pulled out his spyglass.

Emily realized that her focus on James had caused her to lose Katie's voice. She called out again and listened intently for a reply. As she walked through the oversized grass, Emily felt this was hard work. She was dividing her mental attention among the lactic acid building up in her leg muscles, listening for the sound of Katie's voice, and maintaining the mental conversation she was holding with James.

Meanwhile, Peter found he could see the same tree line and because of his height, he didn't have to jump. He thought he might be closer to Katie than Emily and headed off in the direction of her voice. He called out, "Katie I'm coming! Can you hear me?" He waited but heard no response. His intuition told him to get going, so he began to walk faster.

Emily figured out why James was so uneasy. They had heard everyone's voice, except for Charlotte. Where was she?

Charlotte was silently crouched and waiting motionless behind a tuft of grass. She was hiding from what appeared to be a grasshopper the size of a horse. The full moon was like a spotlight on the giant insect as it devoured the grass around it. For the moment it seemed unaware that Charlotte was in proximity, but she was terrified, and didn't dare make a sound or move a muscle. As she listened to the sound of the hopper eating, she felt certain he would eat his way to her in no time.

Peter was surprised when he found Emily first, who was still trying to make her way to Katie. When she told him about Charlotte, he thought for a moment. As he listened to his intuition, it was obvious to him that Charlotte was in trouble. He began to yell, "Charlotte, Charlotte, where are you? Charlotte!"

Then he listened very carefully. He could hear the sound of movement through the grass as the others came to meet them. Still nothing from Charlotte. Again, he called as loudly as he could, "Charlotte! Answer me." Silence.

A visceral fear set into Peter's mind. He wondered what could have happened to Charlotte. Did she make it to wherever they are? Is she hurt? Is she alive? His thoughts imagined all kinds of worse-case scenarios. Overhead, he could see birds flying in a circular pattern. He was fairly certain the birds couldn't see them in the dark, but nonetheless had the feeling the birds were spying on them through the long blades of grass. Every now and then a bird would leave the flock and disappear on a dive to snatch something out of the grass.

Peter's fear escalated and he wondered if they were diving for Charlotte. "Emily, do you see those birds? I'm 99 percent sure that's where Charlotte is. I need to go help her." Without waiting for an answer, he took off in the direction of the circling birds.

Making his way through the dense grass, Peter was grateful for his athletic body. He had large reserves of strength, which sustained him as he pushed forward, calling for Charlotte. He was focused on the circling birds above him. He used them as a guide, until he heard a piercing scream.

Charlotte was right in front of him. The grasshopper she had been hiding from now had her pinned to the ground with its two front legs. Peter grabbed Charlotte by the arms and pulled with all his strength. She kicked her feet as hard as she could at the attacking grasshopper and then moved her feet to the ground to help propel her as Peter pulled.

Their escape was aided as a giant black bird the size of an

airbus dove through the grass. The wind caused by its wingspan knocked Peter on top of Charlotte. As they both hurried to their feet, they turned just in time to watch the black bird snatch the grasshopper in its beak and fly away.

"Are you all right?" Peter gasped for air. "I think we're safe."

Charlotte was in tears and couldn't speak. Peter didn't wait for an answer. He took her by the hand, hugged her, and led her through the trampled path he had made in his attempt to find her.

In a few short minutes Peter and Charlotte were back with Emily, where the others had congregated and were anxiously waiting for them.

They all hugged and the group felt much more relaxed now that they were reunited. "Let's see if we can find a way out of this grass," suggested James. No one argued, and he led the way, pushing the oversized blades aside for the others to follow. Charlotte placed herself in the middle of the group where she felt safe, while Peter brought up the rear. After what seemed like hours, they finally arrived at a clearing.

The night sky had gradually faded with the slow but steady rising of the sun. The increased light provided definition and shape to what before was only shadow. As they looked out, they were standing on the edge of a giant garden. They saw flowers that bloomed in vibrant colors of red, yellow and pink. There were lush, green plants overflowing with oversized fruits, berries and vegetables. It was obvious that whoever owned this garden took great care of it. Dwarfed by the giant grasshopper, vegetables and flowers, it was apparent that they were in a world where they were now the little ones.

Before they could discuss their newly discovered size, Sidney yelled out, "I'm starving!" and ran toward a patch of plump, ripe strawberries that were roughly the size of car tires.

"Great idea!" shouted Peter. The entire group spread out and began helping themselves to the edible berries that were most appealing to them. They momentarily forgot their worries and enjoyed their free, delicious meal.

When he was full, Sidney found a soft, squishy spot of mulch. He made a little nest and relaxed as he looked up at the now blue sky.

James and Emily were speaking in hushed voices next to a watermelon that was the size of a stretch limousine. They were contemplating their next move, bouncing ideas off each other, not paying any attention to the fruit. Charlotte was glued to Peter, who was preoccupied with trying to help Katie lift a giant raspberry. For the moment, all was well.

But their calm was short lived. The earth began to shake and a rumbling tremor could be felt beneath their feet. They looked around to see what was causing the disturbance. The shaking grew in intensity and the noise coming from the earth became louder. Charlotte reverted to fear mode and began looking for a place to hide, "It's an earthquake!"

James quickly put his spyglass to his eye. Sidney reached for his crystal, saw an ugly beast and shouted an urgent warning.

The beast was a giant and he towered over them like a tall oak tree. He could only be described as massive. Everything about him was thick and oversized. He had long sharp teeth, messy red hair, and he spoke an unrecognizable language. His rough-looking body was clothed in some sort of animal skin.

The giant made his way to the garden and now that he was close by, they could distinguish his musty smell. It reminded them of rotten garbage. He carried a large basket made of twigs, grasses, leaves and other debris.

"Hide!" James yelled. It was chaos. They ran, but no one knew where to go. Charlotte hid under a grouping of raspberry leaves she found. She grabbed Emily and pulled her to safety. James joined them in their sanctuary. "Katie! Over here," he called. And she ran quickly to their hiding place.

After Peter saw that Katie was concealed with the others by the raspberries, he made his way to Sidney. The two of them dug into the mulch where Sidney had nested and they covered their bodies in a subterranean shelter. It was musty, dusty and dirty, but an excellent hiding place. Once they were hidden, they smeared mud on their faces and waited for the giant to pass.

Peering out from the leaves, the others could see that the giant was close. Believing the giant could see her, Katie felt vulnerable and pressed deeper into the raspberries to hide behind James.

The giant looked over his garden, his intention was clear. He had come to get food. Like a cook in the kitchen, tasting as he went, the giant surveyed his crops. They watched as he plucked entire plants from the ground, roots and all. He shoved them in his mouth, chewed, then spit out the thorns, stems and an occasional insect.

Charlotte was hyperventilating, certain she would faint. James was gathering all the courage he could find. He instinctively pushed Emily and Charlotte behind him, next to Katie, when the giant glanced in their direction.

"Nobody move. Don't make a sound," he whispered. "I don't think he saw us."

Whether he saw them or not, the giant was drawn to the raspberry bush where they were hiding. He eyed its leafy top, and with a heavy hand pulled it from the ground. The girls let out a blood curdling scream and grabbed the leaves and stems as their entire world shook. The giant began pulling the raspberry bush apart. As he separated the bush, the cage was revealed. All four of them had hidden themselves inside the snare disguised as a raspberry bush. And now, they were trapped!

When James realized what was happening he yelled for everyone to get out. But as they whirled around looking for an escape, they quickly realized one didn't exist. The cage door had already been sealed shut with a small wooden pin. The giant turned and began to walk away from the garden.

The creature was pleased. It almost sounded as if he was humming. Katie was hysterical, her sobbing was uncontrollable. Charlotte had fainted and was lying on the cage floor. Emily stared off in a stupor. James gripped the cage bars that now trapped them and thought, "How are we going to get out of this one?"

Peter and Sidney poked their heads out of the mulch just in time to see the giant disappear on a path that led away from the garden. "Come on Sidney! We've got to rescue them."

"There's no way we can run that fast. We can't keep up!"

"We've got to try! Come on, let's go!" They pulled themselves out of the dirt and began running after the giant as fast as their legs would take them. Peter turned his head to look over his shoulder and saw Sidney struggling to keep up. "Keep running, Sidney! You can do it!"

Even though it seemed impossible, Peter thought only of catching up to the giant, finding their friends and saving them. He didn't have any idea how they would actually do it, but first things first, they had to find them.

Balchazar: *When you have a goal, you need not worry about how to achieve it. Think only of accomplishing the goal. The way will be revealed to you at the time you need it.*

As he ran, Peter remembered that he had no idea how he was going to find his locket at the plantation, but somehow it all worked out. "A way will always appear," thought Peter. His mind began to race, ideas came as fast as his legs were carrying him. "When we needed to get off the bakery ceiling a way appeared. When we had to get out of the quicksand a way appeared." His memories fueled his confidence, and he was now certain. "Once we find them, a way will appear, and we will save them." This time he said it aloud, "Once we find them, a way will appear, and we will save them." He shouted again at the top of his lungs, "Once we find them, a way will appear, and we will save them."

"What did you say?" asked Sidney.

Peter was shocked. Sidney had caught up to him and was running by his side. "How did you catch up to me, Sidney?"

Sidney shouted back, as he gasped for air, "You told me I could do it, and that I had to do it, and you're right. I can do this!"

"Way to go man! Keep it up, we're gaining on them. We're going to make this happen. I don't know how, but we will."

Balchazar: *Peter does not know it, but he is absolutely correct. You see, many people never move past a challenge because they think they have to know every step, from start to finish, before they begin. My friends, that is a false belief. It is not necessary to know how you are going to accomplish something. What is necessary is that you have to start. It seems simple, but for most people, starting is the hardest part. Thomas Carlyle said, "Go as far as you can see. When you get there, you'll see how you can go farther."*

After what felt like hours of running, Sidney began to lose his faith, and as doubt crept into his mind, his legs began to slow and he fell behind Peter. He could not go on.

Realizing Sidney was no longer with him, Peter stopped and turned around to see him bent over with his hands resting on his knees for support, working to catch what little breath he had left. Peter gave up the race and walked back to Sidney, plopping down in the center of the path.

Kindness overtook him, and he began speaking to him in a soft voice. "We're going to save them, Sidney. But I need you to believe and imagine that we're saving them. It worked for you on the beach when you pictured the sand castle. It worked for me in the hurricane, when we had to decide which path to take. I'm sure of this, Sidney. Use your imagination for a good cause. Let your mind come up with ideas to rescue them. Get out your crystal if that'll help. You can do this."

Sidney thought about what Peter said for a couple of seconds and knew he was right. He decided he had nothing to lose, so he fired up his imagination. He was now dressed as a cross country runner in a marathon. His lungs had no problem handling the deep breaths he was taking, providing sufficient oxygen to his muscles. He felt good, strong, and able. He had no difficulty keeping up with Peter and would soon be passing him.

Following the giant turned out to be easy. His extreme weight, and big platypus feet flattened everything in his path, leaving a clear trail for Peter and Sidney to follow. Soon, they found themselves at what they assumed must be the giant's house.

The house, if it could even be called that, was small and primitive-looking, more like a hut. It was built with mossy stones and had a thatched roof. The inside was damp and moldy. Around the room were various animal skins, spears and arrows. A simple stove stood at the far wall, with large pots resting on burners. There wasn't a bed or a couch. On the floor was a rug that probably served as the giant's bed, and opposite of the stove stood a table fashioned from wood, without chairs.

As he made his way inside, the giant placed the basket with the plants he picked on the table and hung the cage from a hook directly above it. Dirt fell from the cage onto the table. Dirt was everywhere. The giant was definitely not tidy.

The constant drone of his unidentifiable language continued, and it seemed, at times, that he was yelling at himself. The deep guttural sounds he made were joined by an occasional lashing out at an invisible opponent, revealing the danger of his sharp teeth. In between all this he busied himself preparing for his next meal. He lit a fire in the stove and placed a large pot of water on it.

The plants, fruits and vegetables that had been collected from the garden were pulled from the basket, shredded and dropped into the pot. No need to clean anything. The giant obviously didn't care about dirt.

A mouse scurried across the floor, and with the precision of a marksman, the giant swatted it with a nearby stick, rendering it unconscious and immobile. He picked it up by the tail and tossed it in the same pot, which now contained boiling water, plants, fruits, vegetables, and one dead mouse.

"James, did you see the size of that mouse?" questioned Katie in a panicked voice, "It's as big as we are!"

"Or, are we as small as it?" James wasn't sure. But it was clear that proportionately the size ratios did not fit. They were tiny in comparison to everything in this oversized environment.

Outside, Peter and Sidney stared at the giant's hut. Despite Peter's encouragement, Sidney had been unable to focus on a plan to get them inside. Sidney hadn't a clue what to do.

"Okay," said Peter. "Now how do we get inside? Is there an opening we can squeeze through? Or do we climb up to the window?"

Resentful of Peter's insistence that he imagine a plan in his mind, and feeling a little guilty about his lack of ideas, he angrily responded, "How am I supposed to know? You're the one who seems to have all the answers."

Peter was startled and slightly offended by Sidney's condescending tone. Why was Sidney questioning him when he had clearly helped them get this far? Peter quickly put the offense out of his mind and asked, "What do you have in your fanny pack that can help us get inside?"

Before Sidney could answer, Peter yelled, "Can you see the

cage? There they are!" He could see the giant through the open window. He was hanging the cage on a hook.

Sidney looked upward and gasped. "It's them! How are we going to get to them? That cage is so high!"

But Peter knew better and was not discouraged. He had lived the impossible at the mansion. "Nothing is impossible!" he said loudly, with conviction, even trying to convince himself a little bit. "We'll figure this out. Every problem has a solution. Stop wasting time. Tell me what's in your nerdy fanny pack." His tone was becoming less and less friendly and more and more urgent. Peter was finished with Sidney's bad attitude.

Sidney complied without saying another word. He had already stepped outside his comfort zone to confront Peter. Now he unzipped his fanny pack. Inside was everything they needed to climb a mountain, including ropes, safety harnesses, helmets, hammers, pulleys, crampons and a rappelling device. They were in business.

"I don't know how this stuff fits inside your tiny bag, but this is our answer," said Peter. "It looks like we're going to climb up the wall and go through the window!" Peter was excited to get going. He didn't know how to climb, but he was about to learn.

Balchazar: *Once you make a committed decision, the universe will supply you with everything you need at the time you need it.*

Sidney went deep into his imagination. He was climbing the face of a mountain, a vertical slab of rock that went straight up. In his mind he was an expert. He knew exactly what to do and scaled the rock as though he was a lizard. He couldn't fail, nor could he fall. He took a quick look in his crystal ball and saw himself with Peter standing on the window ledge high above. Peter's conviction and energy was contagious, and Sidney could feel belief and confidence growing inside him.

They both felt clumsy as they helped each other get into their gear, trying to determine how to make it all work. For every question they asked, they had a solution. And even though they weren't experienced climbers, Peter knew they would make it. His confidence inspired Sidney to stay close and keep trying.

While Sidney finished attaching the crampons to his boots, Peter wrapped a harness around his waist and began to climb the side of the hut. "Hey, Sidney, I think there are enough hand holds here that we can climb without the ropes."

"Okay," answered Sidney. "But why don't we take one up with us just in case."

Peter agreed and continued scaling while Sidney stood on the ground below. He watched how Peter struggled every once in a while to get a solid foot or hand hold. This caused him to worry. He wasn't nearly as strong or athletic as Peter. He could barely do a chin up, how was he going to climb the side of this house? He looked in the crystal ball for reassurance but saw nothing. No image of any kind. Now his stomach was in knots. They still had to make it to the cage, rescue their friends and then get out alive.

Peter made it to the top and peered inside. He could see the cage which held his friends captive. James happened to glance over to the window and caught a glimpse of Peter in the corner of his eye. With a double take, he confirmed Peter was standing in the window. Peter was quick to put a finger to his lips, signaling James to be quiet. He complied.

Peter looked down and could see Sidney still climbing. He was shaking and Peter could tell he was a bundle of nerves.

"I've got this," Sidney said to himself. "I don't have to be as strong as Peter." Just then he lost his footing. His body slamming against the house, he screamed as his cheek scraped against a mossy stone. His frightened scream drew the attention of the giant, who came to the window to see the cause of the commotion.

Peter quickly hid in a crack by the ledge. Sidney heard the clumsy footsteps of the giant and clung to the side of the house, trying desperately to blend in.

"We're busted, so busted. This is bad, oh so very bad," Sidney thought to himself. But then he caught himself. He closed his eyes and climbed into his imagination, where he saw himself standing safely on the window ledge next to Peter. But this wasn't enough to calm his mind. He had to go deep inside himself for this one. "Get a hold of yourself! Do it now!" called the voice inside his head.

Sidney did get a hold of himself and ignored everything going on at the window. He continued climbing, for the only answer was up. Down was not an option. Hand over hand he climbed, planting each footstep deep into the mossy cracks of the rock wall.

Unable to see anything unusual, the giant lost interest, stepped away from the window and walked out the front, and only, door. Sidney quickly reached the ledge where Peter was hidden. He climbed out from his secret spot to join him. Now they were both standing on the ledge. They hurried through the open window and dropped onto the table. Above them, the cage dangled.

"James! Can you hear me!" Peter called.

"Yes! Get us out of here. Hurry!" James was close to panic.

Peter turned to Sidney and instructed him to pull the rope from his fanny pack. Then he yelled to James, "Do you have any idea how to get out of the cage?"

James didn't have a clue. "I don't know, there's a piece of wood that holds the door closed, but I don't know how to get it out."

Peter was attempting to get a good look at how the door of the cage was held shut but couldn't quite see. There wasn't enough time to check it out; the giant was inside again, grunting and growling from his recent distraction.

Walking to the table, the giant noticed Peter standing beneath the cage. He lifted his hand to flatten him. Peter ran as fast as he could, darting left and right to avoid the heavy blows. The giant's hand landed hard on the table. The jolt on the table tipped the basket, and Peter hid under the plant remnants not yet deposited into the boiling pot of water. Sidney climbed back up to the window ledge and watched everything from above. His heart pounded so hard in his chest he thought for sure it would explode. He quickly crammed himself into the hiding place Peter had used just moments earlier.

Fortunately, when Peter disappeared under the leaves, the giant lost interest. His next move was toward the cage. His short, stubby fingers plucked the stick that held the door shut. He swung the door open and reached his hand in for one of the hostages.

Charlotte was pressed against the back of the cage and began to scream hysterically. Katie was too scared to scream. Emily, who was closest to the door, began to run. But with no place to hide, she was an easy target for the giant. It didn't take long for his stubby fingers to catch her and lift her by her upper body.

Emily's initial reaction was fear and shock. She screamed and put up a fight in every way she could. She kicked, bit, and scraped at the giant's fingers, but none of it made any difference. She was in his grasp. Finally, she yelled out in exasperation, "Help me!"

The moment the giant grabbed his sister, James began the fastest sprint of his life. "NOOOOOOOO!" he screamed. He ran toward the giant's hand, but it was already out of the cage. With so much forward momentum, James made the instant decision to jump. He leapt toward the hand but didn't even come close. Instead of grabbing onto one of his club-like fingers, he fell into the tipped basket of vegetables resting on the table below. The leafy greens softened his fall. He completed a quick self-assessment, grateful he was still in one piece, without any broken bones.

The giant was now aware that James was no longer in the cage. He turned his attention away from Emily as he searched the table for his missing hostage. With his free hand he sifted through the plants in and around the basket. But James had already hopped out of the leaves and was running across the table in the opposite direction of Peter.

Angry and annoyed, the giant let out a loud growl and turned his attention back to Emily. She was causing enough irritation to make the giant want to release her, so he made his way to the stove.

Not content with watching anymore, Sidney slid out from hiding, dropped the rope and repelled to the floor. He ran to the giant, who was now at the stove. As he made his way across the hut, his crampons periodically stuck in the floor, requiring an exerted effort to lift one foot in front of the other. When he reached the giant, he grabbed handfuls of coarse leg hair and began climbing up his leg. With each new handful of hair, Sidney pulled as hard as he could and dug the spikes of his crampons as deep as he could into the giant's leathery flesh.

Over and over he yanked the hair and dug his crampons into flesh, slowly slicing the giant's leg. The giant yelled in surprise and anger. He kicked his leg causing Sidney to lose his grip and fly across the room.

The giant reached down to rub his injured leg, inadvertently loosening his grip on Emily. She felt the pressure ease, and with her next kick, she freed herself from his grasp and began falling toward the stove. Fortunately, she was close and her fall was not far. Emily hit her hip against the outside edge of the boiling pot, which thankfully slowed her fall and softened her impact on the scalding burner. She immediately felt the heat of the flames. She wasn't on fire but knew her hair was singed.

From the table, James watched Sidney's run on the giant and Emily's fall. He cheered and shouted to her, "Run Em! Hide!"

Emily scurried into the next burner and shimmied into the area beneath. She was safe for the moment. As she looked herself over she saw that her skin was bright red from the heat of the pot, but she was all right. Her adrenaline was flowing and it masked her pain. She was grateful to have escaped the giant's grasp and still be alive.

Back on the floor of the hut, Sidney lay stunned and dazed, barely able to comprehend what had happened. "Sidney, hide!" yelled James. The giant was coming for Sidney. The floor thundered as he approached. Sidney saw a small fold in the rug and pulled himself in to hide. The giant didn't see where he went. One by one the giant threw objects from the floor he believed might be concealing Sidney. After he had thrown everything, he crouched down on his hands and knees and began to sniff.

Eventually he caught a whiff of Sidney near the rug. He picked it up and shook it violently. Fortunately for Sidney, the giant grabbed the exact fold where he was hiding, allowing him to remain firmly in place as he shook. The force of the shaking made Sidney dizzy. He knew, without the added pressure of the giant's grip he couldn't hold on by himself.

Finally, the giant dropped the rug back onto the floor. Sidney was almost certain he was hurt. Everything looked blurry. He had a headache, and wondered if he had a concussion. As much as he wanted to escape, he had neither the strength nor the will to move.

Meanwhile, Charlotte looked down from the cage and saw an opportunity. In all the confusion, the giant forgot to close the door, allowing her and Katie a chance for escape. The only question was how were they going to land safely on the table?

Charlotte pushed that thought from her mind as she looked at the same pile of leafy greens that had softened James' fall. "If he can land it, then we can too," she told herself, remembering her soft landing from the bakery ceiling. She knew they could do this.

"Katie, come on!" Charlotte called. But Katie was frozen. Her eyes huge, her mind filled with fear. She was in shock, and her brain did not hear or process the command. Charlotte took action, dashed over and pulled her by the arm. "Come on! This is our chance to get out of here." Without even thinking about it, Katie responded to the tug and together they moved toward the open door. "Katie, we have to jump."

She snapped out of her daze, "No! I can't. I can't do that." She could see her legs snapping in two as she landed on the table. Waves of fear caused Katie to cling to the side of the cage.

"Yes, you can do this. Katie, look at me," Charlotte couldn't get her attention, so she raised her voice, and turned her face toward her. In the calmest tone she could muster Charlotte said, "Yes, you can do this. We can do this, and we're going to do it together. The key to this fall is to be completely relaxed. We're going to land on that pile of greens, when you hit them let your legs relax and let your body roll onto the table. You won't get hurt. You'll be safe. Just follow me."

Katie was imagining the perfect gymnastics fall just as she was taught to do when she missed a grip on an apparatus, but for some reason it wasn't calming her. Charlotte caught a glimpse of the giant who was pulling the stove apart while he searched for Emily. She reached for the keys in her pocket and felt the calmness move up her arm. She took hold of herself and willed her mind to leave the cage.

Without saying another word, Charlotte took Katie's hand and moved closer to the open door. She sat down on the ledge, put her legs outside the cage, turned herself around and shimmied until she was hanging outside the cage. Once fully extended, Charlotte dropped to the greens on the table below and rolled, allowing her legs to fold beneath her, and the inertia of the fall to move through her upper body. She was safe and unharmed.

"Ok, Katie, your turn! Do the same thing. I'm right here I'll break your fall. Come on."

Katie followed her lead, sitting on the edge of the cage, she turned to lower herself. She was on her belly and all she had to do was push and let go. But again, she froze. Peter could see what was happening and came closer to offer encouragement.

"Come on, Katie." he yelled. "Don't think about it. We've got you. Just let go. That's all you have to do. Let go!"

Charlotte extended her arms and was instinctively reaching for her while Peter continued his encouraging words. James began to worry, he could see that the giant was quickly losing interest in finding Emily. His attention was now coming back to the cage. He lunged for the rope, still tied where Sidney had attached it to the open window.

"Katie, you have to drop now!" Peter made his demand with such authority and urgency that Katie complied. She forcefully pushed herself out of the cage and screamed as she fell. Peter and Charlotte caught her and they all landed in the pile of greens.

James now had the rope in place and herded them toward it. "Slide down to the floor!" Peter put Katie on the rope first and she slid down with the grace of the gymnast she is. Katie waited at the bottom for Charlotte who followed. Her movements were awkward but she made it. James and Peter were quick to follow, narrowly escaping the slamming of the giant's fist on the table in one last attempt to stop them.

Sidney finally pulled himself together inside the rug and poked his head out to see what was happening. He saw everyone slide down the rope and knew he needed to join them.

Emily had found her way down the piping inside the stove and exited through an opening in the back. She cautiously ran to the front and found herself staring at the matted hair on the giant's legs. He was dangerously close to her friends who had just slid down the rope.

She didn't know where the courage came from but she moved to the giant, grabbed the biggest amount of leg hair she could fit in her hands and pulled as hard as she could, making an intense sound effect as she did. After she pulled, she ran under the table and hid between the wall and a table leg.

Sidney pulled himself out from the fold in the carpet and began moving toward the giant, who was not attempting to see what had bothered his legs.

Katie's mind was racing. She watched Sidney stagger out of the carpet, and put a plan together in an instant. "Peter, can you get back up the rope and release it from the window?"

"What's your plan?" He knew he could climb back up, but was hesitant, knowing that he would have to be fast. The giant was close.

"If Sidney can draw the giant's attention then we can trip him with the rope and drop him to the floor. That should give us enough time to get out of this place." Katie's plan made sense to Peter, and James was willing to try anything. It was time to take action.

Peter began the climb. On the floor, James looped the rope around the table leg several times and knotted it in place. The giant had dropped to his knees so he could see what was going on beneath the table. He saw Emily hiding behind the farthest table leg. He reached for her. She screamed as she ran, but now she was trapped in the corner.

The giant backed out from under the table, drooling and growling as he came. His huge head was right in front of Charlotte and James. They could smell his putrid breath. James abandoned the rope, grabbed hold of Charlotte and ran in the direction of the wall as the giant's jaws snapped shut in an attempt to capture them in his filthy mouth.

Sidney's imagination was in full swing. He wore armor, held a flame thrower in his hand, and in his mind, was setting everything in the house ablaze. He marched into the open room stomping as hard as he could, calling for the giant to come to him. But the giant didn't comply. He saw James and Charlotte running toward the wall. The giant would get them this time.

Peter had released the rope and was at the edge of the table, rope in hand, uncertain what to do next.

Below, Sidney pulled the crampons off his feet and ran with all his might toward the giant shouting out the deepest roar he could bellow. The giant made another attempt to eat James and Charlotte, pushing his oversized head back under the table, his teeth snapping all the way. He missed again, but it was a very close call.

As the giant was dragging himself from under the table the second time, Sidney jumped onto his arm, ran all the way to his shoulder and crawled under the animal skin the giant was wearing. He held on tight to the underside of the clothing as he moved in. The movement on the giant's skin was enough to gain his attention.

The giant stood and backed away clumsily from the table. He began to shrug and move his shoulders in an attempt to dislodge Sidney and end the irritation. He reached behind trying to scratch his upper back, but the giant was not flexible, and Sidney was completely out of reach.

Peter shimmied down the table leg and met up with the others. Katie had spied an opening in the wall where the stones didn't fit together properly. She pointed it out. Peter saw what they could do. While Sidney kept the giant distracted, they could weave the rope around his legs and when the giant tried to move forward, the rope would trip him, buying them the time they needed to escape through the opening in the wall.

The more the giant gyrated, the lower Sidney dropped beneath his animal skin clothing. The image of their plan became clear in Katie's mind. "I can see it!" she proclaimed. "Peter you start weaving the rope around the giant's legs, the rest of us will help guide the rope and keep it free and moving. Eventually, Sidney will cause the giant to move forward, and down he goes. It should work. No, it will work!" The idea scared Katie to death, but there was no other apparent option. She had to do it. "Let's go!" she shouted to everyone.

Peter began to run in and out and around the legs of the giant. James stood near the opposite foot, pulling and feeding the line as quickly as he could. Katie planted herself by the table leg pulling the rope toward James. Emily came out from her corner just as the giant stood on the rope. With no more slack in the rope, Peter was jerked to a sudden stop and fell to the floor. James dropped the rope, stepped between the toes of the giant and tickled. The giant gave a small chuckle and lifted his foot off the floor. The adjustment of his foot sent Sidney falling. Upon seeing that the rope was now free, Emily pulled it away from where the giant had stepped on it. Peter began running again and in no time the lashing had encircled both ankles in a beautiful figure eight pattern with very little slack.

> **Balchazar:** *My students are learning an important lesson, by working together to achieve a common goal. They have now activated the power of the universal mind. As you begin to think about the steps you can take to meet your goal, the universal mind will reveal the ideas and suggestions necessary to make your goal a reality. So while there is no time for the friends to stop and talk in detail about how they will accomplish their escape, it all comes together through the power of the universal mind to make it manifest just as they need it to be.*

James helped Sidney get to his feet. Peter called to the girls, "Run in front of the giant and away from him." Everyone obeyed; James pulled a disoriented Sidney beside him. Emily wasn't sure exactly what Peter meant, but she simply followed his lead. Charlotte only moved because she was too scared to be left behind.

Seeing all his captives in front of him, the giant took two steps forward moving quickly and leaning toward them with out-stretched arms to scoop them up. The slack in the rope was taken up, the bindings tightened and the momentum of the lumbering giant propelled him forward. He fell with full force to the floor hitting his head hard on the landing. He was dazed and stunned but not unconscious.

"To the opening in the wall!" cried Katie. And she took off. She didn't even look behind. She got there first, and then turned to make certain the others were coming. Charlotte was breathless and running, but Peter had her hand. James was still dragging Sidney, whose legs were like jelly, and Emily lagged behind. Katie ran back to help. Soon they'd all squeezed through the opening in the wall and were standing in the fresh air of the outside world.

"Are we all here? Is everyone all right?" James was taking inventory. Sidney was weak and foggy, but he seemed okay. Everyone was out of breath, but the adrenaline was flowing. "We can't stop here; we have to keep moving. There may be others nearby. Let's go."

They kept moving until they could no longer see the house. Following the same path Peter and Sidney had run to the hut, they stayed close to the grassy edges in case they needed a quick hiding place. Charlotte was exhausted and Sidney had no more energy. Charlotte dropped to the ground attempting to recover. Sidney sat cross legged with his elbows on his knees and his head in his hands.

No one said a word for quite a while, until Katie finally broke the silence, "I can't believe we survived that."

Charlotte was so grateful to be alive; tears flowed down her cheeks.

Peter continued, "I can't believe we did what we did. And Sidney, you were superhuman." Although Peter complimenting Sidney was completely out of character, he was happy to acknowledge the contributions Sidney made to their survival.

Sidney felt good, barely looked up, and acknowledged the compliment with a nod of his head.

Ever moving forward, James asked the next obvious question, "So, guys, where do we go from here?"

"You know, every time we're transported, Sidney sees something in his crystal ball and my scales teeter. When that happens, we're gone. It's a pattern." Katie now believed that the answer to the question was in the working of the crystal ball and her scales. "But how does it happen? If we could figure that out, we could get ourselves home. Right?"

Emily was intrigued and she began reviewing in her memory all the events leading up to their transports. "Katie, you might have hit on something. Think about it. What were we doing? What were we talking about? What was happening each time before we left each place?"

Everyone dug deep into their memory. Emily continued, "When we got our gifts at the museum, we were confused and we didn't understand what was going on. The scales were in balance. And Katie you said something about not wanting to stay at the museum because you felt something wasn't right. Do you remember?"

"I do, and the next thing I knew, we had landed in the library at that mansion."

"Yes, and we found the locket, melted the woman, ran to the

barn and got trapped in the tack room. Which was extremely stressful," Peter said, not caring to remember the details.

James continued the memory, "but I could see the escape and pointed to the knot where Charlotte put her keys and we got out."

"You're right, James," replied Emily. "But remember, Charlotte was crying, saying please let us get out, please let us get out. And Katie was skeptical. She didn't believe that you could see the lock in the knot. She said something, something that put her scales out of balance."

"Em, you're right, Katie was skeptical. She was adamant that there was no lock and no way out. She didn't believe me," James remembered, completing Emily's thought.

Katie was beginning to see a pattern developing and guilt was growing in her mind. "Am I the cause of all our troubles?"

Emily continued through her memories of everything that had transpired. "Then we were in the treehouse with Mason and the bird. Mason told Katie the answers are inside you. But you were confused. You wanted more information. And the scales teetered again."

Charlotte could see the pattern now, and she was annoyed by the thought that Katie was the source of all their trouble. "And remember, Katie when we dropped through the quick sand and landed with the parachutes? Mason told us to study our gifts. But you were mad, you snapped at him and complained about the vague instructions."

Emily completed Charlotte's recounting of the story. Her memory was perfect. "You're right, Charlotte. Katie said, 'How are we supposed to know what to do with those vague instructions? Yes, we know our thoughts have power, but give us some direction!' She wasn't satisfied and we were gone again."

Katie was crying and unwilling to accept all the responsibility for their situation.

Peter felt sorry for her. He reached out to grab her hand but she swatted it away.

"I'm not the only one who has had negative thoughts and ideas about all of this stuff. You can't blame all this on me."

Sidney pulled out his crystal ball and peered inside. He saw thunder clouds and the threat of lightning. He used his imagination to see blue sky and warm breezes. The scenario in his crystal settled down. The sky cleared, turned a beautiful pale blue, with wispy clouds slowly moving on the horizon. "That was close," he thought.

"Wait a minute. Let's look at this from the other side. If Katie can think a thought that takes us to a negative world, can she think a thought that takes us to a good world? Can she think a thought that takes us home? What if all along all she had to do was think about being back at the museum?" James was pleased with the direction of his new perspective.

"I like that idea." Charlotte was all in. "What have we got to lose? Let's try it."

James provided the instruction. "Everyone think about being back at the museum. Think about nothing but being safe. We're at the museum. Mason has told us about the coin, and we're ready to head back to school. Don't think any other thoughts."

Sidney began a new scenario in his imagination. They were back at the museum. He was leading an expedition just returning from an archeological find in the sands of the Sahara Desert. He was excited about the artifacts he brought back with him. He was discussing an exhibit with the curators at the museum. It was going very well.

Peter was imagining them back at the museum, but he and Katie were alone. She was looking at him with adoration and her eyes never left his. His heart was full and his arms held her in a close embrace.

James was thinking about getting back to school. He wasn't interested in the museum. He wanted to move on to other things.

Emily was thinking about the book she would write about their adventures all starting with a big, black bird, a coin, and six gifts in a curio cabinet.

Katie thought over and over, "There's no place like home. There's no place like home. Handsome, brave Mason is home. There's no place like home. I want my Dad. There's no place like home."

Charlotte couldn't focus. She couldn't maintain a single thought. She didn't want to be back at the museum. She didn't want any more adventure. She wanted to go home. "This isn't going to work. You guys are stupid. We can't go home simply by thinking about it." And those were the last thoughts she had before it happened.

The ground began to rumble, the dark clouds rolled in, the rain began to fall hard all around them. Sidney opened his eyes and stared into the crystal ball. The storm raged. The most violent storm he had seen in the crystal yet.

Katie opened her eyes and reached for the scales. They were teetering. "We're going! We made it happen!" They all waited with great anticipation and joy to be transported back to the museum. But no one knew what Charlotte had been thinking.

CHAPTER 8

CASTLE CHAOS

The six of them stood outside. Rain was falling and thunder cracked overhead. Lightning flashed, illuminating a dark and foreboding building that was NOT the museum. It was a castle. They were standing in front of its massive doors, being pounded by rain.

"I don't understand what happened," yelled Peter over the thunder. "We should be back at the museum. I'm confused."

Chaos erupted immediately after he spoke. At the same time, each one of them shouted their feelings and disappointment.

Everyone that is, except for Charlotte. The moment Peter finished his question, Charlotte became overwhelmed with guilt. The emotion traveled through her entire body at light speed and settled in her stomach. She was sick, she needed to vomit.

Charlotte knew it was her fault they didn't make it back to the museum. Negative thoughts filled her mind at rapid speed. "I'm the weak one of the group… I'm the one who can't control my thoughts… I didn't imagine us back at the museum."

As the thoughts came, so did tears, which formed in the corner of her eyes as she thought of home. "If only I could have controlled myself, we'd all be in the comfort and warmth of the museum, not this nightmare-come-to-life castle."

Charlotte snapped out of her thoughts only to hear Emily verbalize them verbatim. "Peter's right! We're never going to get home! We're never going to figure this out. We can't seem to do what is required to wake up from all of this."

James grabbed Emily's hand and squeezed it. Secretly he was annoyed with the situation, but even as a teenager, he understood there was no value in being upset. They had to persevere.

"Emily, we can't think that way. We'll figure this out. We have to, there's no other option." James' voice softened just a bit. "We can do this. We just have to be strong a little longer. We're almost there, I can feel it." He let go of her hand, put his arm around her shoulders and squeezed tightly.

His embrace and words comforted Emily. She quieted herself, "You're right. There is no other option. I can do this. I have to do this…but I don't want to."

Katie turned and walked toward the gate that separated them from the outside world. She was ready to get out of this place. But her exit was denied; a rusted chain and massive lock kept the gate from opening as she shook it. She turned around and looked at the castle. There were no lights, making it difficult to see. Her only views were glimpses she caught from the frequent lightning. It felt eerie and creepy here. Katie had goosebumps running up and down her arms. She shivered; she didn't have a good feeling.

Holding her backpack overhead, she walked toward the castle door. Wanting to hide the fear growing inside she snapped, "If we don't get out of this rain, my hair'll be a big wad of frizz." She was wet from head to foot and mascara was smudged beneath her eyes.

"Katie's right, the gates are locked, we have no choice, we're going to have to go inside," said James. They walked along the stone path leading to the castle's massive front doors. The trees that lined the path were dead. However, their skeletal branches were filled with vultures. Hundreds of them were perched, craning their heads, watching the six strangers make their way to the castle doors.

Katie looked to the sky and could see something large flying overhead. "What are those huge birds above us?"

"Those aren't...." began Sidney.

But James cut him off midsentence, "Never mind, Sidney, she doesn't need to know...no one needs to know."

"Know what?" Katie questioned. But James ignored her and moved ahead of the group. He was focused on the castle doors.

Balchazar: *Even though my young students are disappointed in their setback, they must continue to move forward. No matter what the circumstances, no matter what your feelings may be, the answer is to keep moving toward your goal. Do not see a setback as a failure. The only time you fail is when you choose to give up. Just keep moving toward your goal. Persevere.*

If he had to guess, Sidney thought the stone castle appeared to be four to five stories high. The many turrets were tall and pointed sharply to the sky. There were dozens of windows, however, where light would normally be shining out on a stormy night, tonight there was nothing but darkness. As his eyes shifted to the castle's base, he observed that many of the stones were covered in moss, "It must rain a lot here," he thought. Gradually his eyes began adjusting to the darkness and he noticed the grounds were overgrown and unattended, with lots of dead trees. He wondered how long it had been since this place was alive with cheerful activity.

Observing the castle and its grounds was all it took to ignite Sidney's imagination. As king, he sat on a throne inside the castle, which was filled with life and activity. The grounds were well maintained by servants who cared for the bushes and trees. His staff strategically placed feeders, which attracted birds of various shapes and colors. He wandered from his throne room into an open courtyard, where he sat next to a bubbling fountain. The soothing sounds of the water provided him the peace and solace he needed to make the important decisions a king must make. He looked at the water as a bird landed and began to shake its feathers wildly as it bathed.

Suddenly Sidney frowned. He saw his own reflection in the

water. He wasn't the least bit surprised to see that the beautiful jewel encrusted crown he wore on his head was too big and too heavy. He re-centered the crown, stood up, and began to walk around the fountain. His robe was long and lined with an exotic fur. He wore his robe often because he loved the feeling of its weight as he moved. A servant arrived, handing him his scepter. He reached to take it, but before he could grab it, Sidney was jolted back to reality with a loud bang.

Bang, Bang, Bang! The sound of the iron door knocker echoed as it beat against the solid wood doors. Minutes passed and there was no answer. There appeared to be no movement or noise inside.

"I don't hear anything," whispered James. He knocked again, still no answer. He pushed on the door and it gave way with the long, penetrating screech of rusty hinges. Peter could see that James needed help. He leaned his 185 athletic pounds into the door. With the two of them pushing, the doors slowly swung open. As soon as there was enough space, Emily and Katie slipped through. It didn't take long for the rest to join them inside. Now they were out of the rain, but just what had they walked into?

"Man, its cold in here," Charlotte muttered to herself as she began to wring water from her shirt. "So cold and dark!" Her voice trailed as the final traces of light from the stormy night disappeared. James and Peter heaved the heavy doors shut.

Surrounded by darkness, it was Katie who spoke first. "Peter, remember at the bakery when your locket was like a flashlight? Pull it out and see if it lights up now."

"Great idea!" cheered Emily.

Peter put his hand to his chest. He could feel the locket under his shirt. It was warm, just like at the bakery. He thought to himself, "Please work. Please give us the light we need." As he brought the locket out he could see a dim light. "It's working!" Peter was so happy, and the happier he felt, the brighter the light became, until it illuminated the entire room.

Directly in front of them was a long hallway covered with red carpet. Suits of armor were standing guard on each side. They were darkened, not polished. They had swords and helmets adorned with dusty feathers on top.

Lightning struck and a flash of bright light filled the long hallway. Emily screamed as she saw a figure walking in the hall, but once her eyes adjusted from the bright flash she realized it was only James.

"Come in here," yelled James, as he walked through one of the many doorways. They followed, not even questioning where they were going. As they walked by the armor, no one noticed that the helmets slowly turned to follow their movement. Nor did they notice that the armored suits drew their swords and began to slowly march down the hall behind them.

The room they entered was dusty and musty. It must have served as a large parlor or sitting room. The most noticeable item was a gigantic bear skin rug that was perfectly centered in front of the fireplace. The fireplace had a stone hearth with a pile of wood at its side. It was dry and ready to be burned. There was an oddly colored green couch that looked very velvety and extremely worn. Its legs were ornately carved of solid wood. The room had tall bookcases, but the shelves were empty. A tarnished, silver tea service sat on a side table. A grand piano with the top open occupied one entire side of the room.

Charlotte was excited to see the piano. She sat on its creaky bench, and softly played Beethoven's *Fur Elise* on its dusty keys. The piano was in desperate need of tuning, even so, Charlotte felt safe as she played the song she'd memorized for a recital years ago. The others listened in a trance until Katie spoke up, "Stop it Charlotte! You're creeping me out with that song. It's spooky."

Charlotte finished her last notes in a crescendo that caused even Peter to feel a little disturbed. She turned to them and giggled, "C'mon you guys, it's Beethoven. It's a classic. It's not creepy!"

"Maybe not," said Emily, "but these portraits on the wall are definitely creeping me out. Does anyone else feel like we're being watched?"

All eyes moved to the walls and Peter held out his locket for a closer look.

"Do you think the people in these paintings used to live here?" asked Sidney. As they surveyed the portraits they saw couples, children, grandparents and even a small boy with a dog. "No matter where I stand in this room, that boy's eyes are staring at me."

"I feel like the grandpa with the hunting rifle is staring at me!" said Peter. There was life behind the portraits peering at them. The alert eyes of the paintings watched every move the six made.

"You guys are crazy," said James. "There's nothing strange about these paintings. Stop freaking yourselves out. Now let's build a fire, get warmed up and figure out how to get out of here." Reluctantly everyone agreed to sit.

"We need to find matches," said James. And just then the wood Peter had placed inside the fireplace spontaneously burst into a roaring fire.

Charlotte screamed! She was embarrassed and apologized, "Sorry, that scared me."

Peter took a seat on the hearth to warm up.

Katie said "I'm freezing, and I'm so wet I don't know if I will ever get dry." She sat next to Peter on the hearth. The crackle of the fire and the burning heat made her feel warm instantly. Peter inconspicuously looked at Katie, he saw her puffy hair, runny makeup, and sopping wet clothes, but he didn't care. He still thought she was the most beautiful girl in the world. He wanted to put his arms around her to help her get warm. But before he could continue this wrestle in his mind, Katie scooted close to Peter and leaned up against him. Peter got what he wanted.

"How are you so warm?" she asked with a slight shiver. "Share some of the heat with the rest of us!" she laughed.

Peter's stomach immediately started doing acrobatics, but instinct took over, he went with his gut and bravely placed his arm around Katie.

He could feel the goosebumps on her arm. "Man, you are freezing," he said. Peter wanted to pause this moment. He completely forgot about his body temperature and the creepy eyes they thought were staring at them. He could have been sitting in ice and wouldn't have noticed. But he did notice the perspiration that began to bead up on his forehead.

Katie put all her feelings about Peter aside for the moment. She felt comfortable with his arm around her and the warmth she received from being next to him, "He's not as dumb as I think he is," she considered to herself. "Just because you're sitting next to him doesn't mean you have to date him, or even like him," her thoughts continued. "Stop!" She said inside her head. "This doesn't have to be anything more than two friends sitting by the fire getting warmed up." Katie relaxed and ended the confusing thought patterns flowing through her mind.

Balchazar: *As Peter and Katie have demonstrated, in many situations it is easy to lose control of one's mind with useless and confusing banter taking charge. Always bring order to the thoughts in your mind, remembering that order is heaven's first law.*

Meanwhile, Charlotte's thoughts raced a million miles a second as she stared at the fire. She couldn't shake the thoughts she had earlier; they tormented her with guilt, "This is my fault! If I'd been able to control my thoughts we wouldn't be in this creepy castle. Why can't I do this? What's wrong with me? Everyone else can control their thoughts!" She slumped down in her chair and placed her hands in her pockets. She felt for her keys. She gripped them, and almost as fast as the fire started, a warm, calm feeling worked its way up her arm and throughout the rest of her body.

The warmth and calmness that spread also brought relief to her thoughts and mind. She noticed the bear rug stretched out in front of them. His angry mouth was wide open and the sharp teeth glistened in the firelight. "Is that bear creeping anyone else out?" No one answered. "Good thing he's dead." Charlotte had a knack for stating the obvious.

As the calmness from her keys and the warmth from the fire enveloped her, Charlotte let her guard down and decided it was time to confess to the group that she was the person who didn't focus on the goal. She failed to control her thoughts and was to blame for bringing them to this place. "Maybe now that everyone is warm and calm they won't take it so bad," she hoped.

Before she could get the words out, Peter spoke up. "Hey guys I don't want to alarm anyone, but something's not right. The hair on the back of my neck is literally standing up." Peter spoke calmly, but everything inside him was telling him to run and run far.

Immediately everyone stopped what they were doing and slowly looked around the room, not daring to speak or move. Noise was coming from the hallway. There was a rhythmic clanking that was getting louder and closer by the second.

Emily was on the brink of a panic attack. Her breathing had become loud and labored. James motioned for her to calm down. She closed her eyes tightly and concentrated with as much intensity as she could on breathing in through her nose and out through her mouth in a controlled manner. But it wasn't helping. James could feel her struggle. He moved next to her and put his arm around her. Although her fear did not subside, she now felt assurance that she could breathe at a more natural pace.

Suddenly the noise from the hallway stopped, causing the tension in the room to elevate. When nothing happened they relaxed slightly. "Does anyone have any idea what that noise was?" Charlotte whispered.

Sidney instinctively took out his crystal and saw nothing but the six of them in the parlor with the fire roaring in the fireplace. Everyone was dry, warm and unharmed.

James spoke up, "It was probably nothing. I don't hear it anymore. Why don't we forget about the noises for a minute and figure out why we ended up at this place? Why didn't we make it back to the museum? I thought for sure we could transport ourselves back through the combination of our gifts and thoughts."

Charlotte's insides sank. The comfort she had experienced just moments ago about sharing her failure with the group was gone.

Sidney answered and interrupted her thoughts, "I know I can imagine anything, see it in my crystal, and then it happens for real. I've done it several times and I'm convinced I can do it whenever I want. All I have to do is see it in my mind and keep my thoughts focused. But I'm confused, because I did imagine us back at the museum."

Peter was the next to join the analysis, "I imagined being back at the museum. But I didn't see all of us there. Perhaps it was my fault."

"No Peter, I don't think what you did would send us here. My mind couldn't focus on the museum, I jumped ahead of myself and pictured us back at school," James replied.

"I kinda did the same thing as you, James. I tried to think about the museum, but my thoughts were obsessed with wanting to be home. I had this image of my dad saving me." Katie felt remorse over those seemingly selfish thoughts.

Finally Charlotte spoke up, "No, you guys did what you were supposed to do. I'm the one at fault here. I hate to admit it, but I just couldn't focus. I thought it was a good idea, but I didn't believe it was going to work. I didn't believe that we could really get back to the museum just by thinking about it."

Balchazar: *One of the most difficult, but most rewarding lessons one will learn was taught by Napoleon Hill. He brilliantly stated, "What the mind can conceive and believe, the mind can achieve." Not until our six friends wrap their heads around this simple truth will they ever return to the comfort of their museum.*

Charlotte was embarrassed and afraid. She kept telling herself she was the reason they weren't at the museum. She was the reason they failed and she was pretty upset with herself. "I don't understand why we're at this castle though, I know I had a lot going on in my mind, but I really don't remember thinking of this place. I'm so, so sorry."

Katie immediately chastised her, "How could you do that Charlotte? You said it was a good idea! But you didn't help at all?" Katie's anger got the best of her.

Peter's hot head was about to support Katie in her anger, but he didn't get the chance. Emily spoke first, "You guys! It's over and done. We're here. Calm down. We're all right. Yes, it's scary but we're all right. Let's focus and do like we've done every other time: figure out what we're going to do next."

They relaxed a little and began to think. They were concentrating so hard that no one said a word. Katie was starting to feel hot next to the fire. She stood up to move over to the couch. But as she did she felt a cold breeze.

"That's strange," Katie said. "I just felt a rush of cold air blow past me when I stood up. Did you feel that Peter?"

"No" he replied. "I just feel the heat of the fire."

"Maybe it was a ghost," said Sidney. "I read online that ghosts leave a cold breeze as they fly by you. Some people say when you experience an unexplained and sudden drop in temperature it's because a ghost is next to you."

"I'm sorry I brought it up!" said Katie as she rolled her eyes and walked across the bear rug to the sofa. As she stepped across the rug, the sleeping bear awoke. He raised his big head, opened his mouth even wider than it already was, and growled. Everyone screamed, jumped up and took cover throughout the room.

The bear was standing on its hind legs. The saliva dripping from its teeth reflected the light from the fire. His growl was like an engine roaring to life as he reached out to swipe whatever might be in his path with his razor-sharp claws.

Charlotte didn't have to think twice about getting out of the room and quickly ran to the doorway only to find the doors shut and locked.

"We're gonna die! We're gonna die! We're gonna die!" Emily repeated as she crouched behind the couch. Even though her eyes were shut tightly, the tears welled up inside.

"Emily! Stop that!" Peter yelled at her, shaking her by the shoulders.

Charlotte began to fumble for her keys. They had opened locks before; perhaps they'd open these doors as well. But there was no lock on the doors in this room.

As everyone else was frantic and chaotic, an unexpected calm suddenly came over James. He quickly withdrew his spyglass and looked at the bear. But instead of an attacking predator, he saw a little boy. He seemed afraid and was crying for someone to help him. He was standing in place, tears streaming down his face. James removed the spyglass from his eye to confirm what he saw. In front of him was a bear growling and clawing at the air.

As he lifted the spyglass for another look, he saw familiarity in this boy. He was the boy standing with his dog, in the portrait on the wall.

Emily, still frozen behind the couch, could feel James' change in emotion and perspective, "James, what did you see? No never mind, it doesn't matter. Just do it, whatever you're thinking.

Remember back to the island, do the illogical, defy logic. It worked for us on the island; it will work here and now." The island memory was very clear in Emily's mind, and she knew it was what James needed to hear.

He tucked his spyglass away and began to slowly move toward the bear. Although the bear was making a lot of noise and swinging wildly with its paws, it had not taken one step closer to them. Perhaps he didn't intend to hurt them. This bolstered James' confidence somewhat, and he mustered all the courage he could find. Although he was scared, he stepped forward toward the big, brown bear. As he did so, Emily simultaneously moved closer to Peter. She crouched down behind him and peered around his shoulder as she attempted to shield herself from the horror that might soon come to pass. But no matter how badly she didn't want to watch, she couldn't avert her eyes.

"It's all right. Everything's going to be all right." James' voice wasn't much more than a whisper. As he was cautiously moving toward the bear, the animal didn't budge. James walked around the couch and stood directly in front of the growling, threatening bear. He froze, breathing as deeply and steadily as he could. His body was sweating all over, his palms were wet and he felt tears about to burst from his eyes. He calmly and gently spoke to the bear, "Don't be afraid. I'll help you."

Suddenly the bear stopped swiping his paws, quit growling and dropped from his hind legs onto all fours. He stared directly at James.

"Oh James, be careful!" Charlotte could only peek from behind the hand she held in front of her face. She felt sick. Katie had tears rolling down her face, and Emily had finally hidden herself completely behind Peter. She couldn't bear to watch what the bear might do to her brother.

Of course, Sidney was active in his mind. He imagined everything was fine. He pictured James making friends with the bear and gradually earning his trust. He pulled out his crystal and saw the result in the ball. He was confident in what he saw, he believed it, and as he stood next to Katie, he motioned for her attention and showed her what he saw in the crystal.

James reached out and touched the bear's back. He began to pet him as if he were a large dog, but exercised extreme caution. The bear didn't react, so James lowered his head and whispered something into its ear that no one else could hear. "You're not alone. It's ok. You're all right. I'm here to help you."

After a few short moments of whispering, the bear began to transform in front of their eyes. Fur turned to hair, paws to hands and feet, while claws shrunk to fingernails. Soon, the child from the portrait on the wall was standing before them. And now everyone saw the child James had seen through his spyglass.

Once the shock wore off, they began to slowly walk over to James and the boy. The boy sat in a chair next to the fireplace. As he sat, his body sunk through the chair, like he wasn't even there. He silently disappeared, leaving behind a folded bear rug on top of the cushion.

Sidney reached out to grab the rug. With Peter's help, they placed it back in front of the fireplace, smoothing it out as if nothing ever happened.

There was an audible exhale from the group. "Of all the things that have happened to us, that was by far the strangest." James was feeling confident. Everything was coming together for him. The different perspective his spyglass provided empowered him to act, and each time he did, the physical manifestation of that reality was present for everyone to see. As he thought about it, he began to look forward to the next opportunity to use it again. If only he could find a way to do it without feeling the fear.

Balchazar: *Often times all we need to succeed is a change in perspective. James has learned a valuable lesson pertaining to believing in himself. My students must learn to ignore their fear, to press through it to the other side, and then see the good results that come from their actions. Believe in yourself. Take action, and what you dream in your mind will become your reality.*

"Okay," said Charlotte. "I think I've had enough of this room. Let's get out of here and figure out how to get home."

Her statement was met with no argument. As they turned to

exit the parlor, they found the door wide open, just as it had been before the bear-child awoke.

"Who's opening and closing this door?" asked Emily. "Actually, never mind. I probably don't want to know. I really don't like this place." The more Emily thought about it, the more her fears grew.

No one spoke. No one had a clue, and in reality, they knew Emily was right, they were afraid to know the answer.

All six of them cautiously stepped into the hallway. They instinctively turned to go back to the front door. As they hurried along the red carpet in the long corridor, two suits of armor blocked them. The arms of the suits were extended, as if to halt the group, but even more daunting, their swords were drawn and pointing right at them. Charlotte stifled the scream in her throat before it escaped her lips. They wasted no time running down the hall and entering the next open door they could find.

The only light in this room was provided by Peter's locket. As Sidney slammed the door closed behind them, Peter began to aim the locket to see where they were. Suddenly, lightning flashed, brightening the room well enough to see they were standing in a trophy room. Every wall was covered with mounted beasts staring back at them with beady eyes and fang-like teeth.

This time Charlotte couldn't stifle her scream. She was immediately repulsed by the heads and latched onto the door Sidney had just closed behind them. She had no idea what to do. In front of her was a variety of creatures she had never seen before, all staring at her with angry, menacing looks. Outside the doors, the suits of armor stood guard with their swords. Ultimately, Charlotte decided to stay in the room and not leave her friends. There was definitely safety in numbers. But it didn't make her any more comfortable.

"Wow!" exclaimed Sidney, "These are the coolest heads I've ever seen." He marched to the wall with the most heads and stood directly beneath the largest one. He struck a pose as though the kill was his. In his mind, Sidney was on safari. He had bagged the big one.

Peter joined in, "I know, I've seen animals mounted to a wall before, but I don't have a clue what these are." He stood directly underneath one and shined his locket for a better look. It had horns like a ram, the head of a mountain lion, and long straight hair. The look on its face was anything but friendly. Its mouth appeared to be growling, and every tooth looked razor sharp.

Everyone except for Charlotte studied the strange animals. The creatures they saw were not identifiable in the normal animal kingdom. But they did have features of familiar animals. There was a lion-boar combination, an elephant-moose combo, and a tiger-elk.

As they admired the creatures, they could hear a deep, haunting laugh. "Whoever is laughing like that, stop it!" demanded Katie. "Peter, are you doing that? Stop it!" They all looked around to see who it was. It was none of them. They stood frozen, quietly listening. "Maybe it was nothing," Katie continued.

"Or maybe it was Sidney's imagination bringing one of these beasts to life." Peter was trying to lighten the mood, but his comment didn't go over well, as the haunting laughter started again. The very suggestion ignited Sidney's mind. For a fleeting moment, he saw the lion beast reaching down to bite Peter's neck. Sidney was fed up with Peter tormenting and teasing.

Seconds after Sidney had the thought, the lion beast came to life with a deafening roar. Peter jumped and the head reached out to grab him. He ducked just in time, but still the large canine teeth of the beast scraped Peter's shoulder and back.

Balchazar: *One must learn that it does not serve you well to think about what you do not want. Instead, think about what you do want. For that which you focus your mind on is exactly what you will receive.*

Peter cringed. He was bleeding.

"Peter, are you okay?" yelled Sidney, who was immediately feeling regret for his thoughts.

"I'm fine," he said. "It's just a scratch. I'll be okay."

"James, I want to get out of here. Now!" Emily begged.

Charlotte agreed and opened the door that lead to the hallway, and the suits of armor. The suits stood motionless, lifeless.

"Yeah," said James. "Let's go, somewhere, anywhere, but here."

"Over here," motioned Charlotte. "This looks like the dining room and it's the closest. Let's go in there and figure out what to do next."

They all entered the dining room. Now covered in a hazy film of dust, the floor-to-ceiling windows must have provided an amazing view of the grounds when the castle was full of life. Through the windows they could see the storm was still raging.

Although the wind was howling and the rain was falling heavier than before, everyone's eyes were drawn to the massive dining table located dead center in the room. It was the largest table Sidney had ever seen, his quick count revealed seating for twenty-two guests. He looked at the dark wood and used his finger to write his name in a thick layer of dust, while gripping one of the weathered, leather chairs.

"This table setting is beautiful," said Katie. "It looks like they're ready to serve a fancy meal right now." The china was ivory with gold trim. In the center was a family crest which appeared to be of royal heritage. Katie picked up a plate for a closer look, immediately dropping it and retreating from the table. In the crest was a recognizable beast from the trophy room. It snarled at her from the porcelain dish, bringing its huge head within inches of her face.

Charlotte picked up one of the silver utensils and was surprised at how heavy it was in her hand. The goblets were empty, but were etched with a beautiful floral pattern. She unfolded one of the linens. Dust immediately filled the air, causing her to sneeze three times in a row. "Excuse me," she whispered. "This is so pretty, but so dusty. It looks like someone was preparing for a royal celebration. I wonder what happened. Why did they leave?"

Katie noticed a full-length mirror with a gilded frame, leaning against the wall. She knew she must look a mess after being in the rain. Wanting to fix her hair and makeup, she walked over and leaned in for a closer examination of her face. She screamed. The reflection staring back was not hers. In the mirror, Katie saw a skeleton, a skull without eyes, and a jaw chattering with laughter. A boney finger appeared and pointed at her. She screamed again, turned and ran, crashing into Peter, almost knocking him over. He impulsively took hold of her and held her tight. She buried her face in his chest not wanting to see anything else in the room.

He gently placed a hand on the back of her head and asked, "Katie, you're okay. What's wrong? What happened?"

Without lifting her head, Katie told him about the skeleton in the mirror. A shiver ran down Charlotte's spine, and Emily looked to James for reassurance.

Sidney's imagination kicked into overdrive. They were in a haunted castle. That much was certain. He imagined skeletons coming from every direction. Gargoyles were flying into the dining room through the giant windows. He heard the clanking, marching footsteps of the suits of armor. In his mind he saw ghosts and goblins floating around them.

Faster than he could control it, he had created the most frightening, haunted castle his brain could conjure. He was now standing in front of the dining room table, scared because of what he had just imagined, not wanting anyone else to know how much he let his mind take over.

Katie's sobs were quieter now as she hid herself in the protection of Peter's arms. James and Emily stood in a corner whispering to each other, and Charlotte gripped the back of a chair and stared at the door. As Sidney looked around the room, he had the strange sensation they weren't alone. He felt like the master of this castle was with them. He got the feeling that even though these people had passed on, they still followed a routine. Sidney had no idea what time it was, but he knew it had to be close to dinner time.

As he studied the dining table again, he saw that a number of the chairs were now occupied. A ghost family had materialized before his very eyes. These must be the former occupants. He wondered if this was why the table was set; it was ready to serve them. Although they were ready to eat, the spirits at the table did not seem to mind that Sidney and his friends had intruded. It had been so many years since they had dined with entertainment.

James said to the group, "Why don't we sit down and figure a way out of here."

As the living began to sit, Sidney realized that he must be the only one able to see the ghosts. He wondered if he should say something but withheld for fear of being yelled at for his overactive imagination. He quickly chose an unoccupied seat, and so did the rest of the living, except for Charlotte. "No, Charlotte," he said. "Sit here, next to me." Charlotte gave Sidney a strange look but didn't question him. She moved down two spots and pulled out the "empty" chair next to Sidney.

As he looked around the table he could see his friends and seven non-living beings. No one was sitting on top of a ghost. He wasn't sure what would have happened had Charlotte planted herself on the elderly ghost who was already tucked into the chair she had selected.

He pulled out his crystal ball and looked deep inside, hoping for assurance that what he was thinking and seeing would not reveal itself in the ball. Unfortunately, he couldn't have been more wrong. As he gazed, he not only saw the non-living guests at the table, but now ghost servants had entered the room with trays of food. They acted in a formal manner, spreading out and standing directly behind those seated at the table. Sidney saw one of the spirits raise his fork and tap it against his goblet. Sidney heard the tiny ping. Commanded by the sound, each servant placed their tray on the table with precision.

Sidney was salivating; there was ham, turkey, bread, a steaming pot of soup, potatoes, salad, fruit, and a bowl of peas. He could practically smell the food as the non-living began to load their plates from overflowing trays. Staring into his crystal ball, he wondered what they'd serve for dessert. Would it be something chocolate, a pie, or maybe pudding?

But before he could answer that question, Charlotte interrupted his thoughts, "Sidney, what are you staring at in your ball? You've been glued to that thing ever since we sat down. And you have the strangest look on your face!"

"Um, uhh, well, uhh…" Sidney, not wanting to be discovered chose his words carefully and with trepidation. "You're not going to like what I have to say."

James spoke up, "What is it Sidney? It doesn't matter if we like it or not. If something's wrong you need to tell us."

Sidney reluctantly responded. "When we came into this room

I had the distinct feeling that we weren't alone. Then, without even using my crystal, I saw others in the room with us. When I sat down I pulled out my crystal and my hunch was correct."

"What is it? What do you see? I can't see anyone else in the room! Are you sure?" questioned Katie.

"Oh, I'm very sure," said Sidney. He was visibly shaken now that the attention of the group was focused on him.

"What is it Sidney?" questioned Peter cautiously. "Is something bad happening?"

"I don't know if it's necessarily bad," he responded. "But we're not alone."

"What?" stammered Emily as she craned her head looking for someone. "I don't see anyone other than the six of us."

"Me too!" added Charlotte. "Where are these people?"

"They're not people!" responded Sidney impatiently. "This room is crowded with spirits that you can't see. In fact, right now, there are seven of them sitting at this very table. The plates and glasses you see as empty are actually filled with food, and the spirits are enjoying their dinner party. There are also spirit servants standing by ready to wait on them."

Both Peter and Katie continued to look around the room. Unable to see anything Sidney described, Peter asked, "Are you sure it's not just your imagination?"

"I wish it wasn't true," answered Sidney. "But I see it with my own eyes, and I can see them inside my crystal. But lucky for us, they don't seem to mind that we're in the room with them, sitting at their table."

Balchazar: *We have been conditioned and trained to see our world only through the experience of our five senses: taste, touch, smell, sight, and hearing. But there is an entirely unseen world which is invisible to our senses. And although we cannot perceive it, it does exist. For example, there is music all around you. You cannot see it or hear it. But if you tune a radio to the right frequency, you will hear it clearly. My students must learn to recognize that which is undetectable to their senses.*

James reached to the side of his chair and began rummaging through his backpack. Finally, he found it. He pulled out his spyglass, and began to survey the room. "He's right! Every single thing he said is true! I see it. But they seem to be ignoring us. They're just eating."

"What should we do?" asked Emily.

"Well, I think we should get out of here!" said Charlotte.

"Wait!" shouted James abruptly. "Sidney, do you see what I see?"

As he looked out the window, James could see something flying in circles around the castle and in the courtyard, but he had no idea what it was.

"I don't know what it is James. I see them in my crystal too. They're coming from the roof. It looks like... no, it can't be... but it looks like the gargoyles from the roof have come to life."

James looked through the spyglass and focused on the flying creatures. "You're right, that's exactly what's out there, but not for long, it looks like they're trying to find a way inside."

"And it looks like they're coming straight for the window!" yelled Peter.

"Now what?" cried Katie.

"TAKE COVER!" yelled James. "Quick! Everyone, get under the table!"

He threw his chair back, grabbed Emily and pulled her under the table, only to hear the sound of a million pieces of glass shattering and falling to the floor.

Katie screamed as Peter pulled her to the rug and covered her instinctively with his body. Charlotte wasted no time following. She saw something crashing through the glass in front of her but didn't look to see what it was.

Sidney, on the other hand, was completely frozen. He'd moved his focus from the crystal to the shattered windows. He watched as dozens of concrete gargoyles flew into the dining room, smashing everything in their path to pieces.

Charlotte had been yelling at Sidney to move, but he wasn't responding. Finally, she pulled him under the table, as one of the gargoyles flew low, smacked into his chair, splitting it in half.

As they crouched on their hands and knees beneath the table, they listened to the sounds of destruction coming from above. Everything in the room was being demolished. They were grateful the dining room table was not only hiding them, but protecting them from the debris that rained down.

Charlotte yelled to Sidney, wanting to know what was destroying the dining room. But Sidney was in shock. He was lying on the floor in the fetal position, mumbling inaudible words.

Charlotte looked to James for guidance. "What did you see in your spyglass? What just came crashing through the window?"

"I think it's the stone gargoyles."

"Gargoyles?" questioned Charlotte. "Where did they come from?"

"Who cares where they came from," interrupted Katie. "What are we supposed to do now, run?"

"I'm not moving from under this table until those things are gone," said Emily, shaking her head. "I think we're better off staying put until it calms down."

"It's not going to calm down!" yelled Sidney, who finally pulled himself onto his knees and was looking into his crystal.

"What do you see?" demanded Peter. "What's going to happen?"

"Sidney answered. "The hallway is full of suits of armor and they're marching toward us. The beasts mounted to the walls are alive. There are spirits in other rooms of the castle coming our way, and the spirits seated above us are motioning to the gargoyles that we're under the table."

"And in case you haven't noticed," interrupted James. "The storm outside is stronger than ever."

He was right. Lightning was flashing more frequently, and the thunder sounded like a series of exploding bombs.

Before they could wrap their heads around what Sidney just said, one of the gargoyles came crashing into the table, splitting it in half. Their hiding spot had been discovered, and it was time to move.

Charlotte screamed and another gargoyle came straight for her. She rolled to the side, knocking Sidney off his knees. The gargoyle smashed into the table and upended it, pushing it onto its side. The sound of breaking china and crystal added even more confusion to the already chaotic room.

"Hurry!" yelled Peter, "Follow me, take cover behind the table!

We can use it as a shield." In a matter of seconds all six of them were behind the table they had safely been hiding under moments before. It had been moved to allow just enough space between the broken chunk of table and one lone window that was still intact.

"Think fast!" yelled Emily. "We need a plan, NOW!"

"We can't take on all these creatures by ourselves," said James.

"We need to do the illogical!" yelled Charlotte. "It's just like at the other places we've been. Do the illogical."

"You're right," shouted Katie. Her mind was racing; she began to think out loud. "Okay, the logical thing to do is to run away, or to fight. We can't fight these things and win. So, what's the illogical thing?"

"We have to do something different like when we were in the quicksand!" yelled Charlotte.

"Look!" Sidney pointed above them. "The spirits are giving us away again." Sidney started throwing forks at the spirits hovering above them, but it did no good. They flew right through them and landed on the floor.

Without warning, the fractured table was tossed aside, exposing them. They screamed! Swords drawn, the suits of armor had arrived.

Without thinking, Peter jumped up and lunged at the suit of armor directly in front of him. He rammed into him with his bloody shoulder, catching him by surprise. The suit dropped his sword and they both tumbled to the floor and began to wrestle.

"What are you doing?" screamed Katie. "We're not supposed to fight them!"

"Never underestimate the power of surprise!" He called out. Katie was stunned by Peter's actions.

"I think he's trying to get the sword!" yelled Sidney.

As they wrestled on the floor Peter took a blow to his cheek from the suits metal fist. "That's going to leave a mark," said Peter, as he grabbed the suits arm, ripped it from his body, and threw it to the side. He reached for the sword, but so did the now one-armed suit. Peter rammed his elbow hard into the jaw of the suit. He watched the helmet separate from the rest of the armor and fly across the room. With an arm and head missing this suit was now out of the fight. Peter claimed the sword that now belonged to him.

He pushed the sword deep into the chest of the suit. As he did air hissed out like a release valve had just been punctured. The suit shook and rattled and then exploded, disappearing into thin air.

Peter's confidence shot through the roof. His look of pure satisfaction was short lived as he turned to face the next suit and realized there were thirty suits standing in front of him, slowly backing him up against the dining room wall.

"Peter, I have a plan!" yelled Charlotte. "I know what to do!" Charlotte grabbed her keys and gripped them with all her might. She soon felt calmness take over her body; it flowed through her like a wave. She closed her eyes and stood still. It was obvious she was deep in thought. She looked calm and focused. Her lips were moving in a repetitive pattern, like she was saying the same words over and over.

The chaos swirled around her, gargoyles in flight, suits jabbing with their swords, her friends huddled behind the table. But Charlotte was determined. She saw their salvation through her plan, and she wasn't letting it go. Her will was so strong. She held it as if it had already happened. Strongly she stood, focused, using her will to see her plan to fruition despite the chaos around her.

While the others hid in fear, Charlotte stood her ground holding the image of success in her mind. She was not to be moved. She should have been afraid, but she pushed the fear aside and concentrated only on the result she wanted. She knew the answer. She would not be swayed from her mission.

They were all staring at her, but their attention was soon diverted by a loud beeping. It was the "beep, beep, beep" of a construction vehicle's reverse warning system. They looked up to see a cement truck driven by one of the spirits come crashing through the only remaining window, completely annihilating it along with a gargoyle.

The old spirit lady driving the truck was laughing so hard her bun came loose, and silver hair fell over her face. She pushed it out of her eyes and made eye contact with Charlotte.

"NOW!" Charlotte yelled. "Do it NOW!"

The spirit lady used both hands to pull a lever inside the truck. When she did, a familiar river of pink concrete began to flow at an accelerated pace from the truck's chute. Peter saw what was happening and flipped a piece of table and told everyone to get on top. Katie scrambled to get up on the table as a gargoyle dove toward her taking her by the ankle. Peter lifted his sword, and with all his might, swung down hard hitting the gargoyle on the arm, severing the limb. He screamed, "Leave her alone!"

The force of Peter's swing, plunged the gargoyle into the setting pink concrete. Katie was bruised and shaken but safe. The pink concrete hardened in seconds. The suits of armor tried to lift their legs, but they were trapped. They were cemented to the floor, unable to move, frozen in pink concrete in a matter of seconds.

Charlotte smiled and gave two thumbs up to the spirit grandma in the truck. "Thanks grandma spirit!" she yelled. The spirit smiled, laughed, put the truck in drive and disappeared as fast as she came.

"Charlotte, that was amazing!" yelled Peter as he wielded his sword. "How did you do that?"

"The thought just came to me. I remembered what happened to us at the construction site with the concrete and it just came to my mind to use it to stop the suits. Once I had the thought, I saw it in my mind until it happened."

"That was so cool!" howled Sidney. "And the amazing thing is I didn't even see that coming in my crystal ball."

One by one the gargoyles surrounded the group hovering above them in a circle. Katie grabbed Peter's hand. She didn't know what else to do. Emily covered her eyes and James instinctively stood in front of her to block the brunt of whatever was going to happen.

"No, no, no!" muttered Charlotte. "This can't be. We beat the suits of armor; we can beat the gargoyles too." She looked around, but no one heard her. Everyone was too preoccupied with their fear, except for Sidney. He was sitting on the ground, his crystal ball pressed hard to his forehead and his eyes squeezed tightly shut. She watched him and after a moment he opened his eyes, lowered the crystal, looked in it, and smiled.

"Sidney, what is it?" she whispered. "What are you looking at?"

A cracking noise pierced the fear and silence that had overtaken the room. Everyone franticly looked around for the source of the commotion.

Everyone, that is, except for Sidney, who was staring into his crystal. The smirk on his face widened and he started to laugh silently. The noise continued to grow louder. Charlotte noticed Sidney's glee. She pressed her eyebrows together and looked at Sidney. He showed her the scene in his crystal ball.

"Hold this idea, Charlotte. We're going to make it happen." Charlotte, while clasping her keys, held the same image in her mind that she saw in Sidney's crystal ball. They were now of the same mind, same thoughts. Charlotte could feel the strength of the image becoming real and she held onto it tighter and tighter seeing more and more detail in her mind.

"There!" shouted Peter as he pointed to the concrete. "It's the concrete, look at it. It's cracking to pieces. The suits are going to be set free now!"

As the group focused on the cracks that grew increasingly larger, Emily came out from behind James and began to yell, "Something is coming out of the concrete. Now's our chance. Let's run."

"No!" shouted Sidney. "We can't leave. You're going to want to see this."

"Sidney?" questioned Peter. "What have you done?"

Suddenly, the concrete gave way, and eight long tentacles came bursting from deep below the floor. They shot in the air and immediately wrapped around the nearest gargoyles. The gargoyles didn't even have time to react. They were being smashed together and crumbled to pieces.

Quickly, the tentacles wrapped around eight more of the menacing concrete creatures and they were destroyed as they crashed into the suits of armor still shackled to the floor by the pink concrete. Helmets flew in the air, swords clamored to the ground, gargoyle wings fragmented into a million pieces. The destruction was fast and effective.

"Yes!" Sidney screamed jumping up and down with triumph. He clapped his hands in excitement and gave a fist bump to Peter. By now the remaining gargoyles were frantically trying to escape the room, but the tentacles were too fast. They grabbed the last of the gargoyles and thrust them into the remnants of the pink concrete-covered floor.

"Gerry! Is that you?" yelled Emily.

At that moment, Gerry, the soda serving octopus they met in the maze burst through the floor. With a big grin on his face, his tentacles scooped everyone in for a group hug.

"Thank you, Gerry!" said Charlotte. "You're a lifesaver."

"You're welcome, now don't get too comfortable. You've come a long way, and you're almost finished." He reached a tentacle to the sky and asked, "Is anyone thirsty?"

Gerry's tentacle handed each of them a bottle of water. "We're not at the soda fountain, but this will do for now. I've got to go, but I'm sure this won't be the last time we see each other."

"Bye Gerry!" they yelled. "Thank you."

"That was so awesome, Sidney! How did you do that?" asked Katie.

"I can't believe I did that! I was sitting on the floor thinking what are we going to do, when I remembered Gerry and his tentacles. I wished he was here, because I knew he could grab more than one gargoyle at a time. I thought it, I saw it in my mind and then in my crystal ball. I heard the cement start to crack and I just kept focusing. I kept my eyes shut and visualized Gerry smashing the gargoyles with his tentacles. Then it happened. It was so great. I still can't believe it."

"Did anyone else hear Gerry say we're almost done?" asked James.

"Yes!" answered Charlotte. "Does that mean we're going home soon? Oh, I really hope so."

Peter butted in, "He also said not to get too comfortable. Does that mean were not finished fighting off everything in this castle?"

"Speaking of everything in the castle," said James, "What happened to all the ghosts that were in here? I can't see them anymore."

"I can't either," responded Sidney.

"I think I know where they went," said Katie. "Look closely at the paintings on the wall. Does anyone else feel like the eyes are watching us?"

"I guess dinner is over," said Peter.

The tension broke and they all relaxed and laughed a little as they gulped down their water.

"So what's next?" asked Emily.

There was a pretty long pause before Peter finally said, "I know this probably isn't what anyone wants to hear, but I have the feeling that we need to go through the hole Gerry came out of."

"Oh no, that can't be right," sighed Charlotte. "Does anyone have a better idea?"

"I'm sorry Charlotte," said Peter, "But my gut is telling me down is the way. Our journey continues below."

They walked over to the hole. It wasn't large, but it was definitely big enough that each of them could fit through. James dropped his bottle of water down the hole and listened. There was no sound. Nothing.

"Well," said Emily. "Either it's a really, really deep hole, or your bottle landed on a bed of pillows."

"That's it!" said Peter. "A bed of pillows, just like at the bakery. We have to take the risk. We can't see what's down there, but there's no reason we can't create what's down there. Do the illogical."

"What are you talking about?" asked Charlotte. "I think maybe you got hit a little too hard by that suit of armor."

"No, I didn't. I see it all very clearly right now. There's a huge pile of pillows down there. Once we're down, my locket will light the way, and we'll know what to do."

"I can't believe I'm agreeing, but Peter, I think you're right," said Emily.

"So do I," said James. "It makes perfect sense. Let's do it. Are we all in?"

"Yes!" said everyone except Katie.

"Katie? What about you?" asked James. "Can you do it?"

Peter grabbed her hand, "She can do it. Come on Katie. We're almost there. Trust Gerry. Trust me. This is the next step."

She squeezed his hand and said, "Okay, I'm in. But I'm not going first."

"I'll go first," said Peter. "I feel like I'm supposed to do that." He stepped closer to the hole, looked down and saw nothing but black.

"What do you think?" asked Sidney.

"It's now or never." He crossed his arms over his chest and stepped over the side disappearing into the hole.

Charlotte muffled a scream as she bit down on her lip. They waited in silence. Then James knelt down and stuck his head over the hole.

"Peter?" he yelled. "Are you okay?"

The sound of Peter's infectious laugh echoed from below. "I'm great!" he yelled. I'm lying on a huge bed of feather pillows. Here, let me get my locket out." By the light of Peter's locket, James could see a faint glow of light.

"I see your light, Peter. Tell us when you're ready for the next person to come down."

"I'm ready!" he yelled. "Come on down. The water's fine!" he laughed.

"Water?" questioned a still nervous Charlotte.

"He's just joking," Emily reassured.

"Are you sure?"

"Yes," said James. "We're good. Who wants to go next?"

"I'll go," said Sidney. He stepped over and let out a high-pitched scream before he landed on the bed of pillows.

One by one the group jumped, until it was just James and Charlotte, "I don't think I can do this, James, I'm scared."

"You can do it, Charlotte. Just imagine yourself lying on a soft, soft bed of pillows. Focus on the goal, landing on the soft pillows. Get every other image out of your mind."

Charlotte mustered her focus and will, "Keep going. That's helping."

"The pillows are so comfortable. They make you feel like you're floating, they're so light. You're having so much fun, you want to take the pillows and put them on your bed at home."

"I can do this!" said Charlotte. She saw the image in her mind. With her keys in her left hand she felt the calmness. She reached out with her other hand and grabbed James' hand, "Tell me once more."

James started to repeat everything he'd said. By the time he got to the part about her wanting to put the pillows on her own bed,

Charlotte let go of his hand and turned to jump.

Without thinking James reached out, pulled her back and kissed her. Charlotte looked at James in shock.

"Jump!" he said. "Do it. Now!"

Still not comprehending what just happened, Charlotte turned, jumped, and disappeared into the hole. James could hear everyone cheering her on, and then someone yelled that it was clear for him to jump.

James couldn't stop smiling. He had no idea what crazy impulse had caused him to kiss Charlotte. But he didn't care. He did it, and he enjoyed it.

He took one last look around the dining room. It was completely unrecognizable from when they first entered. "What a mess," he thought as he looked at the paintings on the wall. His eyes paused at the painting of the grandma, who with her silver-haired bun looked surprisingly similar to the ghost grandma who drove the cement truck through the dining room window. She winked at him. James gave a quick smile and then disappeared down the hole.

He immediately noticed that the room was completely different from the rest of the castle. It had no furniture. The only thing in it was the huge stack of feather pillows they landed on. Beyond the light of Peter's locket was complete blackness.

Charlotte was waiting for James as he staggered off the pillows. "Excuse me, but what just happened up there?"

James wasn't sure what to say, so he turned the tables on her. "What do you think just happened up there?"

"Well, you kissed me, and I wanna know why!" retorted Charlotte.

James said, "Because I like you."

"You like me?"

"Yeah. Is that okay?"

"Umm, well," Charlotte had no idea how to respond to such honesty. "I guess so."

"Well good," said James. "Now let's figure out where we are."

Charlotte was so confused. What motivated that kiss? Where did these feelings come from? She knew this had been the craziest day of her life. She recalled how much he had helped her and how instrumental he was in coaching her whenever she lost control. She had known James for years. How did she not see this coming?" I'm not even sure I like him that way. He's my friend's brother. Her thoughts flew threw her mind like a whirlwind.

Finally, Charlotte yelled, "STOP!" inside her mind. "Time out! Why don't you just enjoy the moment and see where this goes?" She paused and her mind eased up. "There, that's so much better."

"What did you say?" asked James.

"Nothing," she blushed. "Let's see if they've figured out what we're supposed to do next."

"Peter, what is this place?" asked James. "And do you know why we're supposed to be here?"

"Nope, I was hoping maybe someone else could figure that out."

"It's okay," said Katie. "We'll figure it out."

"Katie, did you hit your head on the way down?" asked Peter.

"Ha Ha, very funny. No, I did not, but I think it's time I start believing. It seems like we go as far as we can go and do as much as we can do, and just when we think were doomed the next step in our journey appears. I guess it's time that I give in to being positive and believing, instead of always doubting."

"Who are you, and what have you done with our Katie?" Emily joked with a huge smile on her face.

"Very funny guys. I'm serious."

"I see something!" yelled Sidney. "Over here, on the other side of the pillows. It's a backpack." He grabbed the bag and brought it over to the group.

"Hey, that's my bag," said Emily. "Here, let me open it."

As she opened the bag, she pulled out a worn book, opened it and shrieked, "My quill! I didn't even know that I didn't have it. Katie, I think there's something in here for you."

She handed the bag to Katie who reached inside and pulled out her scales. "Look the scales are in balance. They're perfectly still, and they're not teetering. That has to be a good sign."

"That's definitely a good sign," said Peter. "And I bet it has something to do with your change of attitude."

"Guys, you're never going to believe this," said James. He was looking through his spyglass, into what appeared to be complete darkness.

"What is it?" asked Emily.

"I think I see our way out."

"How?" shrieked Charlotte.

"I see six weathered doors, but guess what? This time they have door knobs on them."

"Where do you think they go?" asked Sidney.

"I think this is it," said James. "This is our ticket back to the museum. Come with me. Peter, we'll need your locket. Let's go check it out."

They walked for several minutes in the dim light provided by the locket. No one said a word. James stopped. "Here we are, can anyone see the doors beside me?"

"I see one door," said Katie. "I think it's my door. Do you think that's why I can see it?"

"Hold on," said James. He pulled out his spyglass and looked at the doors again. There were names on each door. "Katie, can you see your name on the door?"

"Yes, I couldn't at first, but I can now. Why do you think I can see my door and the others can't?"

"Katie, I think it's because you believe. I think you know that this door is going to take you back, back to the museum, back home."

"I think you're right, James. That feels right."

"I want to see my door," said Charlotte. "What do I need to do?"

"Focus," said Peter. "This is it. We all need to focus, but don't focus on the door. Focus on where you want the door to take you. Focus on being home, at the museum. That's what we have to do."

They all stood in silence. Each one expended every bit of imagination and energy they had thinking of the museum. Emily thought of the small conference room they were in when this all started. She saw each one of them opening their gifts. She felt the excitement as she opened the box that contained her quill.

Charlotte was smiling. She remembered the picture she had Sidney take of her and Katie on the stairs leading up to the museum with the stone lion. She was in the elevator with Katie. They were giggling and pushing the button for the third floor over and over. She thought of being in the museum close to James. It was all good.

Peter was standing in the lobby while Mason was talking to them about the coin. The sun was shining through the window onto the back of Katie's hair. He was thinking of how shiny her hair looked. Then her head turned and he saw her face bathed in the sunlight. She looked angelic. His stomach turned and did the strange exercises it often does whenever he thinks of her.

Sidney was staring into his crystal ball. He saw the museum. It was a large, brick building. It looked old and dignified. He walked through its halls. He was distinguished; he was a curator leading a group tour. He was explaining how he obtained the ancient Egyptian mummy that was on display. People were listening to his explanation, mesmerized by the story he told.

One by one they opened their eyes and small gasps and tiny shrieks escaped as they each saw their own personal door in front of them.

"Does everyone see their door now?" asked James.

Each responded in the affirmative.

"Are we ready?" he asked.

"Yes, I feel it," said Peter. "This is it."

Sidney agreed, "The lightning is striking in my crystal. Katie, what are your scales doing?"

"They're still balanced and that's the way they're going to stay, because we're going back to the museum."

"I love it," said Emily. "Let's do it."

"Charlotte," said James. "What are you thinking?"

"I'm thinking this is definitely the moment. I'm going to put my key in the lock."

She reached forward with an unsteady hand. She paused and let the calmness of the keys spread through her body.

Seeing her nerves, James gently took hold of her free hand. "This is it, Charlotte, you've got this."

Once she was calm, she knew what she needed to do. "I'm going to unlock my door and it's going to unlock all our doors." Her key was drawn to the door knob like a magnet. It slid in smoothly and she turned it effortlessly. A clicking noise sounded in each door.

"Everyone put your hand on your doorknob," said James. He let go of Charlotte's hand and winked at her. "On the count of three open your door and let's go..."

"...back to the museum," Emily finished her brother's sentence.

"One... Two... THREE... Now. Do it now," said James in his ever calm and comforting voice.

All six doors opened. They walked forward. Lighting struck and cracked as they walked through and each door slammed shut behind them. They were no longer in the castle.

CHAPTER 9

THE UNCOMFORTABLE TRUTH REVEALED

No one was brave enough to open their eyes and see if they made it to the museum. The silence was deafening and gave no hints regarding their location. No one said a word, but in her mind Emily was calling out for James. James reached down to feel the furniture in which he was seated. A plain wooden chair held him.

"I think we're all right." James still hadn't opened his eyes.

Sidney took James' comment as fact; he opened his eyes to see the artifact room in the museum where they had begun, "He's right! We did it! We're back at the museum!"

Charlotte screamed a cheer of jubilation and began dancing to the music playing in her mind. Emily hugged James like she hadn't seen him in decades.

"Look," screamed Charlotte. "My phone! Oh, I have missed you so much." She picked it up and frantically began to search for what she had missed while she was gone.

Katie opened her eyes to see the scales in perfect balance.

Directly across from her sat Peter. She wanted to hug him. She saw him differently now, but didn't dare move toward him. Was it because of his bravery at the castle? Did she feel safe and protected when she was with him? Logically, she knew he wasn't right for her, but for some reason he seemed different now, like a few of the rough edges had been knocked off his persona. Her heart was speaking to her head, telling her to be a little more open-minded to what Peter may bring to her life. But her head is stubborn.

Peter stared back at Katie from across the table. His mind flashed to the conversation Katie had with the football captain. That seemed liked ages ago. In his imagination, he had held Katie's hand walking to class. And even though that hadn't happened, he had held her hand. He had cradled her in his arms. He had comforted, protected, and saved her. It was better than he had imagined.

He knew that Katie was stubborn, but that's okay. They had shared amazing moments, and he had a good feeling about the two of them. He could be stubborn too. Peter was willing to exercise patience and persistence. Katie was worth it.

Sidney's imagination began to create an image. He was standing on the steps of the museum in a dark, navy blue suit, with a white shirt bearing French cuffs. His tie, a multi-colored paisley print loosened at the opened collar of his shirt. The paparazzi buzzed around him; photographers all vying for the best shot. Microphones pressed toward his face with reporters shouting out questions about his latest adventures. He placed one hand in the pocket of his suit pants while gesturing with the other as he answered each question, one by one. Sidney was the center of attention. He was finally the cool guy.

In the midst of the celebration and relief to be back at the museum, the door to the artifact room swung open and Mason returned. This time he was dressed in a suit and was holding the small box he'd retrieved earlier from his desk. "You're back!" he grinned. "That was interesting, wasn't it?"

His words caused the room to erupt in utter chaos.

Charlotte lost all control and yelled, "Interesting? Interesting you call that! What's that supposed to mean? Where were we?"

Katie had to shout to be heard over Charlotte, "We were thrust into some kind of alternate world time and time again, and you were there! You were with us, you spoke to us! And you did nothing to help us! What in the world just happened?"

"You owe us an explanation," Emily told him.

Mason looked to Peter, who said, "None of this makes sense. You seem to know this crow. He was with you in these places. But nothing makes any sense."

James was frustrated and wanted to go home. He was getting impatient, "Mason, please explain. Like, how long were we gone? Why didn't you help us? Did you know this was going to happen? Why didn't you stop it?"

Mason was no longer smiling. That is, until he saw Sidney, oblivious to the confusion around him, staring into his crystal ball with a huge grin.

Mason knew he needed to do something fast to gain control. He sat his box on the table, reached into it, and pulled out a glass sphere very similar to Sidney's crystal ball. As he touched it, sparks of electricity surged inside it. This caused enough of a distraction that the group became silent as everyone focused on the curious object Mason was holding.

"I know you guys have a lot of questions. If you'll just be patient and trust me, I can help you. You need to know a couple of things. Years ago, I experienced something very similar to what you just went through. I received a gift too."

Mason held the ball in front of him and the electrical currents inside it surged and grew. All eyes were glued to the ball. "I know what you're feeling right now. Please understand the first time is always the most difficult. It gets easier each time."

"The first time!" said Charlotte. "Oh no, I'm not doing that again. I'm out of here. Come on, let's go."

Sidney was seated to her right. He had gone from staring into his crystal ball to looking at Mason's ball and because his imagination had taken him someplace else, he really had no idea what was going on around him. When he heard Charlotte say, "Let's go," he stood up to leave.

His move emboldened her. Charlotte left her keys on the table, grabbed Sidney's hand, and turned to Katie, who was seated at her left. "Hurry Katie, let's leave before we get trapped inside another nightmare."

This was all happening too quickly for Katie. She tried to reason through the chaos. She wanted to hear Mason out, but she couldn't reason through her fear; it was in control. She agreed with Charlotte, she didn't want to repeat what just happened.

Charlotte took her free hand and latched onto Katie's arm. As Katie walked to the exit with Charlotte and Sidney, she looked at Peter. Her eyes were filled with confusion and doubt, but were clearly telling him to come with them.

Peter shook his head. "Katie, don't leave. Please. We need to hear what Mason has to say. Trust me; it's going to be okay. I know this is what we're supposed to do."

But Charlotte wanted nothing to do with any of this. She turned away from her friends.

In a flash, James leapt from his chair and bolted for the door. He grabbed Charlotte by the arms and looked her in the eyes. He leaned in. Charlotte saw the kiss coming but his lips moved past hers and stopped at her ear.

"Charlotte," he whispered. "I know you're scared. It's okay. We all are. But let's hear what Mason has to say. I want answers, you want answers. Give him a chance to explain. I promise I won't let anything happen to you."

As James hugged Charlotte, she felt like he was pushing out all the fear and anxiety that had been raging in her just moments ago.

"Thank you," she whispered.

"Of course," said James. He knew what Charlotte needed. He took her hand, walked her back to the chair and handed her the keys. As expected, the calming effect traveled up Charlotte's arm and throughout her body. James took the empty chair next to her.

"Katie," Peter coaxed softly. "Come over here and sit by me. Everything's going to be okay."

Katie, along with the rest of the room had no idea what had just happened between James and Charlotte. Katie looked at Charlotte, who was staring at James.

Katie finally looked at Emily who shrugged, "Don't ask me, I'm only his twin sister."

Finally, Katie gave in and looked at Peter. She slowly walked over to him, and apologized to Mason as she stepped past him. She was embarrassed about her reaction. In her mind she had blown any chance of being with this gorgeous, older man.

Sidney seemed unphased by what had just happened, and was already walking back to his seat.

James made eye contact with Peter, and then Peter noticed his phone on the table. He picked it up and texted James, "Operation Everest, phase one accomplished."

James hadn't noticed that he had his phone back until he felt it vibrate in his pocket. He grabbed it, read the text and responded with the thumbs up emoji.

Peter quickly texted back, "Looks like you have your own operation that you failed to share with me. Bro???????"

James smiled and texted, "Stealth mission. Details pending."

This time Peter responded with the thumbs up.

Everyone's eyes were on Mason, "Thank you for staying. I'm sorry I've upset you. But I'm glad your desire for answers has overcome your fear."

"The journey you completed isn't the first of its kind, and won't be your last. You've had the amazing opportunity to see firsthand how the faculties of your mind are used to create, build and shape either the life of your dreams, or that of your nightmares."

"Congratulations! Your first journey can't be completed until you're able to make the connection that your thoughts create the physical world around you. Never forget this important lesson. It's the basic foundation for any subsequent journey you'll have."

"Now that you're back, you must keep experimenting with your thoughts. I want you to learn that your thoughts carry the exact same power in this world as they did in the world you just left. It's essential that you practice and develop your skills. Become familiar with your gifts so you'll be prepared when the time comes for your next lesson. I don't know when your next lesson will take place or where it'll take you. But just like today, when you're ready to be taught, off you'll go."

SIX MONTHS LATER

The bell rang announcing the lunch break and the usual sea of students spilled out the double doors to what had started as a sunlit morning, but was now a cloudy afternoon. Emily and James were already at the picnic table under the tree discovering what was in the plain paper sack for lunch. Sidney joined them with a new-found confidence since surviving the adventures of their minds. Peter approached the table scanning for Katie. Charlotte came wishing in her mind that lunch could be had at the mall, but she didn't dare say it aloud. She sat next to James believing she could convince him to drive her to the mall. Perhaps she would whisper her wish in his ear.

As Peter straddled the bench, he saw Katie. She was with the captain of the football team, but today their conversation was short. He could see her shaking her head indicating no. Soon after, Katie arrived at the worn picnic table and asked, "Hey guys what's up? What are we doing this weekend?"

As they considered all the possibilities, Emily couldn't help but think that nothing could compare to the adventure they lived just a few short months ago. She shuddered and quickly wished for calm, quiet and a good book. Solitude and serenity is what she sought.

Emily's serenity was interrupted as Charlotte screamed, "Hey look in the tree. Isn't that the crow?"

Ever since they got back from their adventure, Charlotte was paranoid that every black crow might trigger their next journey.

Everyone had become tired of her paranoia. However, all eyes followed the crow, as it left its branch and landed directly in front of James. The bird dropped a shiny object on the table and returned to his perch above.

"Oh no, not again!" Charlotte hid her face behind her hand. "This is it, isn't it?"

"Is that our coin?" asked Peter.

James picked it up and recognized it instantly. It was the same coin he'd seen at the museum when Mason returned with the dusty box. "No, this coin belongs to Mason. But why does the crow have it?"

Peter's gut told him the answer. He was sure of it, "James, something's happened to Mason. He needs us. He's in trouble."

The crow gave a loud caw, as if to confirm Peter's intuition.

James pulled out his spyglass. No matter where he was, he kept it with him. He looked at the coin and saw that it was actually the glass ball Mason had said was his gift. The energy inside it was electric and shooting all over, like lightning. "You're right Peter, this is about Mason, and there's lightning. Sidney, do you have your glass ball?"

Of course he did. Like James, Sidney never went anywhere without it. He pulled it out of his bag, looked into it and verified that lighting was striking inside.

"Katie," said James, "Do you have your scales with you?"

"No," she answered guiltily. "They're too big. I can't carry them with me all the time. They're in a safe place in my room."

Peter interrupted, "My guess is if we looked at them right now they'd be teetering out of balance."

"I think this might be what Mason was talking about," said Emily. "Do you think it's time?"

Lightning lit up the sky, thunder cracked, and the six caught one last look at their untouched lunches.

APPENDIX

BALCHAZAR EXPLAINS THE SIX MENTAL FACULTIES

MEMORY

How often do you forget? May I make a suggestion to you? You don't forget. Why? Because you didn't remember in the first place. Did you know you have a perfect memory? I realize that may be difficult for you to believe, but it is true. You just need to develop it. Like the muscles in your body which need constant exercise to be strong and remain in top condition, such is the case with your memory.

The process of developing your memory muscles is easy. You do it through ridiculous associations, silliness, and rhyming. This is how the greatest memory experts can recall hundreds of numbers or names years after memorizing them. By developing your memory muscles, you are able to remember whatever you wish for as long as you want. The key is to LET yourself remember.

You actually know more than you allow yourself to know. And if you would step inside the dreams you have for your life, your future self will tell your current self exactly how to create the life of which you dream. You see, you can use your memory to create future memories, just like you hold onto the memories of your past.

Your memory is valuable. And once you have developed it, you will gain more confidence. You'll want to push yourself into your future as you want it to be. Create a new habit, a new pattern used daily to develop your memory. Memory enables you to take advantage of the other mental faculties. And the stronger your memory, the more able you are to use other gifts you have which will flow to you and through you to enrich your life.

Yes, you have a perfect memory. Tap into this gift and see what it brings to your world.

PERCEPTION

Your perception is how you see the world. Most people don't realize you can see things from more than one point of view. Did you know that if you change the way you look at a situation, you will change the way you see it? You can make anything different based on how you choose to view it.

Let me give you an example. Say you are standing inside a classroom. Looking straight ahead you see desks, chairs, pencils, chalkboards, erasers and white eraser dust. The students are quietly working on a test. Their heads are down, but you see determination and concentration in their eyes. The teacher has complete control of the room as she quietly answers questions when students raise their hands in an orderly manner. Then, if you turn 90 degrees to the right, you are looking at the playground. Here you see sheer pandemonium. Students are running, laughing, screaming, shouting and a couple might even be crying. They are involved in many activities. They chase each other. They hit and kick balls. They climb and hang from jungle gym bars. You're standing in the exact same spot, but your view is completely different.

Similarly, if you shift your perception your whole world can change. Nothing is good or bad until you decide how you are going to perceive it. And you have the power to choose how to see everything. One small shift in perception can change the entire way you think!

INTUITION

Everyone has an intuition, whether or not you believe it. And your intuition is speaking to you all day every day. Has this ever happened to you? You are thinking of a friend when the telephone rings. When you answer it, your friend is greeting you on the other end of the line. Did you think about your friend because he was about to call you? Or did your friend call you because you were thinking of him?

We are all connected through this mighty power of the universal mind. It may be difficult for you to understand, but your subconscious mind is part of a larger, powerful, all knowing mind. And you can tap into it through the development of your intuition.

It is that still, small voice in your head that nudges you forward. The thought that keeps appearing in your mind that says, "do it." It is the voice that answers you when you ask a question about something you have no idea how to approach. Pay attention. It is inspired insight coming to you because you are interested, you want to know and the knowledge is there. Learn to use your intuition, just relax and trust and you will begin to see signs and clues. Thoughts will come to you to guide you to the right answer. Your intuition is your subconscious mind talking to your intellectual, thinking mind.

When you learn to use and trust your intuition, you will have direct contact with the mind that knows everything. It will tell you exactly what you need to know. It will guide you to exactly where you need to be. It helps put you in harmony with that which you seek, and the ideas will come.

You see the first law of the universe is the law of vibration. It says that everything vibrates. That vibration we call a feeling. When you think about a problem or what you want, your thinking sets up a vibration in your body. There are infinite vibrational levels in the universe. Your intuition senses a certain vibration and you feel that in your body. Sometimes your intellectual mind tries to convince you that you are going in the wrong direction. It will encourage you to ignore your intuition.

But how many times have you said, "I always regret it when I ignore my gut feeling?" That is because your gut feeling, your intuition, knows. You get hunches, feelings, random thoughts and it can be challenging to tell the difference between your intuition and your own thinking. How do you know? When your friend calls you, does he have to identify himself? No, you know the sound of his voice. With practice, you will learn the sound of the voice of your intuition.

Your intuition never explains; it just points the way. Tap into your willingness and trust, pay attention and listen. Your intuition is a clear and reliable gift once you learn how to use it.

IMAGINATION

One of the things I find most fascinating about people is how they live through their senses. They judge everything in their lives by their senses. The mistake people make is relying solely on their five senses. There is an entire universe separate from your sensual world, and to dismiss its existence simply because you cannot sense it, is an error to say the least. People who make this mistake live in a very limited and small world.

You can take your thoughts and dreams, apply the laws of the universe and go where you want to go, create what you want to create, give what you want to give, have what you want to have. Know this, the source of results is not in the world. The source is within you.

There is a physical and a non-physical world. The non-physical world is filled with thoughts and thought energy. The physical world is that with which you interact through your senses. These are two different worlds. Engage your higher faculties and you can tap into the power of the non-physical world. You can create the world in which you want to live.

It all starts with your imagination. When you were a child your imagination was active and vivid. You pictured big thoughts, created monsters in your mind, played make believe, maybe even had an imaginary friend or two. But as you grew older, you were encouraged to let go of your imagination and take hold of facts you could verify through your senses. Your imagination is still there packed away in a dust-covered trunk in the attic of your mind.

We often use our imagination in the wrong way. We use it to worry and be fearful. We imagine the worst-case scenario instead of the best case. In doing so we create what we do not want. First in your imagination and second in your reality. Allow yourself to imagine what you do want, and do not focus on what you do not want. Let go of how you think it will happen. You do not have to think about that. The universe will supply all those answers when you ask the question. For now, imagine the life you would love to live. Because we can create anything we can imagine. Napoleon Hill called the imagination the workshop of the mind.

All new ideas are handed to you through your imagination. It causes you to tune into the source of all information. Have you believed that certain people are just "lucky?" Well, there is no such thing. Everything begins with the imagination. Everything created began as a picture, an idea, in the imagination of the one who brought it into being. Get busy in your imagination.

REASON

This is my favorite mental gift. This is the gift of thinking. Every human being has the ability to think. Yet most of them do not. They go through life relying on their five senses to interpret the world around them, accepting whatever happens to blow their way with the wind. They have no idea whatsoever that they have the power to create their circumstances.

But here is the key: What you think about, focus on and talk about the most will become your reality. We become what we think about. Henry Ford said, "Thinking is the hardest work there is." Based on the number of people I know who think, I believe he is correct. Because there is a difference between mental activity and true, proper thinking.

Do you live with a mindset? I am willing to wager you do. People are creatures of habit, doing the same things every day over and over. We think the same thoughts, believe the same ideas, and never dare to step outside of that mindset. But I challenge you to think of your life in different images. Create a new life through the gift of your imagination and then think about how you can make it happen.

How do you do that you ask? Quiet your mind. See how a little thought will pop into your mind and then another, and soon you have an idea. An idea is just a collection of thoughts brought together toward a purpose. Think about what you want, what you really want. Develop a fantasy in your mind of what that might look like. And then think about how you can make it happen. Because you CAN make it happen. Your thinking will make or break you. Dare to use your thinking to create a life you truly want to live.

WILL

The will is the gift you possess that allows you to concentrate with laser focus on any idea you hold on the screen of your mind, to the exclusion of all other thoughts, ideas, and distractions.

This is not will power. For if it was that simple, then every resolution committed to by mankind would succeed. Your will power has no connection to any energy, and you can actually wear out your will power. The more you use will power, the weaker it becomes until finally most give up without success.

The use of your will connects you to a universal power of creation, a vibration, a frequency if you will, that puts you in harmony with universal law. This law attracts to you the very thing that is the focus of your will. It can't be forced. But by using your will to hold the image of what you want on the screen of your mind, that image becomes impressed upon your subconscious. And once in your subconscious mind, things begin to shift as your vibration changes and aligns with the very thing you want to make real in your life.

Use your will to focus on solutions, for every problem you encounter has a solution. Your will is the power central to achieving any goal you choose. Your intuition gives you the thoughts and ideas, your imagination creates the picture in vivid detail and your will provides the focus and concentration to hold that image to the exclusion of all else.

With practice, you can learn to focus your will on anything you desire, any problem you face, any goal you wish to achieve. Learn to harness your mind and become connected to the universal power of creation. For the power of your thinking is immense. Use this power of thought and will to achieve your full potential. Choose what you will think about. Your thoughts either create or destroy. Use this power for good, for your benefit, and engage your will to bring what you think about into your reality.

AFTERWORD

BY PEGGY McCOLL

Forty years ago, I met a wonderful mentor, teacher and friend by the name of Bob Proctor, who started me on the journey of success. Through the teachings of Bob Proctor, I gained the understanding and awareness to create phenomenal results. Bob Proctor wrote the Foreword for this book and his advice is equally valuable. I will say, however, that this book is one of the most unique and incredible books I have ever read. I suspect now that you have read it, your results are also going to change for the better when you apply the wisdom.

Kim Griffith and Paul Kotter have clearly mastered these teachings and have written this astonishing fiction story based on six divinely given faculties. The characters in this book are guided through various messages of how to use these faculties to create the life they truly desire. *Gifted: Unwrapping the Adventure One Magical Thought at a Time*, is a beautifully written and captivating story of self-discovery and self-growth.

This story teaches us about using our minds to focus and expand, to make connections and most importantly, that nothing is impossible. You could also begin declaring that anything is possible and that you are possible.

Now that you have finished this book, here's what I recommend that you do. Go back to the book and read the explanation of the six mental faculties in order to better understand and apply all that your mind is capable of.

I believe this book is destined to become a classic and even a movie! I see this book on everyone's bookshelf. In my mind, I visualize people sharing how THIS book made a difference in their life and the lives of their children.

One of my favorite lines in this book is the following: "*Thoughts are things. You will soon learn you have all the power to create the results you want by carefully choosing the thoughts you think*".

I believe the authors meant that the potential is available to YOU, to all of us. I believe that when you change your perception, move into action and make a decision, you have the answers to achieve your goals. There are many wise teachings to be found on the pages of this wonderful book. Be sure to buy multiple copies of this book and share this book with everyone you love and care about.

Peggy McColl
New York Times Best-Selling Author
aka "The Best Seller Maker"
peggy@peggymccoll.com
http://peggymccoll.com

ABOUT THE AUTHORS

PAUL KOTTER

Paul Kotter is a dreamer with an active imagination. However, like so many others, he knows what if feels like to doubt his way out of a dream. But with the help of the one and only Bob Proctor, Paul's days of doubting are behind him. Now he is fully aware that belief in himself, and his super-sized dreams, is HIS choice; one he is very happy he made.

As an author and business owner, Paul empowers people all over the world to expand their minds so they can live their fullest potential. He considers Gifted, his debut novel, to be a mixed genre of fantasy and self-help. The first in a series, the book explains the six God-given gifts of the mind that every human being possesses, and illustrates how to use them to create a better life.

Although Paul's life isn't as exciting or eventful as the characters in his novel, he does enjoy finding his own adventures in travel. His favorite travel partner is his beautiful wife, Nicole.

KIM GRIFFITH

Life doesn't have to be limited, although you couldn't convince her of that. Kim believed in the chosen elite of which she was not a part. Enter Bob Proctor who opened her mind to a world full of possibilities. Everything you need is in you, and Kim discovered a passion for sharing this truth. She teaches a happiness workshop and seminars on the power of the mind engaging college students in the beliefs required to ensure their own success.

Kim loves the view from the back of a horse, an afternoon in the barn, or a romantic evening with her husband, Randy.

MAGIC IN YOUR MIND

ALL YOU'VE EVER DREAMED OF... *MAGICALLY YOURS!*

THE GIFTED CHARACTERS EXPERIENCED IT, AND NOW YOU CAN TOO!

HOW DO YOU CREATE THOUGHTS THAT WILL PRODUCE THE SUCCESS YOU WANT?

By developing your higher mental faculties and getting in touch with the Magic In Your Mind.

Gifted introduced you to your six mental gifts – Imagination, Intuition, Will, Perception, Memory and Reason. Now, you can tap into their power in the landmark coaching program, **Magic In Your Mind**.

In this program, Bob Proctor, Mary Morrissey and Sandy Gallagher teach you how to develop and properly use your six higher mental gifts.

Expand the magic and power of your marvelous mind today. **Visit ReadGifted.com/magic** to discover more about this innovative program.

The **Magic In Your Mind** program is Balchazar recommended!

Hearts to be Heard

Giving a Voice to Creativity!

Wouldn't you love to help the physically, spiritually, and mentally challenged?

Would you like to make a difference in a child's life?

Imagine giving them:
confidence; self-esteem; pride; and self-respect.
Perhaps a legacy that lives on.

You see, that's what we do.
We give a voice to the creativity in their hearts,
for those who would otherwise not be heard.

Join us by going to

HeartstobeHeard.com

Help us, help others.